SCOTT NAD

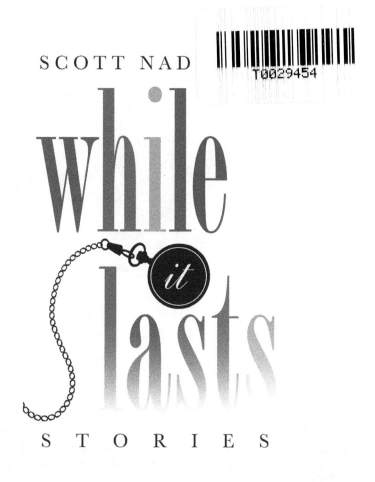

while
it
lasts

STORIES

Columbus State University
PRESS

Library of Congress Control Number: 2022943199

Published by Columbus State University Press

Marketing and distribution by the University of Georgia Press

Cover designed by Peter Selgin

Author photo by Alexandra Opie

For Iona and Alexandra, always

Table of Contents

Gray on Green on Brown

Take Rothko, for instance. At twenty years old, he's a Yale dropout, humiliated by his failures, uncertain about the future. It's the spring of 1924, and he has yet to pick up a brush or touch paint to canvas. He goes by Marcus Rothkowitz still, a name that made him stand out in New Haven, even among his own kind. The Jews who thrived there came from established families of German descent. Recent immigrants like him, those from Eastern Europe on scholarships that covered only tuition and books, lived in packed boarding houses a mile from campus. Locals and fellow students shunned them equally. The few who worked hard enough to hide their accents were rewarded with occasional invitations to parties where no one spoke to them.

Miserable for a year, struggling in classes, demoralized, he left without saying goodbye to anyone. After spending a few months with friends in New York, he made his way west, hitchhiking, hopping trains, sleeping in fields. A traveling salesman agreed to take him over the Rockies all the way to Oregon, so long as Marcus drove the overnight stretch. Now, exhausted, he has arrived back in Portland, where he spent his late childhood and adolescence after emigrating from Dvinsk, a provincial city at the western edge of the Russian Empire. He hopes to find sanctuary here, in the neighborhood to the south of downtown, known by inhabitants as Little Odessa. In a dozen blocks crammed with identical rowhouses live Jews from Hungary, Poland, Lithuania, the Ukraine, all of them equally shabby and loud and comfortable with their coarseness, proud of whatever small achievements they can claim in their new home. As Marcus once was, too, until realizing the rest of the world didn't care that he'd established his own debate club at Neighborhood House, published essays and stories in the community newspaper, ingratiated himself with gentile teachers at Lincoln High School.

But now even here he's no less lost than before. He sees only his neighbors' bad teeth and awkward clothes, cringing whenever they attempt colloquial phrases in English. At the same time, he can no longer listen to Yiddish without looking around to see who else has heard. Above all, he can't bear when people ask what he will do with his life. What should he do? His father, dead ten years, might have given useful advice, but his mother tells him only that he ought to go into business, like his older brother Mish who opened a drugstore some years earlier, or learn a trade like a cousin who'd become a carpenter. It doesn't matter to her that until now his only successes have been intellectual ones, that his big clumsy body has never been much use for practical tasks: his sister jokes that he can't walk down a hallway without bumping against both sides. As a boy he was gifted at Talmud study, believed briefly he might one day become a rabbi, but he has not set foot in a synagogue since the months following his father's funeral, when he decided that devotion to God led only to disappointment.

So what drives him to try acting, of all things? Perhaps he misses speaking in front of an audience, as he did during his debate days, along with the accolades that followed. Or else he has simply run out of other ideas. In either case, he joins a local company that performs at the Little Theatre on Northwest 23rd Avenue. Little Odessa, Little Theatre. Why is everything in Portland little? Maybe because the towering trees diminish everything else, or the colossal mountains that appear when the clouds finally lift in June or July. Or maybe because those who live here are humble about their place in the world, so far from the center of culture and commerce, accepting their insignificance.

Except that the company's manager, who doubles as acting teacher, believes her pupils are capable of greatness. So she says at the beginning of each rehearsal. Her name is Josephine Dillon, a stout, round-faced woman of forty, whose voice carries effortlessly across the small auditorium, even when she speaks to someone standing beside her. She coaches Marcus on his stage presence, his stride, encouraging him to swing his arms whenever he takes a step, though he feels more comfortable with them stiff at his sides. She spends a good bit of time arranging his body, pulling his shoulders, jabbing a small fist into his lower back, kicking at his feet to spread them farther apart. When he reads his lines—Falstaff courting Mistress Page with somber Russian intonations—she smiles without blinking and says nothing.

With her hands on him so often, he might believe Miss Dillon takes a special interest in him, except that she pays even more attention to a young necktie salesman named Will Gable. Gable, too, she harangues about his posture, prodding and bending and lifting his chin. She tells him he is too thin, brings him sandwiches to devour between scenes, and forces him to lower his naturally high-pitched voice. Marcus believes he is a better actor than Gable, or could become one, though Gable, he concedes, has a finer jawline. He learns from another company member that Miss Dillon paid to have Gable's crooked teeth fixed, his hair styled. Now she convinces him to go by his middle name, Clark, which, she says, makes him sound more distinguished.

And yet Marcus can hardly believe what he glimpses one afternoon in late May, two months after coming home. Before rehearsal, he steps backstage to find Gable and Miss Dillon mid-embrace, his tall slender body bent over her squat one, her pudgy fingers tight on his buttocks. Miss Dillon is seventeen years Gable's senior, but that isn't what disgusts Marcus or fills him with shame. Rather, it's the instant bloom of his own envy, along with a stirring in his trousers he can't control. Must he always be someone who wants what others have?

He slips out of the theatre and hurries away, knowing he'll never return. But instead of heading back to Little Odessa, he wanders past the grand Victorian mansions of Nob Hill, up into the wooded canyon that will later become part of Forest Park. He walks without seeing anything. Despondency blinds him to wildflowers and deafens him to birdsong. He wants his life to matter. He has long believed he can become something special, that he can overcome the terror and dislocation and profound sense of smallness he first experienced as a boy on the two-week journey from New York to Portland, rocked from side to side on the shuddering train, wearing an ill-fitting Russian suit and a handwritten sign around his neck that read, *I do not speak English.*

But he is still on that train, he thinks, riding to join his father who will die of colon cancer six months after he arrives, and the same tears spill from his eyes as those that blurred his view out the window of a Pullman car. He stumbles past tree trunks, pushes branches out of his way, stomps ferns and the prickly leaves of Oregon grape. He is sobbing now, breathless, his whole body gripped by a sadness he doesn't understand. His nose fills with smells of sap and loam and mold, sweetness and decay. And when he looks up—couldn't this be the moment when confusion and chaos open into mystery, into possibility?—he can make out nothing distinctly, only a strip of gray sky over a dark blotch of green that must be the needles of Douglas firs. And this green in turn shimmers above trunks and earth that blend together into a complicated but unified field of brown.

These colors don't just reflect his sadness, they *are* his sadness, both a product of feeling and a container for it. He is inside of them now; they surround him, caress him, suffocate him. They are the face of God he turned away from in the synagogue, a God he hates for taking his father from him when he needed him most. But he can no longer run from hatred and heartbreak, or shove them away. Maybe he no longer wants to. Instead, he'll embrace them, the way Miss Dillon embraced Gable, passion barely masking her desperation. He keeps his eyes opened wide even as he weeps. Because now he understands: they're the only things that are all his, these feelings, these colors, at once reuniting him with his departed father, bringing him closer to the death that calls for him louder with every passing day, and making him feel more alive than anything else ever has.

Couldn't it be a moment as simple as this?

Loyalists

The boy comes running across the backyard, hunched oddly, hands pressed to his belly, elbows jutting out. He wears an army surplus jacket and work boots that have been spray-painted black, with silver highlights on the sides that might be misshapen stars or anarchy signs. On his head is a dark purple scarf more fortune-teller than pirate. His legs move quickly but in short steps and close together, as if he's holding in the contents of a full bladder. Though the day is windless, the movement splits the unzipped sides of the army jacket and makes them flap like olive flags, revealing a white t-shirt printed with the blue and red of the RAF roundel. Sunlight catches his face and makes him blink equally round, dumbstruck eyes, and if witnesses were present they might notice the wide nose between freckled cheeks, the sharp chin and small feminine mouth before he slips into the dense shade of a horse chestnut. Once there he slows, edges closer to a wooden fence, and bends low, still holding his belly. If the same witnesses were to watch him now, they might think he is suffering stomach pains, possibly the first symptoms of appendicitis. They might wonder if he has been wounded, stabbed perhaps, or shot. Or they might realize he is hiding an object beneath his t-shirt. If they guess the object is stolen and that the boy worries it will slip down into his jeans before he gets away, they would be correct.

But there are no witnesses, and beneath the chestnut, he adjusts the hidden object until it's secure in the elastic of his briefs. When he's certain it won't slide down, he straightens and peeks over the top of the fence to make sure no one is on the other side. Just another backyard, with the same general configuration as the one he's in, a brick patio giving way to an oval of lawn edged with evergreen shrubs and rhododendrons, though this yard also sports exuberant flower beds blooming with late spring perennials: iris, peony, delphinium, gladioli, none of which he could name if he were asked. The house, too, is just like the one he left, a ranch with two squat wings and a daylight basement, big windows facing his direction. But he spies no faces in any of them, so he pulls himself to the top of the fence, rolls his legs over, and eases himself down. Then he's low again, creeping along the boards until the fence meets another, this one older and silvered, with a gap in the far corner he can squeeze through sideways. Behind it is a stretch of scrubby oak woods that follow the power lines from one electrical tower to the next—stretching out their arms like the skeletons of giant robots—until they cross the freeway half a mile north. When he reaches the concrete sound barriers he breathes easier and takes a moment to congratulate himself, imagining a future as a master thief, pursued futilely by teams of detectives, grudgingly admired by his victims, though the house he's broken into happens to belong to his stepfather, and he happens to have a key.

౧

Those, along with the time and place—May of 1990 in Union Knoll, New Jersey—are the broad strokes. In the absence of witnesses, we might add some details to fill out the picture, such as the small hoop earring the boy wears in his left ear and the red and swollen lobe around it. Or the hand-stitched letters on the back of the army surplus jacket, spelling out "The Jam." Or the overwhelming smell of the bearded irises, their upright petals a lighter shade of purple than the headscarf, the lower draping ones an orange-brown, their layered openings letting loose a scent that makes the boy think of overly sweetened iced tea. We should certainly take note of his seasonal allergies, triggered by the abundant pollen in the flower beds, which causes his eyes to itch and water, his nose to tingle. And we should register the sneeze he tries to muffle in his sleeve, but which escapes before he can smother it, echoing off the weathered fence boards and carrying farther than he imagines, across the flower beds and oval lawn, over the brick patio, and through the sliding glass doors of the daylight basement.

In this last case, we aren't alone. A resident of the house, the only one at home, hears it, too, and sits up straight to listen. She has small pale ears, one of which is made prominent by an asymmetrical haircut, short on the left side, long on the right. The haircut is new, urged on her by an eager young stylist, and she isn't yet used to the way it exposes the left side of her neck to the breeze. Nor does she like the way it shows off the increasing amount of gray close to the scalp. But she refused the coloring the stylist offered, in part because it would have added forty dollars to the bill. Even more, it would have meant another hour in the salon, where the music was loud and insipid, the chatter between another stylist and her client even more so. "I'm forty-nine years old," she told her stylist, waving off the tubes of dye she held up, one reddish-brown, the other a sultry black, neither close to her natural walnut. "I don't need to pretend to be something else."

She has been living with the haircut for three days now, trying her hardest not to let anyone notice how self-conscious it makes her. She has been aware of co-workers glancing at her, though none has said a word. Her husband Jeff has told her, on several occasions, that the style suits her, shows off her attractive jawline, gives her face a look of seriousness and allure. But Jeff's job is to make people feel good about themselves: he directs a private hospital foundation, raising millions every year by shaking hands and doling out compliments. She trusts his judgment only when he's let his guard down—after sex, for instance—but in bed she has yet to ask what he really thinks. Nor has she brought herself to snap Polaroids and send them to either of her daughters, both of whom are away from home, one a freshman at Amherst, the other a recent

Penn graduate now working as a legal secretary while preparing law school applications. Neither has ever held back in their criticism of her, and she suspects they wouldn't now. Her son, on the other hand, would simply shrug and say, "I don't know, Mom. I don't care about your hair." He, too, is off at college, finishing his junior year at a mediocre state school in the Midwest. He has always been her favorite.

Though it's a Tuesday, Dana Millen has stayed home from work due to a runny nose and sore throat, hoping to fend off what will likely turn into a full-blown head cold, though she has spent much of the day typing up reports in her basement office. A trained toxicologist, she works in research and development for one of the large pharmaceutical firms whose sprawling campus takes up several hundred acres of hillside a few miles down Route 10. Much of her work involves convincing executives to put safety ahead of profits, and her reports have gained a reputation for their bluntness. Unlike Jeff, she gives people her honest opinion—what the evidence has shown her—without fear of consequences. Argue with the data all you want, she often tells superiors, but in the end the numbers don't lie. In response to the stylist's hopeful grin and cheerful parting words—"I hope you love it!"—she said, "I think I can live with it."

Now, however, with her throat burning and a headache developing behind her right eye, a chill running down the exposed side of her neck, she isn't sure if even that much is true. And when she hears the sneeze in her backyard, she knows the haircut has been a terrible mistake, one she will remedy as soon as she feels well enough to return to the salon. The sneeze makes her think, briefly, that she is being punished for going to the salon in the first place, for letting a sudden burst of vanity—or rather, a fear that it is too late for her to be vain—get in the way of practical thoughts. For three days, everyone has been staring at her, silently judging her, this woman who has always told people, without hesitation, exactly what she thinks, and now someone is watching her in her bathrobe, in her own home.

She leaves her desk. Through the sliding glass doors she glimpses a purple shape, round, among the blue-gray spikes of her iris leaves, a deeper color than any of the flowers. Then it dashes to the left, disappearing through the gap in her fence she has asked Jeff to fix more times than she can remember. Though she has the heat turned on in the house, she thinks she feels a sudden cold breeze blow in through the glass, creeping under the hem of her short robe and up between her legs.

ॐ

By the time she has dialed the number for the police non-emergency line and described her situation to the dispatcher, the boy, Justin Blankenfein—for the past few months he has introduced himself as J.B.—has made it most of the way to the sound barriers. In their shadow, he slides the object from his jeans and examines it closely. It's dark metal, oiled, a little more than a foot long, pointed at one end, cylindrical at the other, with an elbow two-thirds of the way through. A bayonet. His stepfather, Ivan Shapiro, bought it at auction earlier this year, to add to his collection. He's a history buff, especially partial to the Revolutionary War. After all, they were living just a few miles from Jockey Hollow and Fort Nonsense, he has reminded J.B. on more than one occasion. Washington himself walked these roads. How could anyone not want to own a piece of that? So far he's acquired half a dozen uniform buttons, three musket balls, a belt knife, and a pewter spoon, all of them found within a ten mile radius of Union Knoll, many by people digging pools in their backyards.

None of the items in the collection impressed J.B., not until Ivan shelled out three hundred and fifty bucks for the bayonet, a British make, most likely used by a member of a Loyalist militia. The only history J.B.—seventeen, a junior and solid C+ student—finds interesting is that depicted in *Quadrophenia*, which he has watched more than a dozen times. Whenever Ivan describes the heroism of the patriots who freed themselves from tyranny, J.B. says something along the lines of, "They weren't patriots. They were rebels. Traitors to the King." He argues that they would all be better off if they'd stayed British subjects. Just look at Canada, Australia. They'd have free healthcare, less crime, and better music. Ivan, who listens mostly to Romantic symphonies and show tunes, reminds him that Americans invented the rock 'n' roll he loves so much. There wouldn't have been any Beatles without Buddy Holly, he says. J.B. replies, quoting something he's read in a book about the British Invasion, "Anyone can find a diamond, but it takes skill to polish it till it shines."

As far as stepfathers go, Ivan isn't the worst J.B. has heard of, though he tries too hard to find common ground. He's a balding fifty-year-old marketing executive on his third marriage, this time to a woman more than a decade his junior. J.B.'s mother had him when she was twenty-two and did without a husband for twelve years, preferring boyfriends instead. Why she decided to marry this one, J.B. doesn't understand, though afterward she quickly got pregnant and gave birth to J.B.'s baby sister, who is now four months old. Whether his mother really loves Ivan or not, J.B. isn't sure; she seems annoyed with him most of the time, even though Ivan does everything he can to stay on her good side, including refraining from scolding J.B. for making messes around the house or drinking the six-pack of Lowenbrau Ivan brought home from the grocery, leaving his stepfather not a single can.

Stealing the bayonet might be pushing his luck too far, he knows, so he tells himself as he walks along the sound barriers that he is only borrowing it, that he'll replace it before Ivan even notices it's gone. But it's too perfect a weapon for his needs not to take this chance. For over a year he'd saved up all the money from his job stocking shelves at Bradlees to buy himself a vintage Lambretta, a two-seater 1965 vt200, in almost pristine condition, which he drove to school for six weeks, until someone backed into it yesterday in the parking lot of Union Knoll High School, flattening its rear tire and crushing its rim. It will take him at least another three months to save up for repairs, and in the meantime he has to ride the bus to school again, ignoring, or trying to ignore, the kids who call him Prince Justin and ask in a butchered Oxford accent if he wants a cup of tea.

He doesn't know which of the cars parked across from his spot hit the Lambretta, but he won't take any chances—he hates all the kids who own those cars anyway. When he reaches the parking lot, he starts with the Monte Carlo directly opposite. The edge of the bayonet has no trouble scoring the paint, and its tip slides easily enough into a rubber tire surrounding a chrome hub cap. "For Queen and Country," he says when the Chevy tilts to one side, and then moves on to the jacked-up Bronco beside it. This one has thick, off-road radials that give him more trouble. He has to jab a few times and then kick the socket to make the blade go all the way in. When it does, the tire gives a satisfying hiss, followed by a sound like a sigh when he pulls it out.

 beginbreak

CR

endbreak

It's around this time that the police car pulls up in front of Dana's house. She has tried to return to her report on a recent toxicology screen: a new compound designed to stimulate insulin uptake in Type 2 diabetics has shown some early promise in rats, but it consistently shrinks the testicles of its male subjects. She is recommending against clinical trials, over the objections of her supervisor who has repeatedly tried to convince her to soften her stance. But now, every time she begins to type, she finds herself looking over her shoulder to see if someone is peering through the sliding glass door. She has never been accustomed to people looking at her. No one would call her pretty, though perhaps some would use the word handsome to describe her. She is slender, just shy of medium height, with sharp features that, in recent years, have grown more severe. As a young woman, she was put-together enough to catch men's attention when she wanted it, but she has always preferred to think of herself as forgettably attractive, dressing in a way that keeps people from noticing her. Who would want to peek at her when she's not aware? And why on the only day she has come downstairs in her robe, a knee-length silk one her husband bought her for some anniversary more than ten years earlier?

By the time the officer rings her doorbell, she has changed into work clothes: dark slacks, cream blouse, tweed blazer. The only thing she wouldn't wear to the office or the lab are the fleece slippers she keeps on to avoid scratching the oak floors. The officer is middle-aged and mustached, broad in the shoulders and imposing behind his sunglasses. She immediately feels ridiculous for having called, even more ridiculous as she imagines him scrutinizing her behind his mirrored lenses, the haircut that obviously belongs on someone else, someone younger and prettier and more fashionable. Her nose has grown so stuffy she can hardly pull a breath through it, and her eyes itch, but she doesn't want to rub them and make them any more red. She especially doesn't want him to think she's been crying over what happened.

"So," he says, in a voice that's surprisingly high-pitched and nasal, as he flips open his notebook. "You've got a peeper around. First time, or repeat?"

"First," she says. "As far as I know."

"Usually they've been around a while before anyone notices. Were you in the shower?"

"I was in my office. I'm not home most days, but I've got a cold—"

"He was probably watching before that. Shower, bedroom. They'll do anything to catch the moment you drop your drawers. When did you change into those?" he says, waving his pen at her slacks.

"Just after I saw him. I was in my robe before that. As I said, I'm home sick—"

"There you go, then," he says. "Best defense is good thick curtains. Especially in your bathroom and bedroom."

"I was in my office," she says again.

"Well, let's take a look around and see if our friend left any treasures."

She leads him through the house, and he pauses every few steps to make notes. About which windows have curtains, maybe? About the likelihood of someone wanting to watch this nearly fifty-year-old forgettable woman drop her drawers? She's conscious of the movement of her hips as she walks ahead of him to the stairs, and then suddenly finds it disconcerting to have a strange man with her in the house while her husband's away. How many times has that happened during their marriage? The odd plumber or electrician, some dad come to pick up his kid, never a lover. She and Jeff haven't had sex since she got the haircut, nor for the several weeks prior, so of course she hasn't yet asked what he really thinks. In the basement, she shows the officer where she was sitting with her back to the door when she heard the sneeze, and then where she spotted the purple dome of what she guesses was a baseball cap before it disappeared through the hole in the fence.

"No other details you remember? Skin color, maybe? Hair?"

She can offer him nothing else, and he lets out a long breath as he nods, as if he has expected her to disappoint him. Without asking, he opens the sliding door and steps into the yard. For a moment, she sees it through his eyes—her flower beds bursting with color, the collection of gladioli that gives her such pride, even though no one but she knows how many rare varieties she has gathered—and hopes he might say something that suggests admiration. But he only turns and stares in through the glass, judging the angle, perhaps, and what he might see if he were a peeping Tom in a purple hat. She pictures herself in her chair, facing her computer screen, her thighs exposed when she crosses her legs and the robe hitches up. Does he like what he imagines?

He doesn't say. He's already crossing the yard to the far corner, where the hat disappeared through the fence. "First thing you oughtta do," he calls as she follows, "is fix this. No need to roll out a welcome mat." She doesn't bother to tell him how many times she has asked Jeff to do so.

Because now she sees how many of her irises have been trampled, a huge swath of them, their saber leaves cracked, bent, and bleeding sap.

"Son of a bitch," she says.

The officer lifts his sunglasses, revealing small pale eyes that blink fast in the light. "These types are usually harmless beyond looking. This one's reckless, though. They don't usually leave a trail." He follows it—a trail of destruction; no, devastation—across the beds lining the back fence. Her peonies toppled here, a dozen of her precious gladioli stomped near the bulb. The unease she felt earlier has begun to crimp into rage. If she had it to do over again, she thought, she'd run into the yard in her robe and thrash the creep for abusing her plants. "He came from over here," the officer says, reaching the opposite corner, beneath the neighbors' horse chestnut, the only attractive thing in their yard, which is otherwise functional and ugly, nothing but over-fertilized lawn and bark chips and boxwood hedges trimmed so severely they show more sticks than foliage. "Jumped the fence and went straight across. Doesn't look like he came to your window. If he was peeping, he was doing it next door."

Of course, she thinks, and can't believe her disappointment. Even in her robe, even with the silly haircut, even if she dropped her drawers in the middle of the yard, who would bother to glance in her direction?

ଓ

When he's finished with the Bronco, J.B. crawls over to a red LeBaron to its right. Even though it's unlikely to have been the culprit, given the difficult angle it would have needed to hit the Lambretta with much force, it feels too good to wield the bayonet to stop now. He's punishing traitors to the King, crushing the uprising. He's standing up for the Mods against the greasy Rockers, like his hero Jimmy Cooper, except he has no intention of ending up like Jimmy, wrecked on pills, his Lambretta crushed and gone for good.

This time, however, there *is* a witness, tracking him in the rearview mirror of a little black Celica in the row opposite. She watches him crouch between the cars, run the pointed object the length of the LeBaron's driver's door, and then stick its end into the rear tire, near the pavement, where it might be hard to spot the hole. When he pulls it out, over the hiss he hears someone call, "Hey," which makes him flatten himself against the ground. But the "Hey" isn't alarmed so much as curious. He searches for its source and finds it in the face of a girl hanging out of a car only a few yards across the asphalt. He recognizes her—Jeannie Catanzaro, the younger sister of a kid in his biology class—though he's never spoken to her before. But she waves him over as if they're old friends. When he gets close, he hears that the car is running, and the stereo is on. If she's listening to some hair-metal band—Poison or Ratt or Warrant—he'll split. But the sounds that come out are jaunty quick drums, moody synthesizer, a mournful and agonized voice with an unmistakably British accent. The Cure. He can live with that. "How about you get the one over there?" she says, pointing down the aisle. "The white pick-up."

"Friend of yours?"

"Asshole of the century," she says. She's a pointy-faced girl with frizzy hair that falls in dark ringlets over much of her face. Skinny arms stick out of the loose sleeves of a too-large black t-shirt, the four faces of Depeche Mode screen-printed in white across its front. She chews gum frantically, shifting it from molars to incisors, pushing the start of a bubble out with her tongue, sucking it back before blowing it larger. "Deserves the knife somewhere else. But tires'll do."

"Not a knife," he says, and holds up the bayonet so she can see its full length. "This baby's been taking out traitors since 1776."

"Whatever the fuck it is," she says. "Long as it causes pain."

He pops his head up to make sure no one else is in the lot. He doesn't have a watch but guesses it's still third period, which means another hour before kids start skipping out of study hall and driving aimlessly around town. The white pick-up, a Sierra, is brand new, its paint job perfect. This time he makes Xs on the doors and takes out all four tires. He glances up once to see Jeannie watching him without expression through her curls. She can't be more than fifteen. The Celica is her brother Vic's, a sporty kid in golf shirts and spiked hair, friendly to everyone, including J.B., who can't stand him. She watches until the truck settles on its rims and then pulls her head back in. For good measure, he cuts the wires to the license plate lights.

When he creeps back to her, she's leaning sideways against the seat, eyes closed. Out of the speakers comes Robert Smith's profession of undying love, which nevertheless sounds like a lament. "You want to wait and see how he likes it?" he asks. "Or should we get out of here?"

"I can't drive," she says. "Don't even have my permit yet."

"Slide over."

Instead of doing what he suggests, she opens the driver's door, shoves him aside with the heel of her hand, and walks around the hood to the passenger side. He drops into the seat and looks for a place to stash the bayonet. When she climbs in beside him, she grabs it out of his hand, gouges the dashboard, the armrest, the fabric around the door handle, and lays it across her lap, as if she might soon need it again.

"Not so big on Vic," he says. "Another asshole of the century?"

"Millennium," she says.

"I thought everyone loved him. Isn't he supposed to be all Mr. I'll-do-anything-for-people-even-if-they-think-I'm-a-wanna-be-douche?"

"Including pimping out his sister. To assholes who already have a girlfriend."

Now Robert Smith moans about Spiderman eating him for dinner. "You ever listen to *All Mod Cons*?" he asks as he backs the Celica out of its spot.

"Touch my fucking music," Jeannie says, lifting the bayonet, "and I'll stick this through you, too."

CR

After the officer leaves, telling her as he walks to his car that he'll patrol the neighborhood for a few days, keep an eye out for anything suspicious, Dana goes next door and rings the bell. Despite her headache and sore throat, she thinks it's the right thing to do. And she's already dressed to go out. She doesn't know the neighbors well, though she has lived next to them for most of a decade. Or at least next to one of them. Ivan Shapiro was married to a different woman when he first moved here, but she and her children left three years ago. The new wife appeared not long after, with an odd teenage son who stayed with them half the week, puttering up and down the street on an old scooter, wearing a big round helmet with a clear visor that made him look like the alien from Bugs Bunny cartoons her kids once watched on Saturday mornings. She looked too young to have a teenage son, slender but full-hipped and bosomy, and soon enough she had a baby as well. She's carrying the infant when she opens the door now, her fine features pinched as if she expects to find someone selling vacuum cleaners on her front steps, or a religion that would make her give up drinking wine. Dana has met her on a couple of occasions, but she can't remember her name, and there's no sign of recognition in the woman's eyes. Unlike Dana, whose body always returned to its natural boniness after each of her kids was born, she is still curvy after pregnancy, with wide soft lips and big sleepy eyes, a woman built, it seems, for sex and childbearing. The officer would have no trouble imagining someone peeping at her.

"Sorry to bother you," Dana says. "I'm—you probably don't remember—from next door?"

The woman looks at her strangely, leaning away. The haircut, she thinks. It's even more hideous than she realized.

"We met at the Sambors' barbecue," she goes on. "It was a while ago. And you were still pregnant then." She pauses, glances behind her, half-expecting to see someone in a purple hat watching her. But there's nothing but empty street where the police car has been. When she turns back, the infant has eyes locked on her, its tongue working at its lower lip. "Your baby's lovely," she says. "Is it a boy?"

"Does she look like a boy?" the woman asks.

"She's beautiful," Dana says. "Anyway, I wanted to let you know … there's been an incident in the neighborhood."

"An incident," the woman says, a statement rather than a question.

"I called the police."

The infant starts to squirm, and the woman grips her tighter. "What sort of incident?"

"A pervert," she says. "Looking in windows."

The woman leans back farther. "Are you accusing my kid?"

"No, no," Dana says. She's confused for a moment, thinking the woman means the infant, before remembering the older son, the alien on a scooter. "It wasn't even my window."

"He's a weirdo, but he's no perv. And he's at his dad's till Friday."

"I'm sure it was a stranger," Dana says. "The policeman. He saw footsteps leading to your yard. That's why I wanted to let you know."

"My yard?"

"He was probably peeking in your window. You know, when you were dressing, or in the shower."

"He watched me in the shower?" the woman asks, not horrified, it seems, but puzzled, possibly intrigued. The infant's tongue, meanwhile, works hard now at an absent nipple, nose nuzzling the woman's chest.

"Thick curtains," Dana says. "That's the best defense. But the police'll keep an eye out. I gave a description."

"What did he look like?"

"Well, all I saw was his hat."

"That's it?" the woman asks, and now her look turns to disdain, as if Dana has betrayed her by not seeing more.

"It was purple."

"I have to feed her now," the woman says, taking a step back again, the disgusted look deepening. And now Dana understands why. She feels the drop hanging from her left nostril, and having nothing else to use, swipes it with the sleeve of her blazer. But it's too late. She feels the sneeze coming on even as she tries to hold it back. She swivels away, and it rocks her body, splattering her arm. Behind her, the door slams shut.

ᙀ

J.B. isn't comfortable driving a manual transmission, and he grinds the Celica's gears every time he has to downshift. But Jeannie doesn't seem to care. On their way across town, she occasionally jabs the seat between her knees with the end of the bayonet and digs out a handful of stuffing. While he drives, J.B. grieves out loud over the Lambretta, describing its perfect paint job, not green and red like Jimmy Cooper's—too Christmas, he always thought—but blue and white, everything original but the handlebars. "Those fuckers had to go out of their way to hit it," he says. "I parked it all the way up at the front of the spot, and they backed into it straight on. Took out the basket completely, and the spare, too. I'll never get originals to replace them." Jeannie doesn't answer. She leans forward and reaches for the knob on the stereo. He expects her to jack it up, drown him out, but instead she turns it down. He takes this as an invitation to keep talking. "They won't be backing into anything now, right? But you gotta promise not to tell anyone you saw me. I've already got one suspension this year. They'll boot me for good."

She doesn't promise anything, instead leaning her head against the window and saying, "Let's go down to the lake. I need to look at something calm."

"Scooter people, they're crazy for Vespas," he says. "But Lambrettas are way classier. You ever see *Quadrophenia*? Every time I watch Ace Face's ride go over the cliff at the end, I feel sick to my stomach."

Jeannie doesn't give any sign that she knows what he's talking about, but neither does she tell him to quit talking. "There's a rally in eastern P.A. next month. I'm definitely going. At least if I can get it running again. Scooters from all over the country. It's a great scene." He stops short of inviting her to join him but does add, "It's a two-seater," and gives her a quick glance. Her head is tilted back again, eyes closed, and what look like tear-streaks run from their corners, though they might just be shadows cast by branches of overhead trees. "When it's fixed, I'll give you a spin," he adds. "I could take you home from school in the afternoon, so you don't have to ride with this asshole," he says, tapping a knuckle on the Celica's dashboard. "Except for Thursdays. I got fencing practice right after ninth period."

"You're seriously into swords," she says, twirling the tip of the bayonet in small circles near his shoulder. She says it without inflection, and he can't tell if the words suggest interest or derision.

"It's authentic," he says. "Standard issue for the colonial British army." And then he decides to try out the line that has so far failed to move Ivan. "Think about how much better off we'd be if they won."

"Higher taxes," Jeannie says.

"Free health care."

"You're a fucking turncoat," she says, twirling the bayonet closer to his chin, but this time her voice has some life in it, and it's accompanied by a quick smile, the first he's seen.

"Next year, after I'm done at this turd of a school? I'm going straight to London. I don't care what I have to do to stay. Wash dishes under the table for nothing? I don't care."

"They would've won if the French hadn't helped us," Jeannie says. "No one ever talks about that."

This is more encouragement than he's ever gotten from Ivan, and it spurs him on. "We might not pay as much tax, but look what happens. We end up with shitty schools where assholes of the century get to act like royalty."

They've reached the edge of the lake, and as he downshifts to turn onto Lenape Road and skirt the north shore, J.B. thinks he smells smoke from the Celica's transmission. The trees are denser here, and now that the shadows are stable, he can see that Jeannie's cheeks aren't tear-streaked, but the skin below her eyes is dark, her upper lip and nostrils chapped and raw. "He was nice at first," she says, quietly now. "That's what makes it so awful. The way they trick you into believing they give a shit about you, and then they're off with some fucking—I don't care. I'm done with it now."

Development thins and then peters out at the west end of the lake, and he follows a gravel road to a small clearing at its end. Beer cans are scattered all over the dead leaves where he parks, but on a Tuesday morning, it's otherwise empty. They walk down to the water, Jeannie still holding the bayonet, swinging it at tall weeds and blackberry canes like a machete. He knows his stepfather will notice any nicks or stains or smudges, but he'll never say a word about it to J.B. Maybe it's unfair of J.B. to take advantage of him—or rather, to take advantage of his fear that J.B.'s mother will lose interest in him—but he enjoys the freedom it allows, the power he's never had over anyone, especially not his own father, who doesn't let him get away with anything: knocking five minutes off his curfew for every minute he's late, for example, or making him scrub the driveway when his scooter leaked a few drops of oil on the pavement. Still, he has always planned to return the bayonet before Ivan comes home from work and let them both pretend nothing has happened. Only now does he wonder if he might be able to sell it instead, use the money to fix the Lambretta. If his stepfather paid three-fifty, maybe he could pawn it for two.

But Jeannie is moving quickly down the steep path to the muddy shore. When she gets there, she holds the bayonet by its socket high over her head. "Excalibur," she calls. "I cast thee back into the depths!"

"Wait," J.B. cries, but it's too late. Her arm snaps forward, her fingers separate, and the bayonet flies end over end a dozen yards before slicing the surface and vanishing. The water is deep at this end of the lake, twenty feet easy. "That was two hundred years old," he says when he catches up to her.

"Still is," she says. "But you gotta hide the murder weapon. No way I'm getting expelled over that asshole."

"It cost three hundred and fifty bucks," he says, and feels sorry for Ivan, knowing he'll never say anything about the missing bayonet, will just accept it as part of the payment for a young, beautiful wife who might leave him at any moment.

"The Lady of the Lake will keep it safe," she says. "Until the rightful heir appears."

"For the glory of all England," he says.

"I don't make out with just anyone," she says, turning to him abruptly, her skinny arms crossed over her chest and cutting off half the head of each member of Depeche Mode. "I expect them to stick around."

"I pledge my loyalty to the crown," he says, which seems to satisfy her enough that when he steps toward her, she stays in place.

ॐ

That's where we might leave it: the bayonet in the lake, the couple embracing on its shore. Or perhaps we should add some details about the moment J.B.'s stepfather arrives home. A well-dressed man with thinning gray hair arranged carefully over the exposed areas of his scalp, he exits his car, walks through the garage and into the rec room, notices the open cabinet where he keeps his collectibles. He examines the empty space on the top shelf, billows with anger, and goes upstairs to ask his wife if she's noticed J.B. messing around with this stuff. We might then take note that this time he doesn't hesitate, decides he's finished holding back. He's tired of being married to another woman whose love feels so conditional. If she leaves him, he'll find someone homely and desperate, he thinks, someone who'll appreciate anything he has to offer. But when he reaches the top of the stairs, his wife runs to him, puts the arm not holding their infant around his neck, and says she's so glad he's home, she's been so terrified, someone was peeping in her window when she got out of the shower. Her voice is aghast, though her eyes are wild and sultry. "The neighbor called the police, thank God," she says. "Who knows what would happened otherwise." Before long he has promised to buy new curtains and install a security system, which until now he believed was a waste of money. He doesn't bring up the bayonet.

Or else we might head next door to document the moment Dana's husband returns from work to find her in bed. She is surrounded by used tissues. Her nose is bright red, while the rest of her face is paler than usual. Rather than resting, however, she is sitting up, reading over the report she typed earlier in the day, making edits with a green pen.

"Your hair," he says.

She puts a hand up to feel it. For the last hour she forgot about it but now remembers and is relieved once more. After returning from the neighbor's, she stood in front of the bathroom mirror with a pair of kitchen shears and did away with the asymmetrical swoop. She cut both sides equally short, so that now her style is boyish, perhaps sexless, iron gray all the way through. Even after showering, she still feels little clippings tickling her ears. "I decided it wasn't right," she says, one nostril entirely clogged, her voice sounding hollow in her ears, strangely timid. She sits up, so that the shoulders of the silk robe are visible, the wide opening at the neck and the lace nightgown beneath. "What do you think?"

He nods, loosens his tie, pauses. She thinks he might finally say something honest, tell her what she has long suspected: that he has stopped finding her attractive; that he occasionally reaches for her at night only out of a sense of duty; that if he were a different man—like Ivan Shapiro next door—he might trade her in for someone younger.

Such honesty would be refreshing despite its sting. But he is not one to surprise her after so many years. "Looks like your cold got worse," he says. "I can sleep downstairs tonight. Give you some space."

"I need you to fix the fence," she says.

"More deer?"

"They trampled my irises."

"I'll take care of it this weekend," he says. "Can I get you some tea or something? You sound pretty rough." He changes into jeans and a sweatshirt, says he'll go start dinner. Before leaving the room, he lingers at the door. "I think I like it better this way," he says. "It suits you. Shows off your lovely neck all the way around."

Then he ducks out. Dana reaches for another tissue. And that's where we'll leave her, too, sitting up in her empty bed, in the old robe that has begun to fray. She raises the tissue to her face. We won't wait to see whether she uses it to blow her nose or dab at her eyes.

While It Lasts

Twice divorced, diabetic, all his albums out of print, Albert Matzner pawns the last of his guitars. It's a Kona, Style 3 lap steel, bought in Hawaii twenty-eight years ago, for how much he can no longer remember. That was 1971, at the pinnacle of his so-called career. He was in his early thirties then, recording regularly, performing all over the world. Never a household name, certainly, but with a loyal enough following that he managed to spend six straight months living on royalties, feet in the sand on Kaua'i, picking at the Kona resting across his knees.

It's hard to recall now, as he steps out of the rain into the pawn shop, what it felt like to lie in the sun all day, drunk, with a girl whose name has escaped him. Since he was a small boy, he'd wanted to swim with sea turtles, and suddenly he did exactly that, day after day, in water so clear he could make out the pattern on each section of shell—some like sunsets, others little sepia explosions—and the movement of big sad eyes in ancient heads. He knows he'll never see a turtle like that again, though he does sometimes come across western ponds and the occasional painted while wandering across the train tracks from River Road and south along the slough.

If he had his own place, he might consider taking one home as a pet. He remembers how to care for them, make them comfortable in captivity. He had his first eastern box as a ten-year-old, named Ezzie after the boxer Ezzard Charles, who'd just beat Jersey Joe Walcott for the heavyweight championship left open when Joe Louis retired. His mother made him release the turtle into the woods behind their house when he went away to college, and he wept as he set the crate down beside the little creek that cut across Union Knoll before joining Shale Brook. They'd had a good run together, he told himself, and it was okay to say goodbye. But when he tipped the crate over and watched Ezzie take a first tentative step onto dead oak leaves, he thought he'd never stop crying. The sobs came so fast he feared he'd choke on them, and he ran back to the house without looking to see which direction Ezzie had turned.

The creek is likely paved over now, subdivisions having long filled in the open spaces in the suburban New Jersey town to which he hasn't returned since turning nineteen. But the eastern box could live a hundred years in the wild. He likes to imagine Ezzie following the brook west to its source, and then through the remaining woodlands to the protected spaces of the Delaware Water Gap, fifty miles away. There he finds a mate, sits in the sand beside the grand river, munches worms and grubs and fallen berries, lives out his days in reptile contentment and luxury.

℣

The pawn shop is cluttered and disorganized, stereos stacked on display cases full of hunting knives and binoculars. The broker knows nothing about guitars, can't distinguish a handmade treasure from a factory toy, though he has a rack of them behind the front counter, a couple of acoustic Yamahas, the rest electric: a Rickenbacker, an Ibanez, several Fenders. "Sixty bucks," he says, giving the Kona a dismissive glance, before returning his attention to a tarnished silver flask and a dirty rag. He's a big ex-biker recently reborn, his beard shaved, hair cut short as a soldier's, a gold cross at his throat and fresh tattoos on the backs of his hands: *Once Lost* on the left, *Now Found* on the right, both in the typeface of the Gutenberg Bible.

Matz has sold to him before and has come prepared for a low offer. True, the Kona shows some wear. He was known to be hard on his guitars, not caring for them with the sort of masturbatory reverence he's seen in people who can hardly play a chord. But he always makes sure they'll sound their best, and the Kona's tone is as clear now as when he first bought it, even if there are some nicks on the body, a few burn marks where he absently ashed cigarettes during a show.

Rather than argue, however, he plays a few notes and sets it on the counter. This has the right effect on the broker, who tries hard not to show any sign of wavering as he scrubs the dark grooves of the flask's elaborate engraving. He's never heard any of Matz's albums, but music meant something to him in his pre-saved days; he once tried to talk to Matz about the genius of Jerry Garcia, before Matz faked a coughing fit and excused himself. Now, with the steel strings still vibrating, sound waves echoing through the crowded shop, he says gruffly, "Hundred."

"Thing's worth three-fifty," Matz says, inventing a number he hopes sounds like a reasonable one. "Close to a thousand if you got it mint."

"It's far from mint."

"Didn't say it was."

"Why talk mint when it's beat half to hell."

"I'm saying it's worth three-fifty."

The display case beneath the Kona reminds him of the fish tank he had as a boy, with chrome supports and yellowed glass. Inside are antique watches, women's, mostly, the few men's too fussy for his taste, with gold bezels and pretentious Roman numerals. But there's a brass pocketwatch that catches his attention, with a simple face and long chain. The notecard beside it claims it's nineteenth-century, but Matz knows better. It's a Hamilton from the mid-'20s, a railman's watch, the kind conductors used to swing in the open doors of Pullman cars that rolled through Chatwin when he was a boy, on their way to Penn Station. The sleeping cars he sees now, on the Starlight Express heading north to Portland and Seattle before turning east to Chicago, always have their doors closed. The conductors he's spoken to at the Salem station, impatient as they load passengers during five-minute stops, all wear ugly Casios on their wrists, with tiny calculator buttons he wouldn't be able to press unless he clipped his nails to nothing.

The Hamilton is a real find, something to treasure, and the listed price—$40—is a steal even if it's broken. Lucky for him the broker knows even less about watches than he does about guitars. Electronics are his specialty and how he makes most of his living, so Matz doesn't feel bad taking advantage.

But he tells himself to forget the watch, it's not why he's here. Focus, he thinks, and shuts out the images of himself as a train conductor, a boyhood dream not quite as vivid as that of swimming with sea turtles, but alluring all the same. He needs money to pay the week's rent, or preferably a full month's. What good is a watch if he has nowhere to sleep? Last year he spent two separate six-week stretches at the Union Gospel Mission, on a sagging cot surrounded by wet coughing that kept him up all night, accosted every morning with sermons about Jesus's love and healing power. He warded them off by silently reciting the few Hebrew prayers he remembered from dutiful and torturous years of attending Friday night services—the She'ma, the Adon Olam, the mourner's Kaddish—and thanked the missionaries for their efforts. Toward the end of his second stay, a fellow resident accused him of stealing his stash—of what sort of dope Matz never found out—and punched him hard enough in the kidney to land him in the hospital for three days.

At the time, he told himself he'd rather sleep under the bridge than go back to the shelter, though now, when the possibility looks more likely than it has in months, he shivers at the thought of cold nights, a canvas tent, raccoons and vagrants creeping around him in the dark. He'll do anything to hang onto his room at the Creekside, a motel half a mile east of downtown—where most inhabitants pay either by the hour or by the week—which is why he's decided to let the Kona go.

So instead of asking about the watch, he plays a few notes, the opening bars of "Amazing Grace," and the pawnbroker relaxes his hard stance and closes his eyes. After the sound fades, they lob a few more numbers back and forth, inching closer to two hundred. More than the Kona is actually worth, Matz guesses, though probably not more than the Hamilton. He knows he can probably get the broker to go as high as two-twenty-five, but now he can't help himself. "How about this," he says. "I'll give it to you for a hundred-eighty, if you throw in this junky old pocketwatch."

The pawnbroker, suspicious, squints down into the case. "That's a classic," he says. "Nineteenth-century."

Matz scoffs. "If that's nineteenth-century, so am I."

"Owner said so."

"How long's it been here?"

"Year, maybe. Year and a half."

"You'll never get forty for it."

"What do you want it for?"

"Nephew. He likes tinkering with old mechanical things," Matz says, though he doesn't have a nephew, as far as he knows. He hasn't spoken to his sister in nearly forty years, and she was married but childless when he last heard news of her, just before his mother died in 1979. "Might even get the thing ticking again."

The broker shrugs heavy shoulders, winces, kneads his neck with the *Once Lost* hand. Then he unlocks the case and hands over the Hamilton. Matz winds it while the broker counts bills, licking his thumb too often. To his surprise, the watch isn't broken after all. He can hear it ticking even before he brings it to his ear. He slips the t-bar at the end of its chain through the buttonhole of his jeans, swings it around a finger. It has a pleasant weight as it twirls into his palm. It's almost enough to make up for the pang he suffers as he pats the Kona goodbye, though he can't help choking up, just as he did when he carried Ezzie's crate into the woods. But he won't cry in front of the broker, he swears. He sweeps the stack of bills and the claim ticket from the counter, mutters a quick thanks, and heads for the exit. Behind him, the broker plucks one of the Kona's strings, too hard, snapping it against a fret. It makes a sick, plaintive sound, one Matz covers by jerking the door open with enough force to jangle its bell.

cs

Once back on the drizzling street, he concentrates on the bills in one pocket, the watch in the other, on the fact that he won't soon have to sleep in the mud. His room at the Creekside costs fifty-two dollars a week, and he might convince the manager to cut a ten off if he pays for the full month up front. If he sells the Hamilton, especially to someone who knows what they're looking at, he might manage another month, maybe even two.

But he doesn't want to think about selling the watch yet, not when he's just acquired it, when it sits so comfortably in his pocket, when he's imagining showing it off to conductors at the local station, who've told him Amtrak pays them barely enough to feed their families. Nor does he want to think about handing over the full stack of bills to the Creekside's manager, not when there's a bar on Commercial Street, a block and a half from the pawn shop. What harm is there in a beer or two, when he'll still have a week's rent and plenty to spare?

The place is one he frequents whenever he can afford to, a small, windowless sports pub that serves fish and chips and the big soft pretzels that make him nostalgic for the New York of his childhood. Also for his long-dead father, who yielded to few indulgences but never turned away from a pretzel stand when he took Matz and his sister into the city to visit their grandparents. The TV screens showing basketball and NASCAR he could do without, but the beer is the cheapest in town, and he can walk here from the Creekside. More important, he

WHILE IT LASTS | 33

can walk back to the Creekside without worrying too much about losing his way or stumbling into traffic. Plus, he likes the bartender, a skinny guy in his late thirties, with a rockabilly haircut and a cigarette pack rolled into his sleeve.

"Matz," the bartender says, tipping up his chin. "Long time."

"At least three days," Matz replies.

Unlike the pawnbroker, the bartender is someone whose name he wishes he could remember, though as much as he tries, he can't call it up. He knows more about music than the pawnbroker, even owned one of Matz's early records before he realized who Matz was. Matz has since passed him copies of the later ones, but because the bartender has never mentioned them, he guesses they aren't to his taste. At least he's never sighed and said, "what a long strange trip it's been," as the pawnbroker often did.

On the stereo now he's playing *Sweetheart of the Rodeo*, which works to trick his daytime regulars—laid-off construction workers or off-duty corrections officers, some white, some Mexican, all in cowboy boots—into believing they're in a sports-bar version of a honky-tonk, as they might have hoped. Other times he plays *The Gilded Palace of Sin* or *Grievous Angel*. Matz has told him he once met Graham Parsons, after a show in Austin. What he didn't say was that he was so taken with the girl beside him, her black hair and thick eyebrows and high freckled cheekbones, and even her name, Emmylou, that he didn't say more than four words to Graham. A few months later, he was dead.

"Someone here looking for you," the bartender says, and immediately Matz tries to call up a list of people he owes money, and from that a list of those who might bother to track him down to collect. But before he can come up with a name, he's looking at a shaggy-haired kid in Buddy Holly glasses, a big smile framed by pointy sideburns, arm in brown plaid stuck out for a shake.

"Mr. Matzner," he says. "It's an honor."

"Is it?" Matz pulls out the Hamilton, twirls it around his finger without bothering to check the time. "Then I guess you're buying this round."

&

The kid, whose name might be Randy or Ronnie—when he says it, Matz is too focused on the pitcher of beer the bartender pours to fully take it in—turns out to be a writer: a "music journalist," he calls himself, based out of Portland but on assignment for a New York magazine Matz has never heard of. Nor has he heard of the bands the kid names, or their lead guitarists, all of whom cite Matz as an influence. He's pleased, anyway, when he asks what sort of bands these are—dreading the word "folk," or worse, "roots"—and the kid tells him they're avant-garde, indie-rock, experimental. That's how Matz has always wanted to be understood, as someone who infused new approaches with old traditions, an American Stravinsky or Bartók, combining Delta blues and mountain bluegrass with atonal composition and improvisation on open-tuned acoustic guitar. But who among his audience ever listened to Bartók? Apparently some guy named Thurston Moore, who plays in a band called Sonic Youth, which, according to the kid, is the most important since The Velvet Underground.

So he agrees to the kid's request for an interview, which begins with a second pitcher, continues through a third, and then evolves into a day of wandering around the city with a pint of Bell's they pass back and forth. Matz shows the kid his room at the Creekside, plays him a few old records he's hung onto—West Virginia fiddle, Java gamelan—and then takes him to his favorite thrift stores, where he scours the vinyl racks for rarities he can sell to collectors he knows in Portland and Corvallis and Eugene, and even to some in Los Angeles and New York, as long as they'll let him ship C.O.D. This is largely how he's supported himself since the most recent divorce, after which he ate badly, found his toes going numb and his fingers cramping, played erratically the few times he tried to work on new tunes.

The kid looks forlorn when he tells him he's sold all his guitars. He was hoping to describe Matz in action in his profile—he already planned it for the lede—and maybe record a snippet he could play for his editor to get the article bumped to the cover, or at least to second or third rather than fifth or sixth. Matz pulls out the Hamilton again, examines its face carefully, but its numbers blur every time he gets a fix on them, and he can't tell if it's half past five or six. He wishes the Scotch were the reason but knows it's his blood sugar. He needs to eat, or he'll dip hard. He can already feel the tingling around his mouth and the sweat forming on his temples. But first he passes the kid the bottle, waits until he's taken a long swig, confirms that he's swaying in his ripped jeans and skateboard shoes, then says, "I might know where I can get hold of a guitar. How much did this magazine front you?"

The sign on the pawn shop says it's closed, but there's still a light on inside, and Matz knows the ex-biker never leaves before eight. He, too, is divorced and has no one waiting at home. To fight off the temptation of the nearby bars—or worse, the massage parlor above the liquor store—he stays in the shop and prays. With Matz's encouragement, the kid knocks hard. The broker's head rises from the stool behind his counter. Matz ducks out of sight, against the side of a shuttered brick warehouse that hasn't housed anything in the nearly two decades he's lived here.

"Which guitar's yours?" the kid asks, as the broker shambles toward the door.

Matz fiddles with the claim ticket in his pocket. He's already wished the Kona farewell, and the pain of a second parting would be too much to bear. Plus, he's intrigued by the sounds the kid let him listen to on his portable disc player, this Thurston and his Youth, with all their ragged fuzz and distortion and ecstatic noise. He pictures the guitars hanging behind the counter earlier this afternoon, before the Kona joined them.

"The Stratocaster," he whispers. "The red and black one. And the little Marshall amp."

တ

When the magazine arrives in the mail, with a note from the kid—not Ronnie or Randy but Ryan—saying again what an honor it was to meet him and get to spend the day with him, even with the massive headache he suffered the next morning and the fact that he spent most of what he earned for the article on the guitar and amplifier, Matz experiences a set of emotions he hasn't felt for some time: a mixture of hope, and ambitious yearning, and panic. He thought he put all these things behind him, the desire for accolades and admirers, the curiosity that came with exploring new territory, the thrill of recording and performing. But here it all is again, along with the excruciating pain of possibility, rising up to taunt him at sixty years old, fat and bald and nearly destitute. He doesn't know whether to meet it headlong or run for his life.

The article itself brings equally mixed feelings, but these have more to do with pride and shame. He doesn't particularly care for Ryan's characterization of the Creekside as "a teetering flophouse," though he supposes that's close enough to accurate, nor the details of his room, with "records and clothes and pizza boxes piled on the sagging mattress beside rumpled sheets." The room is hardly wider than the bed, and the closet accommodates no more than a handful of shirts and a few hangers for pants. Where else is he supposed to keep things? He especially dislikes the kid's sentences about his appearance. Why point out his bare feet and purple big toe, his jeans held up with twine? Would it be better if they were constantly falling down?

All told, the kid has made him sound like one of those rediscovered Delta bluesmen from the twenties, some of whom Matz himself rediscovered in the late fifties and early sixties, toothless old men who could still belt out an angry lament to break your heart or haunt your dreams. It's an absurd comparison to make, he born a middle-class Jew who inherited a sizeable sum from his father, an insurance broker, and used it to start a record label he gradually ran into the ground. It's also ironic, given his youthful self-mythologizing. For his first album, he penned sprawling, drunken liner notes written by a fictional guitar master, John One-Eyed Dirt, who described young Albert Matzner's early promise and original style. He meant it as a joke, assumed everyone would see it as such, but at the time, 1959, people interested in folk music took everything too seriously. At his shows, they smiled and clapped politely even when he made up mad field hollers, stomping and shouting about the devil and slave drivers as if he'd worked the cotton fields with whips at his back.

When the article focuses on his music, at least, it's more measured and discerning. The kid—Ryan, he reminds himself, though the name wants to slip through whatever cracks keep widening in his memory— has a reasonable grasp on his intentions, describes his noodling with the Stratocaster in flattering terms, though it couldn't have been more than sloppy, booze-inflected racket. He mentions Bartók, Glenn Branca, Jimmy Giuffre, Cecil Taylor. And Matz's quotes sound unexpectedly articulate, thoughtful, even radical, a mixture of insight and fuck-it-all defiance he can embrace without embarrassment. The article is the second in the issue, right after a piece about the legacy of Dusty Springfield, who died a month earlier.

What's more, almost as soon as it's published, he starts receiving phone calls. Or rather, his ex-wife receives them, since her number is the only one on which he's still listed. She finds him in the downtown sports bar to pass along messages, a still young-looking painter of fifty, with a long braid and tired eyes, bewildered by the turns her life has taken. She married Matz when it was reasonable to believe he'd go on living the good life into his old age, then stuck with him when the record label went under and he suggested they get out of L.A., move to a small city where they could live quietly and cheaply—preferably a state capital, he said, where there'd always be government jobs available—only to have him leave her without warning, soon after his chest pains began and a doctor diagnosed his diabetes.

At the time he told himself he wanted to spare her taking care of him as he declined, but even then he knew he was just sick of answering to anyone, of seeing the disappointment in her face, or worse, her devotion despite his failings. In the bar, he tries to see her as someone he still loves, though he prefers to live apart from her. But even such small generosity he finds challenging as he introduces her to the bartender, whose name he suddenly remembers: Neville. How could he have forgotten a handle with a legacy like that?

That's when his ex, Meredith, hands him her carefully handwritten notes, with the date of each call, names, numbers, the best time to call back. One is from a guitarist Ryan mentioned in the article, interested in having Matz play on a track of his band's new album. Another from a producer at a small label, asking if he has new material he'd like to record. A third from Ryan, saying he's spoken with a booking agent in Portland who wants to set up a show—and that maybe, if it goes well, Matz will consider a tour, with Ryan as his manager.

"Exciting news," Meredith says, but with an edge of concern that never failed to irritate him during their fifteen years of marriage, and doesn't fail now, either. "Are you really up to it?"

"I can still get it up," he says, and winks, which only makes her frown and shake her head. He lifts the beer bottle to his lips and uses it to block her face.

"Your fingers," she says. "The swelling's better?"

He clutches the bottle tighter. "I can play."

"If you don't eat well—"

"You don't need to worry about me anymore. I've released you from your duties, remember?"

She blinks, sniffs, looks down at her feet. Neville opens three more bottles, hands one to Meredith, one to Matz, and raises one in his own bony hand. "To the resurrection of One-Eyed Dirt," he says, and clinks Meredith's bottle.

Matz swivels on his stool as if to check on the cars racing in circles on TV, leaves his back to them. "That fucker stays in the ground," he says. "For good."

♋

Every day for a week, he walks beside the slough, looking for a western painted. It's late spring now, the water still high but not yet clogged with weeds. The mud sucks at his shoes, blackberry thorns snag his hems, willow branches slap his neck. He spots a few newts, a bullfrog, but no turtles. A great blue heron flaps past, close enough for him to feel the breeze from its enormous wings. There's time yet, he thinks. Or if there isn't, at least he won't know until it's already gone.

The show is in the lounge of a Mediterranean restaurant a few blocks from Portland's riverfront. Not the setting he's imagined for experimental, avant-garde, indie-rock, but then who has he been kidding? His name isn't Thurston any more than it's One-Eyed Dirt, and he may be sonic, but he's certainly not youthful. The walls of the lounge are decorated with geometric patterns and photographs of belly dancers, and the chairs are upholstered in red velvet. It's altogether too bright in the room, letting him see the audience as he tunes the Stratocaster, and among them are far too many bald heads and white beards to match his own. Meredith is here, of course, because he needed her to give him a ride, and so, to his surprise, is Neville, flashing a thumb's up and then devil's horns as Ryan takes the mic to deliver a self-aggrandizing introduction, as if he not only discovered Matz in a flophouse but dug him out of a grave and revived the spirit in his lifeless body.

As he speaks, Matz feels the familiar squeezing pain in his chest, the angina that has plagued him for years. He was too distracted today to pay attention to what he ate, and now to stave off the dizziness likely to follow, he slips a piece of candy between gum and cheek, one of the spicy cinnamon balls he's always preferred. He wishes Ryan would quit talking already, quoting at length from their interview, when he said whatever bullshit bobbed into his Bell's-addled head. What do any of his thoughts about music matter now, when he's got a hundred people in front of him, some standing against the walls, with belly-dancer navels beside them, others sitting cross-legged on the floor, just inches from the foot-high stage? He can't believe he's done this to himself, after so much time, when just as easily he could have lived out his remaining days—or years? who knows?—in peaceful obscurity. Instead he's exposed himself for the first time in nearly a decade, set himself up to be assessed and judged, and for what? Does he care what a roomful of bald men pining for MacDougal Street coffeehouses four decades in the past think of him now?

He checks the Hamilton, confirms it's ticking steadily, and lights a cigarette. Ryan finishes and shuffles off stage with hands thrust into his pockets, all confidence gone now that he's not talking. Applause follows, but Matz is done looking at the audience. He starts his first song, which begins as an out-of-tune bossa nova before erupting with feedback he coaxes into a quavering drone, using a pair of effects pedals he talked Ryan into buying for him. He's promised himself he'll play only new material, stuff he's written in a surprising rush of energy over the past two months, starting the day after Ryan's visit. He didn't realize he had so much music left in him, nor that the Stratocaster would draw it out so deliriously, this black and red beast he battles rather than plays. He'd gotten too comfortable with his old guitars, the Gibson Recording King he played for two decades, a Martin D-28 he smashed during a fight with his first wife, the Kona he no longer misses. He's needed something to wrestle with, something to challenge him, and though his fingers aren't as nimble as he wishes, this new music accommodates slow movements, even clumsiness. It's meant to sound as if he's stretching every note to its breaking point, until it turns on itself and hurries in a fresh direction. He wants each sound to linger, so that people forget they've ever been without it, and he brings the song to a close only when he realizes his cigarette is about to burn his fingers.

While feedback still vibrates through his amp, he glances up, sees some people clapping, the white beards looking baffled. Meredith has her hands clasped under her chin, as if all she can do is pray he won't collapse on stage. Someone calls out the name of a tune on his second album, recorded in 1963. Into the microphone, he mutters, "I'm not folk. I'm from the fucking suburbs." And then he launches into another new composition, this one rowdy and dissonant and intended to send those folkies running into the street.

If any of them stay, by the third or fourth song, he has forgotten them. He feels himself sweating, knows he's breathing hard. He glances at the Hamilton, sees that only half an hour has passed. To give himself a rest, he shows the watch to the audience, tells a story about an old conductor who gave it to him on a train to New Orleans, back in '51. "I was twelve years old and run away from home," he says. "After my daddy whupped me something good, and I stole all the money out his wallet." Without meaning to, he's slipped into the voice of One-Eyed Dirt, describing a lady on the train, in pointed shoes and big black hat, who offered to teach him what it meant to be a man. "She almost had me, too," he says, "but then I caught the glint of light in her eye. Fire red, I tell you, like a live coal hidden under ash. I run straight to the front of the train, slept in the engine room till we made it to Memphis. Then I hopped a freight heading back, made it home just in time for my daddy to wake up and beat me down again."

He starts another song while he's still talking, follows it with two more. In the middle of the third, he starts coughing, can't manage to stop, so makes it part of the tune, playing around the syncopated sound of his body as he did with his old stomps and hollers. When he brings it to a close and catches his breath, Ryan asks if he wants to take an intermission. But his vision's going blurry now, and he knows he has to call it a night. He's lasted almost forty-five minutes. Whoever's left in the audience cheers loudly, but whether it's for his new music, or simply for an old man raised from the dead, he doesn't know. A few people come to the stage with albums for him to sign, mostly original pressings from the sixties and seventies, and he does so, politely enough, drawing a little turtle beneath his autograph. A couple of young guys with messy hair talk to him at length, about his pedals, about technical aspects of his playing, and he indulges them with some lines intended to sound like wisdom: don't overthink it, just listen to everything, develop an ear, and play from your guts and your balls. They shake his hand, thank him, and walk away with an eager bounce in their step. He wishes he could tell them to become accountants, to stay away from music, which never gives back as much as it takes.

Except, maybe, for tonight: Ryan hands him his cut from the door, nearly seven hundred bucks, enough to cover his rent for months. If he stays in the Creekside, that is, though now he's wondering if he might get a bigger place, just a couple of rooms, so he has somewhere to practice, get a little stronger, build stamina. The kid adjusts his big goofy glasses and says he's made calls to clubs in Seattle, Denver, Oakland, thinks he can book half a dozen gigs for late spring. And then they can consider an East Coast swing in fall. "If you're game for it," he adds, with a touch of worry, making Matz wonder what the kid sees in front of him, if his gears appear even closer to winding down than he realized. "Why don't you see how you feel in a few days, and we'll talk about it more."

Neville approaches him last, skinny and wan, a curl of greased hair hanging in front of one eye, like a young Elvis who's spent the last year in a concentration camp. He hands Matz a pint of Bell's in a paper bag and says, "You're as folk as they come, my friend. Suburbs or not."

He thinks this over on the way back to Salem, in Meredith's car, pretending to sleep with his forehead against the passenger window. Have those New Jersey subdivisions of his childhood, with their bungalows and ranch houses and daylight basements and garages hung with basketball hoops, where he ambled through thin strips of birch and oak woods and listened to records on a portable RCA, now passed into legend? How would he ever know?

"That first tune was pretty good," Meredith says, believing he's asleep, or maybe knowing he isn't. "The others could use some work."

Her smell is sweet and comfortable and cloying. His fingers cramp, his chest aches. Streetlamps flash behind his closed eyes, leaving a pattern that reminds him of a turtle shell beneath clear water. Maybe he'll ask Meredith to paint it for him, so he can hang it on the wall of his new apartment, if he decides to look for one. The designs are so intricate no one could really replicate them, he knows that, knows that people can never make anything as beautiful as what they see in the world or in their dreams, though that never stopped them from trying.

Have You Seen Stacey?

S he had me up early again, the little monster, so I strapped her into the baby carrier and trudged outside, though it was well before dawn, late February and steadily raining, the creeks swollen close to their banks. As soon as we made it to the sidewalk she quit crying, chortling instead at pigeons on a power line, a row of dark blobs barely visible overhead. Around the corner a pair of orange dots glowed on the porch of a halfway house and then faded, and a pickup hydroplaned down State Street. Otherwise, the world was still. She was content beneath the umbrella, which was too small to cover us both, watching a curtain of droplets and bouncing with my strides while rain soaked through the back of my jacket and rolled into my underwear.

I walked for more than an hour before she fell back asleep. By then I'd made it all the way downtown, and the clouds had begun to gather some light. Cornices of old buildings took shape against the gray sky, and cars pulled into the garage next to the courthouse, lawyers and defendants and sleepy citizens called in for jury duty. I slipped into the nearest coffee shop, one that catered to the pierced and tattooed crowd, which was sparse first thing in the morning. Several tables were open, and I took one in the corner farthest from the counter, easing us down and pulling a paperback from my inside pocket: Turgenev's *Sportsman's Sketches*, which I'd started rereading soon after I'd become a parent and found myself, like the book's narrator, wandering the landscape at all hours. Twenty minutes of peace, I thought, that's all I ask, but before I managed to read more than a page about the beautiful July weather in Bezhin Lea, a voice started up behind me, young and eager and a little desperate even as it tried to sound casual. "Hey, man, how are you, been a long time, haven't seen you over at the square much, things good with you?"

I couldn't see the speaker's face, nor that of the person he was talking to, who responded with a brief, throaty greeting, hardly an acknowledgement, before the first went on. "I been over there every day," he said, "just trying to stay focused, you know, skating like crazy, wearing myself out till my whole body aches. Only way I can sleep, you know? It's been hard, man, ever since shit went down with Stacey. Seen her around? I haven't talked to her since I got out. They told her she can't have any contact with me, but that's bullshit, you know, I got every right to see her. She's got my kid inside her. I know it's mine, man, I don't care what anyone else says."

I kept reading the same sentence and stopping halfway through: *On such days all the colors are softened; they are bright without being gaudy…* Every time I told myself I should quit listening, give him some privacy, his words broke through my concentration, the tight black letters going blurry in my vision. The little monster was breathing that deep whistling breath of contentment I wished she were breathing in her crib, her cheek mashed against my chest. Her hat had slipped back to show the soft crown of her head, skin taut over the fontanel and pulsing like a tiny drum struck from the inside. I tried to crane my neck to see the speaker, but all I could catch was a long skinny arm, a black pattern etched into pale flesh from elbow to wrist.

"If they're right about how far along she is," he said, "and you count back, I mean, that's got to be last September, when we were down in Utah. Things were going really well then. She was happy, hardly using, and man, we were doing it all the time, like five times a day, you know what I mean? Those were the best weeks we ever had. And I swear, the desert, you think there's nothing out there, but it's beautiful, man, all that sand and rock and sky. What's missing is all the bullshit. You could just fucking breathe there, you know, and the sunsets just about made you want to cry. Anyway, if it started last September, then it's definitely mine, there's no doubt about it. I've always know it's mine. But Stacey says she can't be sure, not a hundred percent, says maybe she wants to do a paternity test, which is fine by me, I say let's just do it and get it over with."

The throaty voice said something then, too low for me to distinguish any words. But they made the speaker pause and let out a long breath. When he started up again, his voice was slower and strained. "Thing is, even if it isn't mine, I don't care, I love her, man, I'd take care of her and the kid both. Says it could be Runt's or Adam's. Maybe someone she doesn't even remember. When she's high, she'll open her legs for anyone. That fucking H, man, it messed her up so bad sometimes she didn't even know who I was when we were going at it. And I don't blame those guys, beautiful girl like Stacey gives herself to you, you're not gonna turn it down, even if you know she's been with your friend forever. But I swear, man, the kid's mine, and even if it isn't, I'm the only one gives enough of a shit to take care of it. I still love her, even after all this mess. And we would have gotten through it all, too, everything would've worked out if we hadn't gotten busted, and now her goddamn probation officer telling her she can't have anything to do with me, like he's got the fucking right, like we're in fucking China or something, and he can tell her who she can and can't see."

His voice had sped up at the end, and risen, too, and I moved a hand toward the little monster's ear to block the sound. But then the throaty voice spoke up, and for the first time I heard it clearly. "Easy, man," it said, and from the other came another big breath, followed by a surprising laugh, higher in pitch than I'd expected but humorless.

"You don't get to choose who you love, man. You're just stuck with whatever comes."

He went quiet again, but this time the throaty voice didn't respond. I wished it would offer some words of comfort or support and hoped at least there was a sign of understanding on the face I couldn't see. Either way, the silence was excruciating, and I was relieved when the speaker finally broke it.

"She knows I got clean," he said. "Her PO knows it, too, and so does her fucking mom, but she'll always hate me no matter what I do. Two months now, not a single fix, skating every day. I'm healthy, I'm ready, I'd do anything she needs, even if the kid isn't mine. But I don't know where she is. She's not at her mom's place, and even if she was, that bitch wouldn't let me anywhere near her. I been looking for her at the bus mall every afternoon, riding all the way out to Lancaster and back, hoping I'll just get a glimpse of her, but nothing, and her sister won't tell me, and all her friends keep avoiding me."

He paused once more, but this time there was no sigh, no need to get himself under control. Instead, the silence seemed calculated, a little feint before he spoke again, his words now calm and direct.

"You sure you haven't seen her?"

I suddenly had no doubt that the owner of the throaty voice knew where Stacey was, and no doubt, too, that the speaker had guessed it all along. But we both knew he wouldn't spill now. His response wasn't much more than a grunt, and the speaker went on in a bright, false voice more brittle than his previous laughter. "If you do see her, you gotta tell her to cut the crap and call me. Promise?" This time he didn't wait for an answer. "It's really good to see you, man. Maybe I'll catch you at the square sometime soon. I'll be there every day, riding that shitty bowl. Board's the only thing I got now," he said, and then came the smack of wheels hitting the wooden floor, the churr of them rolling away.

The little monster's head jerked up at the sounds, and before her eyes were all the way open, she let out a squawk. I drained my coffee, tucked the book back in my pocket, and stood. The door had already swung shut, and all I could catch of the speaker was a black hood speeding down the sidewalk and out of sight. I tried bouncing a little, but before long she started howling for real. At the table behind us sat a squat guy in his early twenties, with thick-rimmed glasses and messy auburn hair. He was typing on a laptop. A skateboard leaned against the wall beside him. He glanced up at me as I passed, at the infant crying on my chest, her crinkled red face, tiny bald head covered again by a hat with a fabric rose, and gave a look that was more weary than indifferent, though closed off, I thought, to any further suffering, or maybe immune to it.

I had the umbrella halfway open before we stepped outside. The sky was hardly lighter than before, no hint of the rain letting up any time soon. But the thrum of it overhead quickly settled the little monster down, and I started walking without a thought of direction or destination, knowing only that I'd keep going as long as she needed, and as far.

The Withered Hand

"If you want to do something, do something," Clara says, her accent still heavy after more than seventy years in the country. "I don't see why you're wasting time talking to me."

The young woman explains again: she's researching the history of women in the labor rights movement; it's important to tell Clara's story as a model to women in the workplace now; people need new heroes that align with the rise of feminism and the renewed interest in unions...

"And you? Do you belong to a union?" she asks the young woman, whose hands are slim and soft and free of rings, the nails carefully filed but unpainted.

"I'm a graduate student," she says, and flushes behind her large, brass-rimmed glasses. "At a small institution. We aren't organized."

Clara takes a sip of her tea, sets her cup on the flimsy side table. She finds a tissue in the pocket of her sweater, dabs at the corner of her left eye, the filmier of the two, which leaks unaccountably. All the time now she wipes away tears, she who used to cry only during fits of rage or relief: when searching for her cousin among the remains of those who'd died in the Triangle fire, for example, or later, when she learned the girl had survived. She'd just turned twenty-four then, had already led twenty-thousand garment workers in a general strike. She'd been beaten by men hired by sweatshop owners, had six of her ribs broken, but kept from crying then for fear that her parents would try to talk her out of returning to the picket lines.

Now, in 1970, Clara Shavelson, born Lemlich, is eighty-four years old, and she can still feel the knot beneath her right breast where the bone stitched imperfectly. And yet she is no less prone to anger. She feels it rising as she sits across from this young woman, plain-faced and lank-haired, wearing a shabby dress like a sack and sandals as if she's at the beach. Despite her explanation, Clara still doesn't quite understand what she's doing here, in her apartment in the Jewish Home for the Aged, distracting her from the view out her small window. This is her favorite time to gaze across the jumbled houses of Boyle Heights, when the sun lights up the towers of downtown Los Angeles, and the impossible ocean beyond it, an ocean more mysterious to her than the one she first crossed at seventeen. The city itself she still finds inferior to New York, where she married two husbands and raised four children. Two of those children she has followed to this land of sunshine and smog and movie stars who have a strong union, while the people who clean their trailers and serve their food have none. She stares at those office towers and thinks of all the work still to be done, yet this woman scribbling in a notebook—whose name Clara has already forgotten—wants to talk only about the past.

"Had you planned all along to speak out at the meeting?" she asks. "Did you coordinate with anyone? Or was it really as spontaneous as it's been reported?"

What does it matter? Clara wonders. What happened happened, whether it was spontaneous or planned, though of course the truth is she can't quite remember. She recalls only the rage building as she listened to the men of Local 25 giving tepid speeches in Cooper Union, all of them urging caution. Probably she'd expected this, and expected, too, that she would raise her voice and call for action. She does remember anticipating the crowd's cheers of approval.

"Did you have the pledge in mind all along?" the young woman asks. "Or did that come to you on the spot?"

What she hadn't planned was calling out in Yiddish. It was the anger that prevented her from finding words in English, words she'd learned mostly to talk back to managers, since no one at home spoke them, no one in her tenement on Allen Street, or in the shops below. She was good with languages, had taught herself Russian as a girl in Gorodok, so she could read books she earned by sewing button holes on shirts and writing letters for illiterate mothers with children in America. She found Tolstoy that way, and Turgenev, and Gorky, and eventually a neighbor passed her revolutionary tracts she'd memorized by the time the Kishniev pogrom frightened her parents into booking passage from Hamburg. She had to leave all her novels behind, and her wages from the shirtwaist shop weren't enough to pay for new ones. So instead of reading, she organized the women she knew into the International Ladies Garment Workers Union. She was a sprightly girl with a beautiful singing voice, and she half-charmed, half-bullied her way onto the executive committee of Local 25, which was still run by men.

And in the face of those infuriating men, with their middle-class wives in factory-sewn dresses standing beside them, who claimed that a bunch of young girls couldn't sustain a successful strike, she lost her adopted language and demanded to address the audience in words most of those in attendance understood. "I have listened to all the speakers," she said, "and I have no further patience for talk." Impatience was what drove her to offer the silly pledge, and impatience continues to make her say things before she has thought them through.

"Do you eat lettuce?" she asks, turning back to the window, the light growing peach-colored over the ocean.

"Lettuce?" the young woman replies.

"The green stuff. In a salad."

"I know what lettuce is."

"I didn't ask if you know. I asked if you eat."

"Well, yes. I do. Sometimes. I like salads. And on sandwiches."

"And you know where it comes from?"

"I'm not sure—"

"Fields," Clara says. "Harvested by Mexican workers paid next to nothing. Owned by rich men whose fingers are as clean as yours. You know Chavez?"

"The grape strike. I've read—"

"They won because we boycotted. Everywhere. Cafeterias, restaurants, supermarkets. No grapes from scabs. Even here, the managers finally agreed. After I convinced them."

"Just like in Brighton Beach. When you organized housewives to protest meat prices. That was—"

"Now it's lettuce," Clara says. "Chavez, the Farm Workers, they need another boycott. Will you tell your college to stop serving it?"

"Well, I—"

"Better yet," Clara says, "you can help me here. The managers run away the second they see me coming."

"I don't think—"

"If you want to learn about organizing, you organize," Clara says, pushing herself up with both hands on the arm of her chair, and then steadying herself before taking a step toward the door. Her eye has begun leaking again, and again she dabs it with a tissue. If her vision were better, she might get rid of this girl as quickly as possible and spend the evening with a book. She has always loved reading more than anything else, and only now does she actually have time for it. But her cataracts have made it a struggle to get through more than a few pages in any single sitting.

So instead she grabs her cane and hobbles across the room, as the young woman gathers her notebook and the shapeless cloth sack—a different shade of beige from her dress—that she seems to use as a purse. But before reaching the hallway, Clara hesitates, reconsiders. What is she forgetting? Then she remembers, brushes past the young woman on her way to the closet. A hat. She never goes into battle without one. Her choice today is black, broad-brimmed, with a bit of lace that hangs in front of her eyes. She stops at the bureau, pulls out a drawer, and paws around inside until she feels the shape she's looking for, a cool cylinder as wide as her finger and just slightly shorter. Lipstick, a dark shade that goes well with the hat. She spreads some on, then holds the tube out to the young woman, who backs a step away and raises a hand in front of her. "No, thank you," she says. "I don't need—"

"If you don't look good, they think they can push you around," Clara says. "The shabbiest girls are always the ones who get arrested."

The young woman takes the tube, tentatively dabs on some color as if she's never done so before. It makes her lips look even thinner, so Clara suggests they pin up her hair to create some contrast. If she had a dress that would fit, she would offer that, too, but the young woman tops her by nearly a foot, and though she's slender, her shoulders are surprisingly broad. In any case, now that she has set her mind on a course of action, she is ready to get on with it, wants no further delay. She hustles the young woman out of the apartment and down the hall. On the way, she knocks on several doors, and into those that open, she calls out, "It's time."

"Grapes again?" one shaky voice responds.

"Lettuce."

She isn't the only old radical in the Home. Boyle Heights used to be filled with them. Outside of Brooklyn, it once boasted more Jewish socialists than any neighborhood in the country. Several of her fellow residents were also members of the ILGWU, veterans of the garment workers strike of 1933, and four of them now crowd with her and the young woman into the elevator. She introduces two but can't bring up the names of the others. The young woman is too shy or stunned to introduce herself. "If you want history, you should talk to them," Clara says. "They organized the Mexican dressmakers, when no one else cared."

Now the neighborhood is no longer Jewish, and there are plans to move the Home to Reseda, a bland, charmless place, she guesses, full of complacent capitalists. She'd prefer to stay here, even if the kosher delis have been replaced with bodegas and taco stands. It's still more familiar than the suburbs, an immigrant community like the Brighton Beach where she raised her children, or the Lower East Side where she lived when she was the age of this young woman whose neck is surprisingly elegant now that her limp hair doesn't cover it. Clara has taught herself a bit of Spanish, so she can chat with shop owners, as well as with orderlies and cafeteria staff at the Home, who were paid almost nothing when she arrived in 1967. Now, with her help, they have joined the service employees' union, and their wages have increased by nearly fifty percent.

A pair of those orderlies greet her as they emerge from the elevator. They dote on her, call her their hero, but she wants to tell them, too, that they should focus not on what she's done but on what they should do next. Their fellow workers across the city are still laboring under terrible conditions. Why stop now?

But mostly she doesn't want to engage with them at the moment because she can't remember if this one, handsome, with sad eyes and pocked cheeks, is named Jorge or José. It's embarrassing to have things slip away from her, so instead she keeps moving forward. If something hasn't happened yet, she can't forget it. On their way across the lobby, they pick up a couple of additional supporters, so that by the time they reach the main office, they are a crowd of eight, a tight fit for the anteroom, where the receptionist can't stop herself from snickering as she presses the buzzer and speaks into the intercom: "Mr. Freimauer, some residents are here to speak with you."

"It's Shavelson, isn't it," replies a crackling voice. Before the receptionist can answer, it tells her to send them in.

The inner office is even more cramped, an oversized desk taking up much of the space. Behind it sits Myron Freimauer, the Home's managing director. He is a squat, jowly man in his mid-fifties, with receding gray curls and a tired smile that reminds her of Joe, her first husband, who always said, "Do what you gotta do," whenever she told him she'd be out in the streets, that he shouldn't expect to see her when he came home from work. But she always made sure dinner waited for him and the children, something her daughter-in-law never seems to understand. "I'm too busy to cook, I've got important things to do," she says, and Clara's son and grandchildren are left to eat crackers and cheese and whatever else they can scrounge from mostly empty cupboards.

"Mrs. Shavelson," Freimauer says, and nods at the others, as if they are only here to watch the show. "Ladies. How can I help you today?"

"Lettuce," one of them begins, but before she can say more, Clara clears her throat, pulls the young woman forward, and speaks in the voice that has gone throaty with age but still comes out with a musical lilt.

"Mr. Freimauer. I'd like to introduce you," she says, and on the spot comes up with a name, as well as a plan for what she'll say. "This is Julia," she says, using the Spanish pronunciation. "Julia Morales, with the United Farm Workers."

The young woman stares at her, blinks, and Clara tilts her head to encourage her. She turns to Freimauer, spreads her thin red lips. "Hola," she whispers.

"No habla," Freimauer replies, squinting as if in pain.

Clara nudges her. "She speaks perfect English."

"I'm here because…" the young woman—Julia, Clara reminds herself, call her Julia—begins and then pauses. "You've heard of Cesar Chavez?"

"Shavelson—Mrs. Shavelson told me. We didn't have grapes for a year."

"We're grateful for your support," Julia says, shyly, and Clara tells herself to be patient, not to react, let the girl find her footing.

"You know how many of our residents complained? They live on grapes. Even the ones who supported the boycott, they'd forget from one day to the next and ask where their grapes were."

"And because of your sacrifice," Julia says, with more confidence now, "our vineyard workers have a good contract, for the first time ever. But our brothers and sisters in the lettuce fields—"

"And next after that? Tomatoes? Broccoli? Chicken? Am I going to feed my residents nothing but porridge?"

"It's about making the right choices," Julia goes on, her plain pale face gaining some color now, so that the lipstick no longer makes her look sickly. She seems almost spirited as she leans forward over Freimauer's desk, the front of her sack dress blooming toward the managing director, who edges his chair back a few inches. "Speak to your distributor. Make sure they buy only from companies with UFW contracts. That's all we're asking."

"Listen," Freimauer says, waving hands. "I'm no industrialist. Do you think I got into this business to make money? I'm here because I want to help people. Give them a nice comfortable place to live in their golden years. Why should I also have to save every lettuce-picker from Baja?"

"Because, you foolish man," Clara starts, the surge of rage making her dizzy. But this time it's Julia who holds up a hand and cuts her off.

"Your staff," she says. "I understand they are members of the service employees' union?"

Freimauer, holding his head in both hands, answers, "Thanks to my friends here."

"And if they hear that you're unwilling to support their brothers and sisters in the fields, do you think they might reconsider their contract?"

"And maybe my family will reconsider its donation," says the smallest of the old women, whose son, Clara now recalls, works as a lawyer for movie people.

"Lettuce," Freimauer says. "Tomatoes, potatoes, corn. What do I care? I'll talk to the chef. He's the one who does all the ordering."

"If you want us to talk to him," Clara says. Her rage has dissipated, but the lightheadedness remains. She leans one leg against the desk and uses the cane to prop herself upright, hoping no one will see.

"I'll just let him know you'll come see him if he doesn't go along with it," Freimauer says. "When he hears that, he'll fall in line."

"You might also talk to your local supermarket," Julia says.

"My wife does the shopping," Freimauer says.

"Then talk to her."

"She's the only person who scares me more than Shavelson."

The dizziness is now accompanied by a flash of heat, and Clara knows she has to sit down. She backs up a step, and thinking there's a chair behind her, drops heavily to the floor. Then there's a flurry of activity above her, the old women making clucking noises, Julia waving a hand in front of her face, Freimauer calling into the intercom for the receptionist to send a nurse.

"I just need a little air," she says, but her voice comes out scratchy, and what she really wants is some water, some space to breathe, some time to read and maybe to sleep. She closes her eyes and lies back, and then feels herself lifted by the feet and shoulders, laid on a soft surface, and wheeled out of the office. It's humiliating, having people do these things for her, she who has taken care of herself, two husbands, and four children, not to mention all of the garment workers and housewives she organized. When they reach the lobby, she feels the blast of air conditioning on her scalp and remembers her hat, left behind on Freimauer's floor. And though she's still dizzy, she opens her eyes to ask someone to retrieve it. Above her, the young woman, her Julia, strides along beside her, hair falling out of its pins. "I didn't help with your research," Clara says.

"Not quite how I expected."

She can't see the nurse at the end of the gurney, wheeling her toward the infirmary. Instead she focuses on Julia's dark pursed lips and worried eyes. "You did well," she says. "No more lettuce."

"If I turn traitor to the cause," Julia says, with an eager smile, "may this hand wither from the arm I now raise."

Clara closes her eyes again. She doesn't see the arm Julia raises, doesn't want to see. But it's too late not to hear her repeat the ridiculous pledge Clara made so impulsively all those years ago and which she has wished to take back more times than she can count. Because the truth is, as soon as she released the words, she believed, with superstitious fervor, that to speak such a thing out loud made it binding forever. If she stopped, what punishment would descend on her? What harm to her family? It's fear as much as anything that has kept her going for so long, pushing constantly, never allowing herself to pause. Because if she slows for a moment, she has always been certain, her life will fall apart. And now she has encouraged Julia to suffer the same fate.

"Remember to pace yourself," she says, her throat dry, voice cracked.

"Rest now," Julia says, and Clara feels a smooth hand take hers, now wrinkled and arthritic, unable to lift a needle or make a single stitch.

Driftwood

It's just past dawn on a Tuesday morning in early spring. Dim light filters through heavy clouds above hills to the east. The tide is high in the bay, a light breeze rippling its surface. A pair of harbor seals slip into the water near the inlet, beyond which languid waves lash the sand. Closer to the highway bridge, on the tallest of a trio of volcanic rock stacks, the figure of a woman comes clear as the darkness fades. She sits with knees to chest, hair covering her face, one arm looped around the trunk of a stunted Sitka spruce. If not for the fleece jacket with a waterproof shell, she might be taken for some mythical creature risen out of the sea, one who'd sprout a tail were she to dive back under the surface.

But she is human, cold and tired. She has been on the rock for nearly seven hours. She pulls the jacket tighter but can't stop shivering. Her face feels numb. She no longer knows whether to laugh or cry. She does both and then stops herself to conserve her strength. The seals pass below without glancing up at her.

The woman's name is Andrea Schaffner. Friends and family call her Andi. She is thirty-five years old, straight, unmarried, and childless. For the past year and a half she has carried on an affair with a married co-worker—her direct supervisor—at a Portland nonprofit whose mission is to aid struggling rural communities with economic development, especially those suffering from the loss of logging and fishing industries. Her lover, James, is Program Director, and she is Program Manager. Though his salary is ten thousand dollars a year higher than hers, they work as a team—as equals, she believes—

meeting with mayors and city councils and chambers of commerce to design recovery plans and training programs and otherwise help locals attract business, build up tourism, establish sustainable forestry and fishery practices. They travel to beach and mountain towns all over the Pacific Northwest, always booking two motel rooms but using only one.

From the rock, she can see the motel they checked into last night, just a few hundred yards across the bay, a squat, three-story building with rusty balconies that leave stains whenever rain drips from them onto the stucco below. Their room is on the second floor, near a stairwell, but from this angle she can't be sure which one it is. The lights are off in all of them. She can picture it as she left it, James in bed, naked and snoring, her overnight bag unzipped but not unpacked, her cell charging on the desk. Of all the stupid mistakes she's made over the past day—or over the past two years, the past thirty-five—not carrying her phone is the one for which she'll never forgive herself. That, and leaving her sandals behind a driftwood log on the beach so she could feel the sand between her toes.

The breeze eases, shifts direction. She catches the smell of wood smoke and thinks that maybe people are beginning to wake, early risers heading to work, though she knows there is little work in Lincoln City, or anywhere else on the coast. Ninety percent of the houses here are vacation rentals, and the people who clean them can't afford to live nearby; instead they drive over the Coast Range from Salem, Albany, the shabby outlying suburbs of Portland. Over the regular beat of waves beyond Salishan Spit, she hears wings flapping against water. Geese or gulls, perhaps pelicans.

And then comes the sound of an engine, a loud one, not at all like the hybrid in James's Prius. For the first time in more than an hour, she sees headlights in the distance, heading north around the bay. She stands with difficulty, leaning against the little spruce's trunk, keeping most of her weight on one foot, and gives a big wave. Please see me, she thinks, and immediately recognizes the irony, given how often over the past year and a half she has feared exposure, prayed to stay hidden. She can see the truck now, an eighteen-wheeler hauling an unmarked container. Blankets, she thinks, an entire truck full of thick down comforters. She flings her arms wildly, hops up and down on one foot, nearly loses her balance. The headlights' beams pass a few yards to the west of her stack, and then the truck rounds the curve onto the bridge. It passes the end of the bay without braking, changes gear, and heads uphill into town. Andi sits and shivers.

ભ

She can't believe what she's gotten herself into, but then again, the facts of her life continually astonish her. How can she be a person who regularly sleeps with someone else's spouse, the father of two pre-teen girls? Even while in bed with James, his hands gripping her backside, or her legs straddling his hips, she can't quite square her actions with the image she carries of herself, as someone who does good in the world, who puts others' needs ahead of her own. Last night she said as much to James, not for the first time, and again he agreed: it was crazy, they were completely out of their minds, they couldn't keep on this way indefinitely. But of course the craziness was exactly what turned them both on, and in minutes they went from holding their heads in their hands to holding each other around the waist, pelvis to pelvis.

For James, sex was enough to quell any doubts, at least until their next trip together, two weeks away. But after he grunted, kissed her, and fell promptly asleep, Andi lay listening to his breath and the waves and the rattling heater, once more telling herself this couldn't really be her life, even if she had no other to replace it. An hour passed, and when she knew she wouldn't drift off, she dressed and slipped outside, where a rare break in the clouds revealed a bright moon, the tide far out, the inner bay floor uncovered all the way to the opposite bank. She'd never seen the stacks exposed to their base. On her way toward them, she spotted bubbles in the sand, and with a reflex that surprised her, she dropped to her knees and dug with both hands until she came up with a clam. A small one, with brownish stripes and a purple tip, not like the big razor clams she and James had recently eaten in Vancouver, during a weekend conference they hardly attended. Still, pocketing it gave her a feeling of accomplishment, and she dug up more as she crossed the silty flats, thick with weeds, the sand sucking at her feet with every step.

Her jacket pockets were heavy with shells by the time she reached the stacks. In the morning, she'd build a fire on the beach and steam them for breakfast, surprise James with them just as he was waking up. It would be their farewell meal, she decided, enjoying the drama of such a thought and the way it immediately choked her up. They'd eat and make love one last time, and then it would be over. She'd never steamed clams before, not even on a stove, and didn't know how to do it on open flames. But it was time to learn new things, time to become the person she thought she should be rather than the one who stumbled into careers and love affairs as if she had no control over where her feet carried her. She could always look up directions on her phone when she got back to the room.

Before returning, however, she'd climb the stack, sit for a few minutes looking at the stars, which were far more distinct here than in Portland, even with the moon still high above the horizon. It was the right place to feel lonely and sorry for herself and hopeful about the future, except on the way up she sliced the ball of her foot on a barnacle. It bled, not profusely but steadily, and she lay on her back with her foot in the air, waiting for it to clot. When it finally did, the tide had come back in. The water was already up to her knees by the time she limped down the rock, and it was freezing. The bank was several hundred yards away, and by the time she reached it, she'd be mostly submerged. How long did it take for hypothermia to set in? Her foot throbbed. She'd probably need stitches. A weak swimmer at the best of times, she didn't know if she could kick hard enough to keep invisible currents from yanking her out to sea.

Back atop the rock, she waited for James to wake and realize she was gone, to come looking for her, though only part of her believed he would. He always slept hard after emptying himself into her and rolling to his back, rarely shifting his position all night. Often he didn't hear the alarm in the morning and stirred only when she tickled his feet. And he usually woke cranky, yawning and rubbing eyes, already distracted by thoughts of work or the drive home, uninterested in her affection. What was she doing with this forty-seven-year-old boy, selfish and inconsiderate, with graying chest hair and the beginning of a paunch? What did it matter that his smell made her salivate?

If he didn't come looking for her, she assured herself, it was definitely over between them. But if he did, that was another matter. She imagined it, his swimming through the frigid water to save her, then cooking the clams while she warmed in a bath he'd drawn. He might tell her how precious she was to him, that she meant more to him than anyone else in the world—including his daughters—and if she wanted, he would leave his wife for her. And then she would say, as she had before, that of course he should stay with his family, at least until the girls were in high school and didn't care what he did, that she was a big enough person to recognize what priorities mattered most, and who said she wanted a full-time relationship anyway?

Yes, if he saved her, it would be okay to put off any decisions about parting until some other time.

CR

Now, as mist thickens into drizzle, she no longer cares who rescues her. She no longer cares how embarrassing it will be to have someone discover her here. But a dog? Yes, somehow, despite the cold and discomfort, she's still capable of being insulted, she who has only ever had cats, including a calico who currently punishes her for her frequent trips by pissing in a corner of her office closet. Yet it's a lanky black mutt that spots her, flapping a long pink tongue. It yaps at her from the beach, runs into the shallows and back out, shaking freezing water from its fur.

And then she feels more shame than relief when a man follows, materializing out of the gloom. His legs are thin but his top half is surprisingly broad and oddly shaped, a huge hump on his back. It takes her a moment to realize it must be a backpack beneath a poncho, but before she does, she thinks of an old crone from storybooks, the kind who might help her but only for a price. Her first instinct is to hide. She huddles against the bent trunk of the wind-battered spruce, hopes she looks like a bundle of roots silhouetted against the brightening clouds. But the dog keeps barking, splashing now into the bay, swimming a few yards in her direction, and then turning and swimming back. Before the man reaches the water's edge, he raises his head, pulls back the hood. She can't see features, only the outline of a gaunt face topped with wispy hair blown back by the breeze. But the voice comes to her clearly, throaty and loud.

"The accommodations are cheap," it says, "but not much in the way of comfort."

"The heater's broken," she calls back. The shivering makes her voice tremble, but otherwise she tries to sound stoic. "And no one answers at the front desk."

"Next time you might want to book somewhere with amenities. Like a roof."

"Good idea," she says, and wonders how long he plans to go on this way. The dog has calmed now, sitting beside his leg, glancing up at him and then back toward her. "Maybe walls, too."

"Do you see any driftwood up there?" he asks, and now she begins to question whether he was joking after all. Does he believe she chose to stay here all night?

"Driftwood?"

"Small pieces. Size of your foot's ideal."

"I can look."

"Best time to find them. Right when the water drops."

"Do you happen to know when it's due to go all the way out again?"

"Low point's around eleven," he says, "but it'll still be about four feet then. Won't be dry again until tonight."

"Maybe you could call somebody then? Police, I guess?"

"They'll take longer than the tide. I can get hold of a boat. Just take a few minutes."

"I'm not going anywhere," she says.

"Meantime, look around for small bits," he calls. "Size of your foot down to size of your hand. Nothing too fresh. Old and beat-to-hell is good."

Without another word, he turns and starts back the way he came, toward the old wooden pier sticking partway into the water before petering out in a staggered grid of rotten pillars, and beyond it the dunes covered in grass and salal. She almost calls him back. Even more important than being taken off this rock is not being left alone on it again; she'd rather have him there talking to her for the rest of the day than spend another moment with nothing but her thoughts and the sound of her chattering teeth. But without seeming to hasten, he's moving quickly away. The dog barks at her once more and then races after him. Past them, she can see the waves clearly now, white crests forming out of the fog and then spewing up spray to become part of it again. On the spit, the harbor seals, dozens of them, huddle together, lump against lump against lump. The droplets coming through the spruce are larger now, loud against her hood. The sound scares her, makes her feel even more isolated, and before the man and dog reach the pier, she calls out to them, "Please hurry!"

If they hear, they give no sign.

CR

Then she's on her own again. A few lights have come on in the motel, on the first floor, on the third, but not on the second. One of the dark rooms is the one she booked, that the agency is paying for, but in which she hasn't set foot. How different the job would be if she were to sleep on her own every night, get up and meet with local officials, and not feel a secret tingling between her legs. Would she care at all about the mild successes they had, bringing small investments to towns that would never thrive again, only limping forward as the world continued to leave them behind?

The truth is, she's never cared much about the plight of out-of-work loggers or fishermen—like the old man with the dog, maybe—except in a distant, abstract way, like caring about people with prostate cancer. Unlike James, who came from a dying rural community in the Midwest, studied political philosophy as an undergraduate, and earned a master's in policy and planning, Andi didn't arrive here as a result of passion. She grew up in an affluent Boston suburb, majored in European history, and then worked for a series of nonprofits, some arts-related, others social service, sometimes doing publicity, sometimes program management. As long as the organization's mission was generally to make a positive impact on the world, she felt reasonably satisfied at the end of the day, though the work was largely tedious, and she never felt particularly tied to any position. She followed a boyfriend to Chicago, and then another to Seattle. She'd come to Portland to pursue an online flirtation that never bloomed into a relationship. She took the job because it was the first one that offered her health benefits.

On the phone with her parents, who don't understand why she has to live so far away, she talks about the importance of helping workers whose livelihoods have dried up. They built the country, she says, made it what it is, and shouldn't be abandoned just because those who control the wealth have moved it elsewhere. But with James she never talks about the people they serve, except in practical terms: whether they'll sign on to agreements to manage their forests and fisheries in a manner that won't deplete them for good; whether they'll provide useful data she and James can report on upcoming grant applications; whether their stories are compelling enough to appear on press releases and promotional pamphlets.

The people themselves are irritants, distractions from the pleasure they derive only when they are alone. Their daytime meetings she has come to think of as punishment they must suffer in order to reward themselves when they are finally free in the evening. Whether these communities recover or collapse is all the same to her, so long as she has a reason to keep driving to mountains and beaches and tearing off her clothes in darkened motel rooms. If she ends things with James, the job will lose all meaning for her. She might as well take a corporate position that will further exploit and undermine these communities and double—or triple—her salary.

More lights are coming on in the motel, some on the second floor. She's now quite sure that the fourth one from the beach side is James's, that he has woken and found her gone, has checked the bathroom and perhaps called her cell phone only to discover it on the laminate desk. And then what? Does he call her room, the one she's never entered? Or the front desk, asking if the clerk has seen her, if she's left a message? Does he check to make sure the car is still in the parking lot? Maybe he guesses she's gone out for coffee, that she'll surprise him with pastries, believing he deserves it. At what point will he begin to worry? She wants to imagine the moment when he thinks she has really decided to leave him, when he'll suffer an exquisite pain and longing for what they've shared, and even more, the moment when she returns and he's so relieved he knows he'll never take their time together for granted.

Any second, she thinks, he might step onto the balcony and see her, and then the brief hold loss has on him will loosen. So she ducks behind the spruce and hopes to prolong his worry for as long as possible, and thus to seal herself in his heart for good. Because of course the real reason she has considered ending the affair isn't because she has come to believe what they are doing is crazy—she knows it is, has known all along—but because she anticipates that James will eventually come to his senses and decide he can live without her.

ℭ

That's when she hears the boat engine, a soft stuttering above the rain. The fog has grown denser, and she can't see anything yet, can't tell what direction it's coming from. But she remembers she is supposed to look for driftwood and does so while she waits. There's nothing on top of the stack, though of course the tide hasn't been this high, so she lowers herself carefully over the side and begins to climb down. She watches out for barnacles now, but her foot slips on a weedy spot, and she has to grab hard with her numb fingertips to keep from sliding. The clams in her pockets bounce against her hips. The engine grows louder, but still no sign of a boat. A couple of feet above the waterline she does find a silvered stick, as thick around as her wrist and a little longer than her forearm. She hugs it to herself, crouches, and thinks the boat isn't coming for her after all. Just then the dog yelps, directly below her, followed by the gravelly voice: "Check-out time."

"Kind of early, isn't it?"

"You get what you pay for."

The dog barks continuously as she descends the rest of the way, and only when she's right above it can she make out the aluminum boat with a small outboard motor, the lanky figure with a hump beneath his poncho, his hood up again so she can't see his face. He makes no move to help her down, just stays seated, with a hand on the tiller. The look of him calls up another image from a childhood storybook, of Charon and the river Styx, which in turn makes her think of the band Styx, her older sister's favorite when they were growing up. Every night through her bedroom wall she'd listen to ballads that went on far too long, growing increasingly frenetic but also oddly seductive: *Come sail away, come sail away, come sail away with me!*

She lowers herself as far as she can and drops the last few inches into the hull. The boat wobbles. Her cut foot hits cold metal, a shriek of pain rises up her leg, and she clamps her teeth to keep from crying out. She falls onto the seat, and the dog barks in her face, licks her hands. The boat eases backward, away from the stack, before turning and heading slowly toward shore. Over the dog's head, she finally catches a glimpse of the man's face—not quite as skeletal as Charon, but gaunt and weathered, eyes set deeply beneath wild eyebrows. It's the kind of face she's used to seeing at open community meetings, off in the corner, skeptical and unmoved by her work on his behalf. She passes him the stick of driftwood. He holds it up with his free hand, still steering through the fog with the other. The light is diffuse all around them, but he shifts position as if he can get a better view by angling closer to the sun. He squints, turns the stick end over end. Then he tosses it over the side of the boat. "Needs a couple more decades," he says, sounding not disappointed so much as confirmed in his low expectations.

She wants to show her appreciation, feels he should be compensated for his effort, but her wallet is on the desk along with her phone. All she has in her pockets are the key to James's room and the clams, so she pulls out the latter and holds them out in both hands. There are nine of them in total, hardly enough for an appetizer. The dog sniffs them and looks to its owner. "Not sure what the exchange rate is," she says, "but I think this is more than I paid for the ride out."

This time he doesn't take up the banter. Instead, he peers intently at her hands, the creases on his forehead unfolding as his brows lower. "You didn't eat any, did you?"

"I usually wait until after dawn for breakfast."

"Don't you know about the ban?"

"Ban?"

"All of Oregon. Southwest Washington, too. No clams. Blue-green algae."

She doesn't understand what he's saying but answers anyway, "I hadn't heard."

"It's dangerous," he says. "Causes brain damage. Permanent."

The thought of it, that she might have poisoned James rather than indulged him, horrifies her but also makes her laugh. An idiot's version of a suicide pact: Juliet too stupid to know she shouldn't eat clams or serve them to her forbidden lover. Now it's her turn to toss them over the side. Nine little splashes she can't hear over the sputtering engine, each shell visible for the first few inches beneath the water and then gone.

Sooner than she expects, the boat skids into the soft sand on the north shore of the bay, right in front of her motel, but now she's reluctant to get out. She wants to say something to explain herself but doesn't know what. The light in the room she believes is James's is still on, but the curtain is also still drawn. "I'm actually staying there," she says, gesturing at the rust-stained stucco. "But those accommodations aren't much better."

"Crappy bed?"

"More the company. Complicated." And then, as if to justify being here at all—or else to justify her very existence—she tells him about her job, what she's trying to do to make the place vibrant again for people like him, not just wealthy Californians with second homes.

"People like me?"

"You know, whose livelihoods—" She pauses, shrugs, juts her chin toward the inlet, then in the direction of the single hillside visible through the fog, barely recovering from a decade-old clearcut. "Fishermen, loggers, whose industries—"

"I'm a sculptor," he says, and shifts the backpack from beneath the poncho so he can open the zipper. He pulls out a piece of driftwood the size of his hand, pronged and gnarled, worm-eaten. "This is what

I'm after. Got to get out just when the tide starts back to beat the competition."

"Sculptures? Out of these?"

He hands her a card. It has the name of a gallery on it, and beneath, an image she has to look at carefully before she understands what she's seeing. A chunk of driftwood on a metal stand, a face carved into one end—a woman's face, sultry and blissful, surrounded by waves of silvered hair. It's so hideous and absurd she instantly wants to own it.

"When I moved here in '73," he says, "it was all hippies this end of town. Great place to raise the kids. Music every night. You could live on nothing."

She pockets the card and thanks him, says she's sorry to have taken him away from his hunt. The dog yaps when she gets out of the boat, jumps after her, tears up the beach before she can grab its collar.

"Don't worry about her. She knows where to go. I better get this back before the owner notices it's missing." He doesn't look at her as he backs the boat away. "You find any good pieces, bring them by the gallery."

She listens to the boat's motor even after she can no longer see it. The dog's also out of view, and the beach is once again empty and still. She searches for her sandals behind all the nearby logs but can't find them. After a few minutes she gives up and limps to the motel.

ॐ

She was wrong about James's room. It's the fifth from the end, and its lights are still off when she finally makes her way back inside. James is still asleep on the sagging mattress, rolled onto his side now, with his back to the spot where she should have been. The alarms on the clock and his phone are sounding—the former set to a jazz radio station, the latter electronic birdsong—but he snores through both. Seven and a half hours, and he hasn't known she was gone, hasn't suspected anything might be wrong. She strips out of her jacket and wet jeans, out of sweater, tee-shirt, and underwear, and slides under the blanket, shivering. If only she can get warm, she'll fall asleep, too, despite the music and chattering birds, but the cold is so deep in her she thinks it will take hours to dissipate. In the meantime, she studies the moles on James's back, most light brown, a few pink, one alarmingly dark and misshapen.

Is there something about this stretch of pale skin that makes it matter so much to her? Are its qualities particularly suited to excite or comfort her? Or is it just what happened to fall into her path? She's sure she would tire of this back if she had to see it every day, or if its owner's beard trimmings clogged her sink, his dirty clothes filled her laundry basket. It's strange to think that she is actually content with her tentative existence, her small rented apartment, her disgruntled cat, her borrowed lover, that she'd do anything to hang onto these things. Her foot aches, but she will hide the cut from James, pretend she has been with him all night, that nothing has shaken her faith in him or their ridiculous affair. The best thing to do is to hold perfectly still, listen to the waves crashing in her mind, since she can't hear them over the sound of alarms and snoring. And she is beginning to warm after all, her eyes are beginning to close, she will stay right where she is all morning, or all week, or for as long as the tides move in and out of the bay.

But then James's snore chokes off into a loud snort, and he stirs. That cranky groan, the beleaguered yawn and shake of his head. He pushes onto an elbow and looks at the clock before turning to her. "You let us sleep in," he says, and shuts off both alarms. "We've got to be downtown in twenty minutes." He slides out of bed, and she watches his lovely hairless buttocks move across the room and disappear behind the bathroom door. There won't be time for both of them to shower. She wants to join him under the hot stream but knows he doesn't like to see her naked if they won't have time for sex; it distracts him too much, gets in the way of practical thoughts. So she stays where she is until the shower turns off. She should wash her cut foot, keep it from getting infected, but there's no time for that, either. She gets out of bed, dresses in her work outfit—slacks, blouse, flats—fixes her hair in the mirror over the desk, packs her bag, and is ready to go by the time he comes out, wrapped in a towel, still scowling.

"If neither of us can wake up, we'll have to jack the volume."

"Next time," she says, and opens the curtain so she can look out at the rock where she spent the night, twice pulling down her pants to pee off the side. To her surprise, though, their balcony doesn't face the bay, only the parking lot, the blue bubble of James's Prius a short drop below.

"I'll change it back to the buzzer instead of birds."

He says it without hesitation or doubt, without any question that there will be a next time. In two weeks they'll drive to the high desert, will lie together on another motel bed beneath a greasy headboard. And then she'll watch him pull on his boxer shorts as she does now, watch him button his shirt over the broad chest and soft belly, watch him stuff the ends into his chinos and cinch the belt. Until then, she needs nothing else. Or almost nothing. "You should go to the dermatologist," she says. "There's a dark mole on your back. It looks angry."

"I know," he says. "Beth told me."

"Oh. Good. I'm glad she's paying attention."

"I've got an appointment next week."

"On our way home," she says, surprised at the catch in her voice, "there's a gallery I want to check out."

"I've got to take the girls to jujitsu at four."

"It won't take long."

His expression is tight, pinched, full of aggravation, but also certain of her devotion. "Can we just do our job and worry about other things later?"

"I'll lead the meeting today," she says, trying to match his confidence, and then waits until he has passed through the door to shuffle behind him, favoring her wounded foot. She's on the verge of a decision, she's sure of it. She just needs some sleep, and then she'll be ready to take firm hold of her life. For now, she limps to the stairs. The smell of the ocean ought to be invigorating, but she wishes it didn't always come with a hint of something dead and rotting on the beach. Beyond the parking lot, fog obscures everything.

A Theory of Harmony

1.

He misses the Vienna of his youth, when music was everywhere, and all of it excited him. Or else he simply misses youth, and the person he was when he knew nothing other than what he could learn by listening. As a boy of twelve, thirteen, he wandered the city for hours. With friends from Leopoldstadt—known also as Mazzensinsel, or Matzo Island—he would stand in the Prater's main alley, behind a dividing hedge that separated them from the bandstand of the Erste Kaffeehaus, where a small orchestra played military songs and snippets from Wagner. None had ever been to a real concert. They were the sons of craftsmen, shopkeepers, office clerks, and their families had no extra money for frivolities. Some had received lessons in violin or piano, playing on instruments handed down by a grandfather or great-uncle. But most, like Erwin Lemberg—now a composer of some small renown—were entirely self-taught. He didn't yet know the words "counterpoint" or "polyphony." He listened carefully to the interplay of violin and viola and imitated what he heard. Later, when he worked as a junior teller for a private bank, he scraped together three guldens for a cello, which he played with the same fingering as for the violin, not knowing any better. There was such freedom in knowing nothing, in simply creating, without concern for innovation or success.

If it weren't for his friend Heinrich Krantz, he might have remained ignorant for longer. Krantz, a virtuoso who now performs with the best orchestras in Austria, heard him playing with a quartet in the Aurgarten and showed him the correct fingering for the cello. Later, he introduced him to the music of Brahms, as well as to his younger sister Lottie, whom Lemberg married after she became pregnant. He would have found Brahms on his own, eventually, and maybe he would have married on his own, too—though he put off doing so until he was past thirty—but he likes to blame Krantz for making him grow up too fast. His family and his brother-in-law's both have flats in the same house on Liechtensteinstrasse, across the canal from the Leopoldstadt of his childhood. Instead of Jewish peddlers, he is surrounded by artists, poets, philosophers. He and Krantz together have established the Society for New Music and have convinced Mahler himself to conduct their concerts. They spend hours discussing fresh directions in composition, as well as the difficulty of shedding old approaches, especially in a city of philistines who treat any hint of change—especially coming from a Jew—with suspicion and judgment followed by swift dismissal.

The year is 1908. Lemberg is thirty-nine years old but looks older, already bald except for a fringe of dark hair ringing the back of his head. His father, the proprietor of a shoe shop, had a full head of thick hair until his early death, and a dense mustache, too, twirled at the ends like the Archduke's. But Lemberg has inherited his mother's features and those of her Bohemian relations. Large downturned nose, bulbous forehead and narrow chin, enormous ears. He hopes his appearance makes him look distinguished enough to secure a position at the Imperial and Royal Academy of Music, though as yet he has had no success. He earns a living by teaching private pupils, the more talented of whom often struggle to pay. Lottie, not yet thirty, would like a larger flat and one not so near her brother, who, she often complains, takes too much of her husband's time. Lemberg, too, would like more space, especially if it would mean a room to work far away from the cries of his children, who find new ways to distract him every day. Grete is six, sly like her mother though easier to laugh. Klaus, four, weeps when he doesn't get what he wants and grumbles for hours afterward. Lemberg adores them both.

And yet he wants them to go silent when he's working in the small windowless room behind the kitchen, what was once a pantry now turned into his study. How can he hear the music in his head when Grete calls out, Papa, will you read another story? and Klaus asks if he can have a strawberry, though it is still late winter, and none will be ripe for months?

Even more distracting, though, is all the music he has ever heard, all the harmonies of Wagner and Brahms and Mahler that crowd his mind and make it so difficult to create something no one has heard before. He is currently at work on two compositions, one a cycle of songs pairing the mystical poems of Yehuda Halevi with soprano and piano, the second a string quartet with which he has struggled for months. In the latter he is attempting to loosen the hold of keys on harmonic progression, allow for asymmetry, and achieve new freedom in melodic structure and rhythm. He believes in these choices, knows that they are the appropriate development for a music that for too long has been bound by convention. Dissonance need not always find balance in the comfort of tonality, and yet every time he tries to write the third and fourth movement, he finds conventions reasserting themselves, as insistently as his daughter's sweet, sly voice outside the door of his study: Papa? Won't you come out and tell me if I have spelled my name correctly?

ça

Beyond its technical challenges, what makes the quartet especially difficult is his desire to convey in it what he has been unable to express in words. Namely, the combination of ecstasy and bafflement and frustration he has experienced in love, which he likens to his religious experience, filling him at times with reverence, at other times with rage. Seven years ago, he could hardly believe that Lottie responded in any way to his smile, and then to his words of affection—and in fact responded by giving herself to him without restraint, with an eagerness that suggested she'd been waiting to do so all her life. She was just twenty-two then, red-cheeked and mischievous, always humming out loud when people were trying to talk about serious matters. Almost as soon as her brother introduced Lemberg, she began to call him Lemmy, to joke about his thinning hair and threadbare suits, and when it was clear to everyone that he was smitten, to taunt him with casual musings about the various men she might one day marry.

He was afraid of disappointing her then and tried hard to please her: bringing gifts and flowers, composing solo pieces he knew she would enjoy, agreeing to convert so they could be married in the Lutheran church of her family. Now he is tired of disappointing her so often and also tired of trying. She wishes he were more successful, but she also wishes he wouldn't work so many hours, wouldn't take on so many students, wouldn't spend so much time talking with her brother. Your children need you, she says, but when he plays with Grete and Klaus, she scolds him for being idle and useless when they have hardly enough to eat. Even when he makes an effort to spend time in the evening talking with her, telling Krantz he is not available to listen to him practice and provide critique, she tells him she is too busy for his chatter, that he should go bother someone else.

Nothing he does pleases her now, he understands that and has made peace with it, or has tried to. And yet some nights she turns to him in bed with a hunger that astonishes him, muttering expressions of desire, even love, that he cannot reconcile with his understanding of her during daylight. And the touch of her body has never once failed to stir him, leaving him both delighted and forlorn.

And so he has come to think of love as being like the unpredictable hand of God. Worship no one but Me, and I will torment you at My whim. This is what all the music he has ever heard has so far failed to convey, and he has glimpsed it only in the poems of Halevi, which he reads every night Lottie graces him with her caresses, rising after she has fallen asleep and retreating to his study, the words of the long-dead mystic the only thing to provide him any solace:

I wander from you—and die alive;
the closer I cling—I live to die.
How to approach I still don't know,
nor on what words I might rely.
Instruct me, Lord: advise and guide me.
Free me from my prison of lies.

He finds sleep only late, sitting up in his chair, and in the morning Lottie shakes him awake, reproaching him for his laziness. There is no sign of last night's passion in her voice, no sign that she has found any satisfaction in his arms, only irritation and shortcomings. And yet he still feels her breasts against him, her thighs pressing around his waist; he is still full of longing for what he had and does not know if he will ever have again. He dresses, cleans himself, kisses the children, and goes to work. The music should be as double-minded as he is, as contradictory and changeable as love, as mysterious as God's plan. And yet harmony keeps imposing itself, oversimplifying and providing too much structure. He does not know if it can ever do otherwise.

ॐ

In early February, he sets the quartet aside. The young painter appears in the middle of March. As with so many things, he owes the introduction to Krantz, who knows everyone. It was Krantz who first brought him to Mahler's parlor, where he inadvertently insulted the great man, expressing impatience with the slow pace of progress, with the dullness of audiences who wanted to hear only what made them comfortable. I deliver too much comfort? Mahler asked, smiling awkwardly, while Krantz, in his periphery, put a hand over his eyes and shook his head. Is that what you're saying? Lemberg expected never to be invited back, but Mahler turned out to have a forgiving nature, as well as a soft spot for fellow Jews. Even Lemberg's irascibility didn't put him off for long.

The painter approached Krantz after one of his concerts. He was interested in musicians' faces, he said, wanted to make portraits of all the best performers in Vienna. Krantz agreed to look at the young man's canvases and came away impressed. And then insisted Lemberg would be ideal for a sitting. Why me? Lemberg asked. Because the sunlight reflects so brightly from your scalp, Krantz answered.

The painter's name is Josef Huber. He is only twenty-five, but his work is luminous and strange, suggesting the merest edge of control. He works primarily in portraiture, and the faces of his subjects are expressive without being exacting, reminiscent of El Greco. The painter himself looks as if he might have stepped out of an El Greco canvas, with his long neck and arms, his sunken cheeks and wisp of a mustache. He, like Lemberg, is largely self-taught—he left the Academy after rejecting the approaches of both classicists and the Vienna Secession—but unlike the composer he has only just begun to grasp the nuances of technique and the theories that guide them, has only scratched the surface of knowledge which will both enhance and complicate his talent. At this stage, he works purely by instinct, and as such his paintings are full of life, if not yet fully realized.

Huber himself is quietly charming and humble, though also with a brooding quality Lemberg admires. He does not associate with other painters on principle, he says, though what that principle is he cannot articulate. Musicians, on the other hand, he can more easily abide, because they have no valid opinion about his work. His opinion about theirs, however, he offers freely: he appreciates what modern composers are trying to accomplish, he says, but after Bach, no music is really worth listening to. Still, he seems to enjoy sitting silently to the side as Krantz and Lemberg argue about harmony and the value of an audience's pleasure.

Pleasure is best left to the bedroom, Lemberg says.

How dare you speak about my sister that way, Krantz says, shaking a fist with delight.

Huber titters like a child. Lottie, in the next room with Grete and Klaus, does not respond. Perhaps she hasn't heard. Lemberg decides he prefers not to know what she'd say if she has.

2.

Huber paints two portraits of him. Neither is as appealing as those he saw in the painter's studio, both making him look squat and miserable, his suit too tight, his eyes bulging. The sittings fill him with impatience, and after the second, he tells Huber he must find another subject, one who has more time to squander. Paint Lottie, he says, and to his surprise, Huber agrees. His interest in musicians' faces has faded, he says. Women's are more interesting. He poses Lottie in the parlor of the Liechtensteinstrasse flat, and for hours the children watch in amazement as Huber's quick, stabbing strokes bring their mother to life on the canvas before their eyes.

Suddenly Huber is with them all the time, as if he has become another member of the family. He sketches the children, he sketches Krantz's wife Mathilde, he sketches Lottie in every room of the flat, as well as in several different spots in the Stadpark. Lemberg likes having the young man around, in part because his youthfulness burnishes everything around him. Lottie no longer seems concerned about their finances or the future. She laughs more often, pays closer attention to her hair and the drape of her dress on days when she knows Huber will pose her. In the portraits she looks matronly and dignified, though less attractive, Lemberg thinks, than she appears in the flesh.

But even more than the cheer Huber brings, what Lemberg appreciates is the distraction. The young man keeps Lottie and the children busy for hours, not only with their portraits but visits to his studio and outings to the Prater and the Natural History Museum. The Kunsthistoriches Museum he refuses to enter: he won't have his vision corrupted by the work of other painters, he says, especially not those celebrated by the art establishment, which supports only mediocrity. He is determined to remain untainted, he says, even if it means toiling permanently in obscurity.

Lemberg, meanwhile, is able to work in peace, without interruption or guilt, and for the first time in months makes significant progress on his song-cycle. With spring comes the chatter of birds and new buoyancy, and he finds himself allowing surprising turns to enter his melodies. When harmony follows, he does not resist.

જી

In April, Huber moves into a new studio, just a few houses down the street from the Lembergs' flat. It's on the top floor of a once-grand house now dusty and squalid compared to the newly built structures on either side. The attic space has slanted ceilings and windows that rattle when the wind blows. But it is large enough for Huber to store his canvases, some of which are as tall as he. Other than his easel and brushes, he has only a bed, a chest, a drafting table. He makes little money from his paintings, if any. But he never wants for supplies, and his clothing, if plain, is well made. He never speaks of his parents, except to say that they do not approve of his life. But it occurs to Lemberg now that they must provide for him all the same. He may be self-taught but not because he lacked resources, as Lemberg did. He hides his comforts well.

But having him live nearby is a boon for everyone. Huber is good with the children, a playmate and confidante, and he helps Lottie carry items home from the market and up the steep stairs to the flat. He brings them all to the studio with him to work on a new portrait of Lottie, this one even less flattering, Lemberg thinks, than the previous.

But she seems pleased with it and enjoys the rest she gets while sitting in a soft chair and gazing at one of the studio's windows, which by mid-morning is too fogged to see through. With his family out of the flat, Lemberg works hard on his compositions and spends extra time with his most talented students, even when they can't afford to pay him. He feels music coursing through him at all hours.

One day Huber offers to teach him to paint, which makes him feel as young and inept and open to discovery as he'd once been writing notes on a score. Moving color over canvas excites him in a way he hasn't experienced since his first juvenile attempts at composition, and he takes to it quickly, not with much skill but with an instinct for shading and perspective that has somehow been inside him all along. But as soon as he begins to take the endeavor seriously, Huber loses interest in guiding him through it, mutters about painters stealing his techniques and failing to give him credit. He returns to the kitchen, where he talks to Grete about fairies and compliments Lottie on the wonderful smell of her Tafelspitz as it cooks. He goes home to his attic studio only when it's time for everyone to sleep.

Lottie, too, is infected by the presence of youth, and in bed she reaches for Lemberg almost every night, as she hasn't since the earliest days of their marriage. If he wakes early, he finds her body close beside him as he turns on his pillow, her arms sliding around his back. In seven years he has grown accustomed to her movements and the rhythm of her breath, as well as her unpredictably ardent desire, but now her sudden enjoyment of his body surprises him anew. She lets out sounds he's never heard before, and her face contorts as she grips him close. Afterward she quickly falls asleep, but Lemberg remains alert, feeling the sweat drying on his torso and thinking about satisfaction. Is he wrong, as Krantz argues, to ignore his listeners' pleasure? Should he give them more of what they want?

He'd rather give them what they need, even if they don't know what that is. What he needs he failed to find in the dry liturgy of his childhood, the rote Jewish practice of his family, who treated matters of the spirit as nothing more than tasks to be accomplished and forgotten until the next began. He has been seeking the expansion of soul he encountered only by accident—the first time he heard Wagner, and then the first time he heard Brahms. But now, to his trained ear, Wagner and Brahms and even Mahler no longer carry him to such ecstasies, nor, sadly, does making love with his wife, even when she is so eager and affectionate. He needs something new, something that surprises him. He, of course, is his first listener and perhaps his most important—so yes, he thinks about the pleasure of an audience of one. Now that he hears everything, only precision can lead him out of himself and into the ineffable, the kind of precision he finds in Halevi's poems. When Lottie's breath slips into a deeper rhythm, meaning nothing will wake her, he gets out of bed, wraps himself in a dressing gown, and returns to his windowless study. There, under a small lamp, he reads:

> *I sought your nearness.*
> *With all my heart I called you.*
> *And in my going out to meet you,*
> *I found you coming toward me,*
> *As in the wonders of your might*
> *And holy works I saw you.*

℟

And yet, he is not blind. He knows what he has encouraged. Knows, too, the moment flirtation turns to affair, infatuation to adoration. He sees it in her face, the distracted smiles, the sudden pinching of brows, and in her movements, too, at moments light and airy, but also secretive, as if she is preparing to sneak away. Above all, she is kinder toward him, more tolerant. For weeks she does not utter one word of criticism for the amount of time he works or the amount of time he plays with the children or the amount of money he earns for the family. He is relieved that she no longer complains about their flat. Why would I want to live anywhere else? she asks. Everyone important is close, and we can walk everywhere.

Soon she stops reaching for him in bed, and for that, too, he is relieved, though also filled with a new longing he tries to quench by watching Lottie and Huber together, their failed attempts to keep others from noticing their glances and surreptitious caresses. He recognizes the ache in their expressions when others are present, the effort they undertake to pretend they aren't trying, at every moment, to keep from touching each other. He takes a strange delight in the beads of sweat that form above the wisp of Huber's mustache as he paints the curve of Lottie's hip, and the shallowness of her breath as she lifts her chin to gaze at him, fixing her eyes on the tilt of his narrow head on its long stem of a neck. Huber shows her less patience now, snaps at her when she rustles too much, says, Can't you keep your hands still for even a minute? He gets cranky with the children, too, telling them they make too much noise when he is trying to get his shading right. Once, he reprimands Klaus for bumping against his easel, and the boy runs off crying, sobs in his room until the painter, nearly in tears himself, hurries after, calling out apologies and pledging to bring sweets the next time he visits.

Lemberg isn't the only one to notice a change. Krantz knocks on his study door one afternoon when Lottie and the children are out. For once his face has been drained of its playful look of irony and amusement, and instead his lips are pressed tightly together, his eyes tired. You have to put an end to it, he says, before Lemberg can ask what the matter is. It's gone far enough.

What am I supposed to do?

You're her husband. She's betrayed you.

She can only betray me if I believed her lies. I never have.

I'll talk to her, Krantz says. She's disgracing my family.

The only truth I hear is the one that sounds in my head, Lemberg says.

You are a fool, Krantz replies.

You knew that when we met.

And still you surprise me with the depth of your foolishness.

Talk to her if you want, Lemberg says. As long as you make her think I know nothing.

I never should have introduced you.

You are to blame for most things, my friend.

3.

Whether Krantz speaks to Lottie or Huber or both, he doesn't know. Whatever the case, his intervention does not stop the affair, only charges it with a new illicit passion that makes it increasingly difficult for Lemberg to pretend he hasn't noticed. Lottie leaves the children with Mathilde—ordinarily warm and loquacious, now silent and derisive in Lemberg's presence—and disappears for half a day, then returns angry, scolding Grete for soiling her dress with jam. At night he hears her weeping when she thinks he's asleep. At unexpected moments she smiles and flushes deeply, recalling some private moment he can't help but imagine. When Huber is with them, she is subdued, quieter than usual, often morose. Huber, on the other hand, speaks with new confidence about his painting. He has arranged a studio visit with a gallery owner who has not only expressed interest in his work but a belief that it will be easy to sell. He knows he is due for recognition and has spent all day arranging canvases. He put a portrait of Lemberg in a place of prominence, he says. But he has left out the three finished paintings of Lottie, he adds, with unabashed cruelty, because no collectors would be interested in decorating their walls with the face of an ordinary housefrau. Lottie, holding back tears, nods and says, True, no one would.

In June, the Lembergs travel to Gmunden, where the Krantz family has vacationed every summer since Lottie was a girl. The children spend all day swimming in the lake, while Lemberg walks the paths beneath the Traunstein. Overhead, birds flutter in treetops, and beyond them, thin clouds drift toward the mountain's slopes, but Lemberg's eyes are mostly focused on the ground to keep from tripping. Thick roots snake through dark soil and make patterns similar to those made by veins in his wrists and on the backs of his hand. He is days away from his fortieth birthday.

Lottie, of course, is made despondent by the absence of Huber, though she will not say so. She sulks and yells at the children. Despite the beautiful scenery and mild weather, she spends most of her time indoors, lying on their bed in the dark, complaining of headaches. But when she emerges, she seems strangely at peace, as if she has decided important matters while she rested. Husband, she says stiffly at lunch, and then pauses. He braces himself for something momentous. Then she continues: Will you please pass the bread?

Lemberg, too, misses Huber, his subtle wit and enthusiasm, but he also finds himself studying Lottie's moods with renewed interest. They are easy to explain on the surface though also more mysterious than ever. She loves and is loved, she is in the presence of God's majesty, with the mountain looming so high above them clouds cling to its peak, and yet she sees nothing but her own misery, her thoughts a constant whirl. He recalls experiencing such feelings as if they exist only in the past, and he wonders if the spell, for him, has finally been broken. His wife loves another, and he feels nothing. Does that mean he is free?

Only now, in the face of her suffering, does he return to work on his quartet. Viewing it from the outside, he can take in the full range of ecstasy and despair that love engenders, and it almost makes him giddy to find such dissonance making its way into notes on a page. He can hear violins struggling against each other, the cello attempting to reassert itself, the lonely viola brooding in solitude. But something is still missing in the third movement, a gap that neither violin, nor viola, nor cello can seem to fill. What else is there? He wants an element as erratic but necessary as the wind through the branches overhead, or the birds that call out warnings when he approaches too close to their nests. He believes music is capable of such things, if stretched to its limits, though so far he feels he is only stretching himself, his patience, which frustrates him anew.

Finally, at the end of the month, Huber joins them for several days, taking a room at a hotel on the east side of the Traunsee, with a view across the water to the castle on its island. The hotel is one of the finest in the region, a place Lemberg could never possibly afford. So Huber is even wealthier than he imagined, and briefly he comforts himself by believing it is the young man's money that draws Lottie, the potential for a more comfortable life. Married to Huber, she can have whatever she wants while also maintaining the pretense of a life committed to art. Or else, he thinks, what attracts her is that Huber is a true Austrian. She has made a mistake in marrying a Jew, no matter that he converted for her, no matter that he has lived his entire life in Vienna, no matter that he is as devoted as any citizen to the Empire and its ideals.

But when he sees Huber again, he knows neither of these things is true. What appeals to Lottie is simply that the painter is young, beautiful, unique, charming, and talented, and that he is not Lemberg.

And the instant he sees them together again, Lemberg knows that he is not free in the least. He was deluded to believe otherwise. Lottie's smiles at the young man pain him as if he is being stabbed. They make no effort to hide their delight, heading off together immediately after meals, Huber striding in his awkward, hunched way, Lottie bouncing on her toes beside him. Krantz tells Lemberg again he must end it, it is his obligation; to do otherwise is to thumb his nose at the church that married him. Lemberg doesn't care about the church any more than he cares about the synagogue of his childhood. But he says, Yes, because he wants his friend to stop talking. Yes, you are right. I will go now.

Instead, he retreats to his own room, returns to the quartet. What he earlier thought was a breakthrough now strikes him as cold and lifeless, the result of intellect cut off from heart and loins. He keeps hearing the soprano line from his song-cycle repeating in his head, calling him away with Halevi's words of longing. And in the midst of the quartet he adds that voice, a sudden intrusion that jerks all of the earthly desire of the strings upward toward the divine. This is the missing piece, the element that will make the music new. The voice enters when harmony breaks down, yearns for it through the third movement, and disappears when it begins to repair itself in the fourth. He writes feverishly through the day, ignores the sunlight through the window. He feels himself pouring onto the page, the lament of a Leopoldstadt shoe-salesman's son lost in the forests of Austria. The trees surround him. He can't find his way through them. He is all alone. Only occasional glimpses of the mountain guide his steps.

His children come in with Mathilde, their hair wet and fingers pruned. Where is Mama? Klaus asks. Grete shivers and gazes at her wrinkled feet. When he doesn't answer, Mathilde gives him a hard stare. He hugs the children close. She is walking around the lake, he says. She will be back soon.

When they leave, he returns to work. By nightfall, the quartet is finished.

ᛒ

The next morning, Lottie and Huber are gone. They have fled back to Vienna, to Huber's studio down the street from their house on Liechtensteinstrasse. It was Mathilde who finally confronted them, telling Krantz it was unacceptable, she could no longer sit idle while spineless men dithered. She went to Huber's hotel, demanded the clerk show him to the painter's room, and without knocking flung open the door to find them tangled together. And then, according to Krantz, staid Mathilde flew at them, shouting and cursing and flailing her fists until the clerk dragged her away.

Now he is alone with the children. He tells them their mother has gone for a holiday, a cure. She is ill, he says, and must rest. He does not write, hears no music, only the voice of Grete saying, Will she die, Papa?

Of course not, he tells her. She will be waiting for us when we arrive at home.

But she isn't waiting. She has taken most of her clothes to Huber's studio. Krantz goes there to plead with her, returns shaking his head. Mathilde takes the children to visit her, and when they come back, Klaus says, Mama is still sick. She couldn't get out of bed. Uncle Josef is taking care of her.

A day later Huber himself comes to see Lemberg, his long face suddenly looking exhausted and older than his twenty-five years. He stammers words of apology, says that he never meant to cause any harm, but that it is not his fault if Lottie has been unhappy in her marriage, though the truth is, he goes on, she seems no more happy with him. Happiness, in fact, seems beyond her capacity, and instead what she seeks is constant strife. He did not realize it before, and if he had, he never would have encouraged her attention, but now that he has it, he does not know how he can ever do without it.

Lemberg sees the suffering in his face, just as he saw it in Lottie's, and in his own face in the mirror, and despite himself he feels pity for all of them equally. But picturing Mathilde's outrage as she barged into the hotel room, he forces himself to say, You are no longer welcome here.

Through July and August he spends his days caring for the children. They bring him joy, they worry him, they irritate him; they make him despair, they give him a reason to get out of bed. His students spend much of their lessons entertaining Klaus, who cannot obey Lemberg's instructions to stay in his room until they have gone. At night, Lemberg puts the final touches on the quartet, and when that is done, writes his will: he gives all his unpublished compositions to Krantz, his father's watch to Klaus, his opera glasses to Grete. He explains that he will leave Lottie nothing, because she is not his wife, never has been. His wife would not betray him, therefore she cannot be his wife. But she has not actually betrayed him, he goes on, because that would mean he believed her lies, but in fact he heard every lie for what it was the moment she spoke it. He believes only the truth in himself, he scribbles, and therefore he is the one who has done the betraying, accepting the lies even as he saw them for what they were. Therefore he will leave his wife whatever money remains in his accounts, even if she is no longer his wife, or never was.

When he began writing the will, he thought he might hang himself when he finished. But when he is finally done, just before dawn, he is too tired to desire anything, even death. He sleeps an hour before Klaus wakes him, shouting that Grete has cut holes in all his socks.

ര

At the start of September, Lottie returns, carrying a suitcase full of clothing Lemberg has never seen before. She walks in breezily, as if she really has been on holiday, nothing more. She hugs the children, comments on the filthy state of the kitchen, disappears into the bathroom for an hour. When they are alone, she tells Lemberg, Some people are more difficult than they are worth. But later that night he finds her weeping in bed. It feels almost natural to hold her and attempt to console her about the failure of her affair, though nothing he says seems to help. Two days later, she returns to Huber.

For the next two months, this becomes the pattern. Lottie has two homes now, spending a few days with Lemberg and the children, then a week with Huber. Perhaps they will all be content with this arrangement, Lemberg thinks, except that he is miserable, both when Lottie is away and when she is back, pretending that she never left. Mathilde, disgusted, won't speak to either of them, and Krantz only visits him in secret, when his wife isn't present to chastise him. You've landed yourself in quite the tangled web, he says, with his old ironic tone, tired, it seems, of his brief period of judgment and scorn.

Lemberg replies, Life makes art seem simple.

When Lottie is home, they occasionally make love again, and he is horrified to think of himself in the exact same place where Huber rested hours earlier. Yet he cannot resist the touch of her small hands, the smell of her powdered skin. Only afterward does he assess her coolly, with a scrutinizing eye. He wants to detect every change, determine whether she is no longer the woman he married. She has grown thinner, more pale. Her mouth hangs open against the pillow, and a trickle of saliva leaks out. She sleeps for twelve hours at a stretch. She gives the children sweets when they should be eating meals. He tries to gather up the strength to tell her to stay away for good, but before he manages it, she leaves once more.

In October, his quartet gets its first performance at the Musikverein. He sits in the balcony, right above the musicians, the new organ pipes just to his right. The gaudy gold ceiling reflects the chandeliers too brightly in his eyes, so he closes them as the music begins. But he can't help opening them to watch as nearly half the audience gets up and leaves during the first movement, which is also the most straightforward, in the form of a Lisztian sonata, with clear themes emerging from dissonance. Many of those who remain laugh through the scherzo of the second movement, and others shout when the soprano steps onto the stage halfway through the third and begins to sing. By then, Lemberg cares about no one's reaction but his own. He closes his eyes again as Halevi's words rise to him, his audience of one:

> *Heart's grief, cloud*
> *the sky with dark so they'll*
> *not see the light of morning.*

But when the quartet reaches the instrumental coda, the laughter and grumbling die down. It remains quiet in the hall for the final minutes, until the instruments return to the original key, F-sharp minor, ending on the chord with which they began. After the last note fades, scattered applause ripples through the hall, but mostly there is silence, which Lemberg takes as a higher form of praise. Perhaps someone has been moved. In the program notes, he made sure to indicate that the quartet is dedicated to his beloved wife.

But Lottie is not in attendance, nor has she heard any rehearsals. Whether she would admire the result of his many hours of effort, hours away from her, he doesn't yet know. The performance takes place during a week she spends with Huber, who has given up all interest in music, he has told Krantz, unless it accompanies dance. He has begun to paint portraits of dancers, Krantz reports, but his paintings have become even stranger than before, losing definition, the figures hardly recognizable. The gallery owner who earlier expressed interest questioned the new direction of his work, and immediately Huber canceled the show that hadn't yet been scheduled, saying he would never collaborate with someone who doubted his vision.

I don't care to know anything about him, Lemberg says, though when she is home Lottie tells him about her lover in great detail, complaining about his snores, his unpredictable temper, the strands of his hair appearing mysteriously in her food. You have no such worries with me, Lemberg says, patting his smooth scalp, and for the first time in months they share a laugh.

4.

She returns for good at the end of October. It's over, she says simply, and pats Lemberg on the chest. He does not know whether to believe her, or whether he should be pleased or infuriated. He has forgotten entirely how a person ought to feel and instead experiences simple bewilderment, allowing feelings to rush over him without questioning or attempting to control them. He has begun to compose music this way, too, and hears it coming directly from his unconscious, with no need to find a tonal center or rely on received structure. One day he works on a piece for solo piano, the next on an opera. The ghost of a key—D minor, his favorite—haunts both, but it is never more than a ghost, like the ghost of his naïve youth, when he believed that love was something he might one day understand.

Lottie spends Reformation Sunday at the church where they were married. She returns with a new, somber resolve. From now on, she will be a good wife, she says, and a good mother. He remembers writing that she is not his wife and thinks, she is herself and always has been. How can he fail to admire her for that?

But when Huber appears at the flat to plead with her to return, she refuses to come to the door. I'm finished, she says, decisively if not coldly, and then leaves it to Lemberg to walk the young painter down the stairs. Huber is distraught, babbling, telling Lemberg how much he has valued their friendship. His breath smells of schnapps, his clothes of smoke and mineral spirits and sewage. He has shaved off his mustache, which makes him look his age again, but his hair is long and unruly, his eyes rimmed red. I don't mean to cause any harm, he says quietly, and then cranes his neck to call up the stairs: I deserve an audience!

Krantz, who must have been listening at his door, slips out of his flat and joins them. He and Lemberg accompany Huber down Liechtensteinstrasse, the painter lurching and stumbling, pedestrians stepping far out of range as they pass. At the door of his studio, the young man puts an arm around each of them, invites them inside for a drink. Lemberg almost accepts, but Krantz speaks first. We cannot come in, he says. We can no longer be your family. You must understand.

Huber runs a hand over his face, nods curtly, and hurries inside.

CR

They learn of his suicide in the middle of November. That is, Krantz hears about it from another acquaintance and tells Lemberg. They debate whether to pass the news on to Lottie, fearing for her fragile health, but once again Mathilde is the one to take a definitive stance, saying, Of course, she must know, and immediately. Lemberg remains in Krantz's flat while Mathilde goes upstairs. He expects to hear a scream through the ceiling, or the flinging of furniture, but there is only an extended hush. Lottie spends a day in the bedroom and comes out worn but dry-eyed. She refuses to go to the funeral. I was already done, she says.

Before Lemberg can ask if he should attend, Krantz advises against it. I will represent us all, he says. But when he returns, he explains that the family—Huber's parents, a brother they have never heard of—suggests that he and Lemberg come to the studio, examine the canvases, assess which ought to be kept. Why me? Lemberg asks, to which Krantz responds vaguely, You have a keen eye. But when they enter the studio, he understands instantly. There are two new paintings of Lottie he hasn't seen before, along with dozens of sketches, all nude: Lottie lounging in bed, draped across a chair, standing in front of a mirror.

This same mirror is the one in front of which Huber hanged himself, thrusting a knife into his belly as he dropped from the chair. A dark stain remains on the floorboards. And beside it, another canvas, this one a self-portrait. In it, Huber, too, is naked, but the image is not sensuous like those of Lottie. Painted in blue tones, with heavy shading, the figure is emaciated, sneering, seeming to wither into a corpse as Lemberg watches. It is the painter's best work, a true sign of his emerging genius. Lemberg wishes for one more chance to speak with the young man, to tell him that the agonies of youth will pass, that further agonies await, that all can be endured if only one continues to create. He might tell him to imagine God's agony in witnessing the disappointment of Creation, a vision he has sought but hasn't quite glimpsed in Halevi's poems: for God, too, the only solace must be found in knowing He can create anew. But for Huber there is no more solace, and Lemberg feels responsible for not having offered whatever wisdom he had to impart when he still had the chance.

Meanwhile, Krantz lights the stove, burns all the nudes of Lottie. The rest of the paintings they leave for the family to collect.

⚮

On a bright day in December, Lemberg and his family bundle against the cold and stroll through the Stadpark. Lemberg and Lottie walk side by side, though a foot of space separates them, and they refrain from holding hands. Klaus runs circles around them, while Grete, now seven and eager to sound mature, comments on the beauty of the trees without their leaves. They pass the frozen pond and pause in front of the Schubert monument. The old master, with his perfect curls and dimpled chin, gazes skyward, a notebook open on his lap, a marble pen forever hovering above the page. Lemberg experiences a moment of bitterness and thinks that easy praise is as empty as love for which one doesn't have to struggle.

He looks like Uncle Josef, Klaus says.

Yes, a bit, Lemberg says.

Where is he? Klaus asks.

Gone, Lottie says.

Will he come back? Grete asks.

No, Lottie says, with the slightest tremble in her voice. I don't think so.

I miss him, Klaus says.

We all do, Lemberg says before Lottie has to reply. And perhaps in gratitude, she takes his arm. After struggling for long enough, maybe one deserves at least a moment of ease. The children stay close now, and with the wind rustling their coats, the four of them pass beneath the bare trees to make their way home.

Inspection

His host smiled and chattered, without suspicion, it seemed, that this visit was anything but routine. He was a large man, gregarious and unguarded, youthful despite his silver hair, which was cropped closely on the sides and swept in a dramatic wave across a high forehead. His full name was something complicated and Germanic, though his accent was nearly undetectable. "Please call me Rex," he said and laughed. "Not that I pretend to be king around here. I'm just a lowly vice president. One of twenty-six, last time I checked."

The lead auditor, Eric Saltzman, had dealt with plenty of vice presidents in his eight years with the agency. Many were feckless and incompetent, some were savvy, a few brilliant. What they all shared, however, was a common talent for obfuscation. Saltz, as he was known by his colleagues, was practiced at sniffing out smokescreens and signs of deception. His team had already set to work in the labs, checking data and running samples. Whatever was hidden would soon come to light.

Rex leaned back in his oversized chair and propped one leg atop the opposite knee, revealing a sock with a surprisingly bright pattern, red and yellow diamonds on a burgundy field. It didn't match his suit or tie, the former charcoal gray, the latter solid blue with a subtle, grid-like texture. On his desk sat several three-ring binders, quality assurance protocols Saltz had already seen. There were copies at the local field office, in a room full of similar protocols from firms around the region. He would find nothing interesting in them, though he would make a show of paging through and taking notes before leaving the office. But

Rex was in no hurry to let him get on with his work, and Saltz knew better than to show his eagerness.

"I gather this is your first time at Elistra," Rex said. "I've been here only two years, but I haven't seen your name on any of the earlier reports."

"First time," Saltz agreed.

"I was at Reinhardt before this. Not a V.P. then. Just a department director. I didn't see you there, either."

"I was out west until recently. Colorado. Transferred in June."

"Colorado," Rex said, wistfully. "I imagine you miss the mountains."

"Every day."

"Our summers take some getting used to."

"I grew up here," Saltz said. "I don't mind the humidity. It's only the traffic that bothers me. And every time I walk outside, I expect the trees to be taller."

Rex laughed again. Saltz tried to detect a hint of disingenuousness in his expression, but he seemed sincerely amused. Perhaps he enjoyed a bit of banter to break up his day. It wasn't uncommon for a V.P. to have little actual work to occupy him. An inspection—a routine one, at least—might come as a welcome interlude, relief from the monotony of his otherwise empty days. Or maybe he was simply naïve. "It's true," he said. "No one moves here for the scenery. But we certainly have the culture. And of course, you go where the jobs are."

"The office does keep me a lot busier here," Saltz said, hoping this might prompt a return to the work at hand without making him seem impatient. It was crucial to appear unhurried—and to be so, as well, in order to avoid making sloppy mistakes. "Last month they had me running all over the state. Even had two inspections in a single week. First time I've ever been asked to finish one in fewer than four days."

"Our previous auditor often did them in two and a half," Rex said, a touch of superiority now creeping into his voice. "When a place runs as efficiently as ours, it isn't difficult. And we've had no violations, nothing but minor infractions for a decade. Did you know your predecessor? Renshaw? Rennie, we called him. A real professional. We were sorry to see him go."

"I hear he's enjoying retirement," Saltz said. "Bought himself a kayak."

"Not that we aren't glad to have you in his place," Rex said, the tone of mild condescension congealing, as if he'd decided only now on the proper attitude with which to address a newcomer. "It's just complicated to have a big change like this after such a long time. When you have a routine, a set of expectations … I'm sure we'll get there. The first time is always the hardest."

"That's why they've given us the full week. To allow us space to feel our way forward."

"Completely understandable," Rex said. "Though it is a bit of a disruption. I just wish they would have let us know sooner. It was quite a scramble to rearrange so many schedules on such short notice."

"I agree with you on that," Saltz replied, adopting in turn the hint of obsequiousness he knew was called for. And yet he maintained the fixed neutral expression he'd mastered for such encounters, one he'd practiced in front of mirrors during his first year with the agency. In the lab, he hadn't needed to wonder what emotions showed on his face, and during his years as a researcher he'd often been frustrated enough to kick over stools. Once, when he thought his results were so far off he wouldn't pass his defense, he hurled a beaker against a blackboard and spent half the night picking up shards. "Believe me," he went on. "I gave our scheduling office an earful when I heard. No reason to take you by surprise this way."

"It happens, I understand," Rex said, curtly, waving a hand. "I don't blame you."

"I promise to keep the disruption to a minimum. My team knows how to stay out of the way. And once I get started, you'll hardly realize I'm here."

"That was always the case with Rennie," Rex said. "He was like a ghost when he visited. I'd forget he was on the premises until he appeared with his report. That's due in part, of course, to our terrific staff. They provided everything he needed without his having to ask. And in return, he made their jobs easy for them." He glanced over Saltz's shoulder, toward the open office door, and Saltz guessed this was the cue for someone to escort him out. He kept himself from turning to look but listened carefully for the sound of footsteps. When none arrived, Rex laughed again, this time with noticeable effort. "Once he'd filed, that's another story. He'd loosen his tie then, so to speak. Or rather, his belt. He was an eater, Rennie. And he enjoyed a good Scotch as much as anyone. After his work was done, of course."

Rex went on to describe the restaurant to which he and some others on his staff took Rennie and his team following their inspections. A classic, dark-wood steakhouse a few miles down Route 10. Rennie was a connoisseur when it came to sirloin, Rex said. "Myself, I prefer flank," he added. "And a nice lager. You?"

"I'm afraid I'm vegetarian," Saltz said, noting the disappointment in his host's face, one he tried but failed to hide, his smile growing stiff and pained. "But I'm a big fan of steak fries."

"And I suppose you don't drink, either," Rex said, with an edge of sadness, or perhaps disdain.

"On occasion. I like to keep myself under control."

He meant it as a joke, but this time Rex replied sternly. "Some of us can manage both." To this Saltz didn't respond, and Rex adjusted his tie, reset his smile. "It was all above board," he said. "The meals came out of my expense account, but Rennie cleared it with the field office ahead of time." As long as he'd filed his report first, his supervisors saw no issues, and of course, Rex continued, Rennie was the consummate professional. "There was never anything to worry about where integrity was concerned," he said, and for the first time Saltz sensed that perhaps Rex understood this inspection after all, knew what had triggered it.

"But it was nice for everyone to let loose a bit afterward," Rex said. "To enjoy each other's company." Because even a routine inspection carried a certain amount of gravity, he added. It made everyone a little tense, no matter how well prepared they were. How could it not? His staff took great pride in their work, everyone at Elistra did, and the internal personnel review process was quite rigorous. Still, being evaluated by peers and supervisors was a very different matter than being scrutinized by representatives of a government agency, even by a team who'd visited enough times to understand the firm's unique culture—to understand and accept, that is, its particular quirks and oddities, which every firm has and which its employees no longer notice or simply take for granted.

While he spoke, he leaned back farther, placing hands behind his head and uncrossing his legs so that the colorful sock was swallowed by the cuff of his slacks. Because his gaze had drifted away, Saltz allowed himself to shift his own just slightly, keeping Rex in view but focusing instead on the horizontal blinds partly covering the wall, made entirely of glass, behind him. It was a big airy office at the top floor of a six-story building, not the tallest on Elistra's campus—that one housed the CEO and other top executives, along with the sales team—nor the newest—that was devoted to research and development—but slightly downhill from those, closer to the road. Quality assurance departments were always the plain-Janes of pharmaceutical companies, respected only slightly more than manufacturing units.

Still, it was an office that suggested accomplishment and dignity, enormous compared to Saltz's cubicle in the agency field office. He could imagine Renshaw sitting in his place, filled with resentment and envy after a long career that had amounted to little. Anyone in his position might waver, at least for a moment. But Renshaw had been reckless, abruptly changing his spending habits—buying a new Audi, taking his family to the Caribbean three times in two years—and failing to cover his tracks with evidence of an inheritance, an investment windfall.

Where exactly the money had come from the Inspector General's office hadn't yet found out, except that it had been paid in cash. And now they were sending Saltz and his team to all the firms in the region to discover whose violations Renshaw might have deigned to overlook.

The blinds were turned at an angle that made it difficult to see much beyond them, though they did let in a significant amount of light. He could make out the loose foliage of an ash tree, and beyond, the slope of lawn leading to the main gate, which he'd passed through half an hour earlier, after showing his credentials to a guard whose uniform was neatly pressed, badge polished. Tall hedges hid the fences topped with barbed wire that encircled the campus, as well as the traffic on Route 10. Saltz had always hated that road, which he found treacherous, jammed with trucks and impatient commuters trying to get to the freeway, and before pulling off the exit this morning he'd nearly collided with an SUV. He did miss Colorado, even more than he'd let on to Rex—or to his parents, with whom he was currently living—and would head back there as soon as he could. He'd laid on the horn and shouted at the other driver, and then did his best to compose himself before approaching the gate. But the guard likely noticed his trembling hands as he passed over his identification.

If so, perhaps he reported it to Rex's assistant, who now strode into the office on loud heels and handed Rex a slip of paper. While he read it, she shook Saltz's hand and introduced herself. Her name, Ellery, made Saltz think of a crunchy green vegetable, bright, springy, refreshing, and bland. She was, of course, young and attractive in an aggressively feminine way: thick sandy hair curled around an oval, small-featured face, carefully made up to appear natural, though he could spot the artificially extended eyelashes, brows plucked and darkened to give them gravity. Her suit had been cut to accentuate her hips, and as she stood beside the desk she gave off a muted scent of daphne. All carefully calculated, he thought, though to her such attention to detail may have seemed instinctive. On Renshaw, at least from what Saltz knew of him—as unsubtle in his desires as most aging men reckoning with disappointments and the little time they had left to make up for them—her appearance would have had the intended effect, disarming him just when he should have been sharpening his attention. It was hard not to feel stirred by her animated lips and dimpled chin as she described the various cafeterias on Elistra's campus, though Saltz determined to steel himself against her charms. "My favorite's in the executive building," she said, tilting her head to let a soft curl fall across her cheek. "There's a sushi bar. Everything's really fresh. I can show you the way later, if you like."

Rex scrawled something on the slip of paper and held it out to her, and without turning away from Saltz, she reached behind and folded it into her slender fingers. Then she flashed Saltz her guileless smile, said he should ask her for anything he needed, and strode out, heels clacking, hips swinging her fitted slacks. "Those dinners always felt celebratory," Rex said, and the sudden return to a conversation he'd nearly forgotten startled Saltz. He chastised himself for his mistake, having turned to watch Ellery until she was out of sight. Now Rex's gaze was fixed on him, a curious series of expressions working over his face, first one of deliberation, then doubt, then determination. "We ate more than we should have. Drank more, too."

Rennie, it turned out, was a real talker once he started on his third Scotch, Rex went on. By then the other members of his team would have headed home to their families, but Rennie's kids were grown and out of the house, and his wife did some sort of volunteer work in the evening. Maybe there were other reasons he didn't want to go home, or maybe he just enjoyed the company of fellow scientists.

Eventually just the two of them would be left in the restaurant, and they'd move from their table in the dining room to stools at the bar. Rennie would tell him all sorts of things—about various personalities at the field office, about intra-agency politics, about sordid details of private lives. Maybe he heard some gossip not meant for his ears, but it was harmless, wasn't it? He was very discreet, never told anyone what Rennie said, except of course Rennie himself, who afterward often didn't remember what he'd disclosed. But on the phone, say a day or two later, when Rennie was good and sober, he'd remind him of certain details, and Rennie would express how mortified he was, how much he appreciated Rex's tact, and on one occasion he might have asked how he could show his appreciation, though Rex assured him no such display was necessary.

In any case, he and Rennie always got along beautifully, and he was glad to know his old friend was enjoying retirement. "You would have liked him, I'm sure," Rex said, smiling shyly now, his chin tucked toward his chest. "Though it's probably best that he didn't know you very well. Or else he might have told me all your secrets."

"Yes," Saltz said, and couldn't help smiling in return. Rex had turned out to be craftier than he'd first imagined, offering a feint or two but largely keeping his strategy to himself. "Good thing."

"Of course you'd met on occasion. A national conference or two."

"Could be," Saltz said. "Those things are always a blur."

"Especially if you like Scotch as much as Rennie does."

"Never been a fan."

"No? Was it bourbon, then?"

Saltz didn't answer.

"Of course, he'd also heard about you from others. Enough to form a general impression."

"Oh? And how did he describe me?"

"Young and eager. A rising star in the agency. Someone who fancies himself a real detective, rooting out nefarious behavior in the most unlikely places. More ambitious than upstanding."

"Sounds like a bore."

"A workaholic, too. Puts the job before everything else. Hard on a marriage."

"Flattering profile."

"Possibly an anger problem."

"I see."

"Does that sound like you?"

"Sounds like a lot of people."

"True enough," Rex said, leaning forward and folding his hands at the edge of his desk, which extended around him in a vast gray expanse. "In this field, it's not uncommon to struggle with a range of issues. Drinking problems. Other substances. A few years ago, one of our research chemists—this was at Reinhardt, not here—was caught making Ecstasy in the lab after everyone went home in the evening. When there's a lot of pressure, it affects the personal life. Relationships suffer. I'm not immune to it. Early in my career, I went through a painful divorce. It was for the best. My current wife understands me far better. But in retrospect, I could have avoided a lot of suffering if I'd recognized that the job didn't need everything I was giving it, that it would never give back nearly as much."

"Seems to have treated you pretty well," Saltz said, offering a lazy gesture to indicate the office's expensive furniture, as well as Rex's appearance of fit and pampered comfort.

"I have no complaints," Rex said, and patted his hair with a touch of self-consciousness. "This is exactly where I want to be. But there was a time when I'd had my sights set higher. There was no amount of success that would have been satisfying."

"Sounds exhausting."

"It was. It ground me down. Almost sent me to the hospital. And if I kept going, probably an early grave."

"So you think I should take it easy," Saltz said. Now he, too, leaned forward, just far enough to pull one of the protocol binders toward him with a single extended finger. He flipped open the cover, scanned the words of the title page without taking note of what they said.

Rex laughed once more, earnestly this time, a laugh directed at himself. "Apparently I'm just becoming an old man who thinks he ought to give advice to strangers," he said. "Perhaps I'm just envious of your energy. There are times when I wish I still had the sort of fire that drove me when I was your age. But mostly, I assure you, I'm content to ride out the rest of my time right here. I do important work, and I'm proud of it. And in a few years, I'll be as happy as Rennie to hang up my lab coat for good."

"And you'll be able to afford more than a kayak. A schooner, maybe."

Laughter again, but strained this time, impatient. "I've never cared much for boats. A sensitive stomach."

"Well," Saltz said. "If you ever want a second career, you'd make a good counselor. I'd come to you with all my problems. That is, if I had any."

And then, as if he really were a counselor, and their time had just run out, Rex abruptly pushed himself back from the desk, flung his hands behind his head. "Of course, one person's word alone doesn't mean much. Especially Rennie's. A disgusting drunk who, as you know—" Rex paused, closed his eyes, and nodded somberly. "As you obviously know, was easily persuaded to put his own interests ahead of the agency's."

"Obviously," Saltz said, though the admission he'd been looking forward to, the definitive moment of exposure, now left him deflated. It had come too soon, too easily. He knew better than to trust it as a victory.

"So I did a little research," Rex said, opening his eyes only to slits. "An inspection of my own, let's say."

"And? Find anything interesting?"

"A police report. Payments to a law firm. Your temporary transfer request."

"You'd make a good auditor, too," Saltz said.

"I'm sure I would," Rex agreed, "though the salary, unfortunately, isn't quite what I'm used to."

"So you've learned a few things about me. And you think that's going to keep me from reporting—"

"I can't guess what the future will bring," Rex said. "All I can do is try to make sense of the past. Gather fragments and try to put together a story."

"And I suppose you're going to recite it now."

"Don't you want to hear it?"

"I'm not sure I have a choice."

"We always have choices," Rex said, "though it's true our options are usually limited by what we've decided before. That's what I always said to Rennie."

"Go ahead, then."

"It goes something like this," Rex said, staring up at the ceiling, so the skin stretched taut over his Adam's apple, his pulse visible in a vein near the surface of his neck. "There was once a young, hotshot auditor, a rising star at the FDA. He was from New Jersey, originally, but worked out of the Colorado field office. Made a big splash in his first few years with the agency, caught out a couple of major violations that no one else spotted, quickly rose up the ranks. So he was in demand all the time, put on high-stakes jobs, worked extra long hours. His wife wasn't very happy about it, and being the straightforward type, she made it abundantly clear, even though she knew he had a temper. As a result, they often fought, sometimes bitterly." Without shifting his gaze from the ceiling, Rex let out a long breath and asked, "How do you like it so far?"

"A little dull."

"The good part is still coming," he said, lowering his eyes now, settling them securely, straight ahead, until Saltz glanced down at the open binder. His hands cramped on the arms of the chair, and he forced himself to unclench his jaw and steady his breathing without letting it show. "One day, the young man goes off to a conference. In Phoenix, I believe. Drinks more bourbon than is good for him, yaks it up with some fellow auditors, including a disgusting drunk from his home state who's already sold himself out for a pittance. Then the young man goes up to his hotel room with a woman from his field office. A brunette with a runner's body and a nice tan, who happens to be under his direct supervision. When he comes home, his wife suspects but can't prove anything. She tells him to move out. There's a domestic disturbance, a neighbor calls the police, but no one is charged. A contentious divorce proceeding follows. Soon after, a co-worker files a complaint. A female co-worker, that is, alleging mistreatment. An investigation opens. It's unlikely to lead anywhere without further documentation, but to be safe, the young man gets himself transferred to New Jersey so he can live with his parents until all is resolved. Another account of impropriety, however, and his superiors will have no choice but to take action. Similarly, all the wife needs to get the settlement she wants is evidence of infidelity. An eyewitness statement, perhaps. Or maybe two."

Saltz waited for Rex to go on, studying the logo at the top of the binder's front page, an elaborate letter E inside a double ring. When Rex stayed silent, he said, "An intriguing story."

"A sad one," Rex said. "But not atypical in our industry."

"It needs an ending," Saltz said.

"Yes," Rex agreed. "I'm still working on that. But I've kept you long enough. As much as I've enjoyed our chat, I know you've got plenty to do, and I'm sure you're ready to get going. You'll be in good hands with my staff. And if there's anything you need, don't hesitate to ask."

Rex stood, with arms outstretched in the direction of the office door. Ellery had reappeared there, silently, it seemed, though when Saltz glanced down, expecting to glimpse bare feet, he saw that she still wore the pointy pumps, and above them the tight black suit, white blouse open at the collar to reveal prominent clavicles and a swath of smooth freckled skin. He pulled himself to his feet. Sweat rolled down his sides. "I think we can finish in three days," he said. "I don't see any reason to be here longer."

"I'm glad to hear it," Rex said. "And once your report is in, we'd love to treat you and your team to dinner."

"I'm sure we'd all enjoy that."

"Ellery can find a restaurant that accommodates your dietary needs."

"Just let me know what you like," she said, her smile no less open and welcoming.

"Anywhere's fine. There's always something on the menu I can eat."

"Don't forget these," Rex said, gesturing at the protocol binders. Saltz managed to pick them up only by pressing them awkwardly against his chest. At another time, he might have flung them across the room. But Rex was right, he knew: each choice impacted the next, narrowing the path forward. That he'd failed to realize how narrow it had grown before he'd even arrived was a mistake he wouldn't make again. But now it was done, and he worried he'd pay for it dearly and for a long time. How many years before he'd feel free again, unbeholden to anyone? How long before he could stare someone like Rex down with the certainty that he held all the best cards in any deck he played?

"Coming?" Ellery called over her shoulder. In her voice he tried to detect a hint of judgment or scorn. That was what he expected, whether he deserved it or not. But instead he heard only lighthearted indifference, which he took—or wanted to take—as a sign that consequences need not be punishment, that he could eventually come out of all this ahead, if he kept calm and tread carefully. Compromise could mean more than just survival, especially for someone shrewder than Renshaw. There were worse things, he assured himself, than going to dinner at a restaurant where he had nothing to eat. He adjusted the binders as well as he could, their edges digging into his forearms, and followed her faint scent, the harsh clack of her heels, into the hall.

Depth of Field

I met Harold Kantor in the early spring of 2000. He was in his mid-fifties by then, balding and heavyset, with sad dark eyes beneath wiry brows going white. As a young man he'd shown his photographs in fine art galleries, but now he made his living as a freelancer, shooting advertising spreads, mostly, along with what he termed "glamour nudes"—soft-core porn images of women in showers or sprawled on mattresses, which he sold to European websites. These I'd find out about only after we'd known each other a while, long enough for him to come to trust me.

The marketing agency I worked for in Chatwin, New Jersey, hired him for various contracts, and as the newest graphic designer in the office, I was often given the most tedious tasks, including touching up photographs. Harold would step into my cubicle to chat when he delivered his images, which he still preferred to shoot on film, though our account managers urged everyone to go digital. If he was working with another designer, he'd come with a CD, but because he knew I didn't mind, or at least didn't feel empowered to object, he always brought me color slides. Then he'd sit by my desk as I scanned them, and we talked through the edits I planned to make. He hated Photoshop, claimed it was the death of real photography, and tried to talk me out of using the airbrush tool to soften clouds in a backyard scene. Outwardly I agreed with him that the manipulated images were cheesier and less compelling than the originals, but I knew better than to follow his suggestions. The backyard shot, with dresses and shirts billowing on a clothesline, was for a magazine spread selling dryer sheets, and the clouds were supposed to resemble cotton balls.

"It looks like a fucking cartoon," he'd say about most of the finished work we sent to print. "Might as well have the machine generate the whole thing and cut the camera out altogether." Then he'd shrug, and his voice would drop in both volume and pitch. "Not that I'm complaining about the paycheck, mind you."

He added that last part hastily, afraid, maybe, that he'd gone too far. Did he think I had any say over whether he kept getting hired? I was twenty-two, a college drop-out, and this was my first job outside food service. Before working here, I'd waited tables in a hotel, covering weddings and bar mitzvahs on weekends and teaching myself editing and design software during the week. I'd always had a sharp visual sense, though not much talent for original artwork. During my two years at Rutgers I'd taken a couple of drawing classes but had planned to major in business. Now, though, because the economy was hot and qualified applicants hard to come by, the agency took me on without a degree. I had no authority whatsoever but was flattered that Harold saw me as someone important enough to check his tone, and maybe it teased me with a sense of power, even one that was purely imaginary.

"Better let me get back to work," I'd say after we'd gone through a few images, not because I was tired of talking to him, but because I took secret pleasure in the way it made him jump out of his chair, or try to, though his bulk made standing quickly a challenge. I was used to taking orders, never giving them, but now I started to fantasize about moving up in the agency, one day becoming an account manager, telling people where to go and what to do.

"Hey, just so you know," Harold said on his way out. "I appreciate your effort, even if you do drain all the life out of my shots."

 os

It was a surprise, then, when he asked, quietly, about four months after we'd started working together, whether I might want to do some freelance photo editing on the side, make a bit of extra cash. He needed someone to clean up a series of images he'd recently taken. Nothing he cared much about aesthetically, just a little thing he did to supplement his income, and he wouldn't harass me about making them too clean. In fact, he needed them as clean as possible. I could make them really slick and lifeless, because that's what the client wanted. "You up for it?" he asked, and those sad eyes of his seemed even sadder than usual—an acknowledgment, I guessed later, of how much he'd had to compromise in his career, how little he'd managed to stand on principle.

"Sure," I said. "I could give it some time in the evenings."

He glanced around to make sure no one was watching, then slipped me a CD. "Don't open it here," he said. "And don't let your boss know about it, okay?"

Even his hushed voice and nervous glances to the side didn't prepare me for what I'd find when I put the CD into my computer that night. I still lived with my parents then, in the aftermath of my college meltdown, and heard my mother putting dishes away downstairs as I opened the first file. I nearly fell off my chair and then rushed to shut the door before pulling up more images. Naked female bodies, one after another, in poses of seduction or simulated ecstasy. When I got over the shock, I tallied up: six different women, ranging from college-age to mid-thirties, I guessed, rail-thin to voluptuous. Where had he found them, and how had he gotten them to take their clothes off for him? That, I suppose, was what shocked me most. Not that Harold took these photographs to make money, but that such beautiful women would willingly bare themselves for a middle-aged fat guy with a camera.

I asked him as much, though not in quite those terms, the next time he came by the office. "You'd be surprised," he answered, with a dismissive shrug. "A lot more exhibitionists around than you'd think." He put ads in the back of a weekly circular and on a jobs board at a local college, and he had more models than he could handle. And then what shocked me even more than the fact of six women stripping down and writhing on a bed as Harold snapped pictures of them was how casual he seemed about the whole thing, as if those legs and hips and buttocks and breasts had no effect on him whatsoever.

And this, I'm sure, says more about me at that stage of my life—hardly out of childhood—than it does about Harold. I'd had only one serious girlfriend up to that point, during my second year at Rutgers, and it was her naked body that led to my leaving school. We dated for a few weeks before getting intimate, during which time I fantasized constantly about undressing her. But when it finally happened—she was the one to tug off her jeans and then mine—I was completely undone by it. Once we'd taken our clothes off the first time, she had no inhibitions about taking them off again. When my roommate was out, she'd walk around my tiny dorm room in the buff, as if it were no big deal for me to see her that way. And yet to me, it was more than a big deal; it was earth-shattering, even more than the sex we had, which was generally awkward and only superficially satisfying.

What amazed me was how comfortable she must have felt to be so open in front of me, so vulnerable, nothing at all between us. I was overwhelmed by my good fortune, and I wanted so badly to protect what I had, to preserve it, that I couldn't think about anything else. I stopped going to classes. I stopped doing homework and studying for tests. I even stopped sleeping much when she was with me, instead spending whole nights staring at the exposed curves of her neck and shoulder and lifting a corner of the sheet to peek at what was beneath. I failed everything that semester, and at the end of it, she told me she thought I was sweet but that she couldn't handle the responsibility of being with me. It was too much to make sure I was keeping up with my obligations while also trying to have fun, so she'd have to let me go. She actually used that phrase, "let you go," as if she were firing me for shoddy work. I went home for the summer and stayed when everyone else went back in the fall. I heard from a friend that within a few weeks of returning she started dating someone new, and because the idea of her parading naked around another dorm room was too hard for me to take, I stopped talking to all the people I'd met during those two years.

I knew Harold was divorced and lived alone, and I couldn't help asking if it was tough for him to be around those naked women and "not, you know, get attached…"

"Hey," he said, sharply, but also with such an immediate look of insult I had the feeling he'd been preparing for questions like this and had rehearsed his answer. "I'm no pervert. I'm very respectful. I know how to keep my hands to myself."

"I didn't mean—"

"Plus, I prefer women my own age. And with pubic hair, if you want to know the truth."

I apologized, but the offended set of his jaw remained. His chin stayed close to his chest, brows pinched even when I handed over a new CD with the images I'd edited, erasing all pimples and stray hairs, scars and birthmarks, bruises and razor burn. He took it without a word, pulled himself up with difficulty, and said, "If I'd thought you couldn't be a professional about it, I wouldn't have asked."

He handed me an envelope with bills inside. I waited for him to ask for the original CD back as well, but he didn't. It wouldn't have mattered anyway—I'd already saved the images on my hard drive and burned an extra copy.

ଛ

I expected that to be the end of our friendship, such as it was, but the next time I saw him he seemed to have forgotten any insinuations I'd made about his treatment of models, or else he'd gotten over it. In either case, he was no longer defensive. "You did terrific work," he said. "Really terrific. Client doubled the last order."

He'd keep passing me jobs if I wanted them, he said. And I did. Over the next year he gave me discs every couple of weeks. Each time there were pictures of new women, along with some I'd seen before, and each time I was astonished to discover another set of willing participants, who not only took their clothes off for Harold but must have known there were men in front of computers around the world, stroking themselves as they ogled taut nipples and bare asses and shaved vulvas. It was horrifying to think about, even as I was one of those men, pulling up the images on my computer after I was done editing them, after I'd handed off polished versions to Harold. I always went back to the originals for my own pleasure. I preferred the women in their natural state, before I'd messed with them, blemished and a little lopsided, oblivious, it seemed, to whoever might be watching as they knelt, face in pillow, backside in the air.

The more I looked at them, the more I recognized Harold's skill as a photographer, and the more I agreed with him that my fiddling took all the life out of his work. His composition was impeccable, as was his lighting, and even though the images were meant to be simplistic, serving only to arouse, there was often a hint of mystery in a model's glance over her shoulder as she soaped herself in the shower, or in the arch of her back as she stretched across the new cream-colored leather couch he'd bought with some of the supplemental income and then wrote off on his taxes. These were the images his client usually turned down, opting instead for the straightforward beaver shots, but they were the ones I returned to most often, the ones I saw when I closed my eyes at night.

I didn't tell him this, exactly, but as we grew to consider each other partners, or at least members of a team, I did praise his skill and point out features of the photos I particularly appreciated. All this in a hushed voice in my cubicle, so none of my co-workers could hear. "I like what you did with the series on the couch," I'd say. "The short-haired blonde in black boots?"

"Adrianne. A real pro."

"The way you blurred out the background. So it looks like the whole couch is floating."

"Just used a shallow depth of field," he said. "Opened up the aperture a couple of stops."

"It's a cool effect. I could do something similar with the software, but it wouldn't be the same. Not even close."

"I use it all the time in my real work," he said. "The stuff no one ever wants to look at."

"I'd like to see it."

"You should drop by the studio sometime," he said. "I could teach you how to use a camera." Then he waved disdainfully at my computer screen. "Machine that captures reality instead of erasing it. Or whatever the hell you do to kill my photos."

ର

I took him up on his offer a week later. His studio was in the basement of his house, a small bungalow half a mile south of downtown Chatwin, in a neighborhood that was on the rise after a long decline. Three of the houses on his street were getting new roofs, another new siding. Harold's needed both, or at least a fresh paint job, but it was tidy inside, especially, I thought, for the home of a middle-aged man living on his own: wooden dining table with magazines stacked in one corner, a single plate and a pair of coffee cups in the sink, a sweater draped over an armchair. It looked like a lonely existence but not a desperate one, and taking it in brought me relief I hadn't realized I'd needed.

Harold greeted me with a big handshake and offered me a beer. He was dressed the same as usual, in fresh jeans and a button down stretched over his big belly, except instead of loafers he wore suede slippers with fleece lining. "Nice to see you out of cubicle-land," he said. "The lighting in that place, I swear. Makes everyone look like a corpse. And here it turns out you're alive after all."

He showed me around his darkroom and let me look at his current project, a series of black and white landscapes that, I have to admit, didn't do much for me. Most were taken on foggy hillsides and incorporated ruins of some sort: a falling-down barn, the stone foundation of a house long-gone, a rusted-out water tank. They were moody and menacing but heavy-handed, I thought, and overly romantic, not as striking as his advertising shots, and certainly nothing close to the nudes. Still, I praised them, said it was a shame no galleries were interested in showing them. He was clearly excited to talk to someone about his work, describing technical aspects of his printing in minute detail, none of which I understood. But I enjoyed seeing him so animated. And it made me feel important to be treated as a fellow artist, though I had only six college credits in drawing and a year's experience as a graphic designer. We both took enough pleasure in the conversation that I stayed longer than I meant to, and while I was working on a second beer, the doorbell rang.

"My next shoot," he said. "Didn't realize it got so late."

"I better split," I said, but he was already on his way upstairs, moving fast despite his size. By the time I made it to the landing, he'd opened the door and ushered in a young woman wearing designer sweatpants and hoodie, with a big shopping bag slung over her back. I recognized her right away, though in the images I'd seen, her dark reddish hair was up in a bun instead of down at her shoulders, as it was now. Her name was Kaitlyn, or at least that was the name on the CD. She'd shot only one set with Harold so far, or at least only one since I'd started working with him. She was probably two or three years older than me, small and athletic, with big lips and sleepy eyes. In the pictures on my computer she'd worn nothing but ballet slippers while doing splits and handstands. It seemed all wrong for Harold to introduce me—"my retoucher," he said—and for me to shake her hand as if I hadn't recently zoomed in to a close-up of her clitoris to soften a shadow. "I was just leaving," I said, but Harold gestured at my half-finished beer and gave a disappointed look.

"Why don't you stick around and see how the magic happens. You don't mind, do you?" he asked Kaitlyn.

"Of course not." She smiled an innocent, toothy smile, then reached into her bag and pulled out a fedora and trenchcoat. "What do you think?"

"Perfect," Harold said.

Kaitlyn led the way downstairs, clearly at ease in the space, and Harold followed. By the time I joined them in the studio, she was already out of her sweats. Beneath them she wore a blue lace bra and matching thong, and while Harold arranged his lights in front of a gray backdrop, she donned the trenchcoat and hat, along with a pair of tall black heels that followed out of her bag. While she posed—pretending first to be a private eye, then a flasher, her underwear disappearing somewhere in the process—and Harold snapped his shutter, I tried to keep out of view. But there was nowhere I could stand and still see her without being in her line of sight. Did she notice the sweat on my face as more of her was exposed under the heat of all those blaring lamps? Between shots she'd relax her pout and posture and bedroom eyes and chat with Harold about his family—he had a grandchild I'd never heard about—and in turn he asked about her day job, as a receptionist at an optometrist's office.

"Doc's on vacation for a week," she said. "Kayaking in Chesapeake Bay. But he still wants me there to schedule appointments. All day, no one comes in, and I get maybe two calls. Totally losing my mind."

This as she flung the trenchcoat onto the couch. She used the hat to cover her crotch, gave a few flashes, then set it back on her head, turned, and bent over, so it reappeared between her legs. Harold crouched and shot.

"Got to get going," I said, and hurried up the stairs, flushed and furious. It was a lie, I thought. There was no reality in his photographs, in the sultry expressions of the models, their seductive glances. Those things were as far from the truth as possible. Yet when Harold handed me a CD a week later, I spent hours with the images of Kaitlyn in and out of the trenchcoat, imagining her lips were pursed for me, that she bent over so I could come to her with the swelling she must have spotted in my jeans.

ભ

I considered quitting after that, telling Harold I was too busy with work and social life to take on anything extra. By then I'd moved out of my parents' house, into an apartment with two of the agency's newest employees, both in sales. I did go out more, even had a few dates with a copywriter, but I still spent most evenings looking at the bodies of women who'd stripped down in Harold's basement, who'd let him take their pictures in exchange for cash. I was disgusted with myself but made no effort to stop. And then September 11 happened, the economy went to shit, and my housemates and I all got laid off. To keep from moving back in with my parents, I returned to shift work with the hotel banqueting department. I put in long hours on weekends and made enough to pay my rent. But my weekdays were still free, and the money I earned editing Harold's images kept me comfortable.

Even though the internet bubble had burst, demand for his product remained high. In fact, business was booming, he said. He took on only occasional advertising contracts now. And with so many young people out of work, he had models lined up a month out. Diligent girls, he said, willing to work for modest pay while they learned how to pose. "Hey, I'm sorry you lost your steady gig, but you know what? It's a blessing. Kill your soul to work under those lights for much longer. You're an artist. Freelance is the only way to live."

He'd stop by my apartment with a CD once a week, and with so much free time I'd turn them around in two days. I had to buy an external hard drive to store all the images, which I catalogued by year and by name. Sometimes, in a nostalgic mood, I'd scroll through by date, as if I were searching memories, reliving those innocent days before planes had slammed into towers. Other times, I'd want to spend nights, even weeks, with just one woman, imagining she put on and took off each new outfit for me. It was a kind of sickness, I know, and it went on this way for far too long.

I'm not proud of any of this. It confuses me to go over it all these years later. I'm married now, have been since 2010. I see my wife's body coming out of the shower every day. We have a normal enough sex life, and I don't keep any pictures of her to look at when she's not around.

I check out other women sometimes, but only in a distracted sort of way, half-conscious of what I'm taking in: a pair of legs passing by a coffee shop window, nice shoulders in a tank top getting into a car, a flat stomach with puckered navel beside a pool. I no longer burrow myself in fantasy, and I don't quite understand why I needed it so badly at the time. But the way I gave it up is the thing I find most puzzling now.

If my emotional life was stagnant then, my professional life did keep evolving. After about six more months at the hotel, I was promoted to banqueting supervisor, overseeing all the waiters and bartenders at a given event. Instead of serving food, I made sure it all got plated up and out of the kitchen on time. I prodded the lazier members of the staff into taking fewer breaks. And I enjoyed the work, much more so than graphic design, even if it seemed somehow less prestigious. I was making better money, too, and moved into an apartment of my own, where it was a relief not to have to worry about my roommates finding Harold's images, though I was still careful to change my passwords every month or two. The hotel work kept my mind engaged, so I was less likely to fantasize during my shifts. I also liked the feeling that came with other staff looking up to me, even if they were sometimes afraid of me. I gave out praise sparingly, so no one could mistake it for bullshit, and those who received it motivated others to work harder. It was the kind of work I was meant to do, I felt, and nothing made me happier than seeing a bar mitzvah boy or a newlywed couple leaving the hotel so satisfied they didn't even think to complain that the appetizers ran out too soon.

Then, as the economy started to bounce back, it was my task to bring on new staff. Jobs were still hard to come by, and we took in dozens of applications for every call. I had my pick of qualified people, many with years of experience. But on my second day of interviewing I hired a young woman with almost none. She was a year and a half out of college, and the only food service work she'd done was during chore rotation at her sorority house. Otherwise, her previous job history included summers as a camp counselor and three semesters as a Spanish tutor. According to her résumé, since graduating she'd found only unpaid work, as an intern at a children's book publisher and as a volunteer at an animal shelter. She gave a good enough interview, was honest about her lack of experience, said she was a fast learner and ready to work hard. Her references were solid, too, but that wasn't why I hired her. Nor was it simply because she was petite and attractive, with nicely shaped cheekbones shown off by her French braid.

I'm sure the reason is easy enough to guess, and I'm ashamed to admit it. But it's true: the moment she walked into the room, I recognized her. The name on her résumé was Erica, but I knew her as Daphne. In Harold's photo set, shot just a few weeks earlier, she appeared in a bodysuit—red, with sheer panels on the sides—that gradually slipped down to reveal surprisingly full breasts and a carefully clipped heart-shaped patch of pubic hair. I'd spent several nights with her since, and when she took the seat across from me I flinched, convinced at first she was there to accuse me of violating her privacy. I'm sure I stuttered through my questions, but if she noticed, she didn't let on. We spent fifteen minutes talking, and I said I'd be in touch soon. Her handshake was firm, her fingers smooth against my knuckles.

I told myself I hired her because I didn't want her to have to go back to Harold. If she earned a decent amount at the hotel, she could keep her clothes on. But of course this didn't stop me from looking at her with her clothes off as soon as I got home from work the night after her interview, and every night afterward until her first shift. Then, seeing her at the hotel in her uniform—white shirt, black skirt, black tights, clogs—made me oddly impatient as I trained the new staff. I knew every curve beneath that drab fabric, every freckle on her chest and neck. I just wanted the shift to end so I could go back to studying them. But it was close to Christmas, and we were doing big corporate parties every evening. Once the event got going, I was too busy to pay much attention to Erica, though I did notice she was less adept than most of the other new waiters, getting her tables served slower, nearly dropping a tray of salads on her way out of the kitchen.

After work, the staff often went to an Irish pub at the top of the Heritage Mall next door, and though I usually begged off, preferring instead to spend time alone with Harold's girls, that night I joined them. We were all in our early to mid-twenties, none married or with kids, and as you might expect after people got tipsy, the talk grew raunchy. Some of the staff detailed recent hook-ups, others partners' preferences in bed. One described a one-night stand with a guest at the hotel. I just sat there and smiled at them all, benevolently, listening like a wise but distant elder, though several had a few years on me. Erica said nothing, either, just laughed at the others' stories and sipped from a frothy pink cocktail. The shift had clearly worn her out. Wisps of hair had come loose from her braid and fluttered over her ears. She yawned several times, once in the middle of a bartender's story about losing his virginity to an older sister's best friend. "Am I that boring?" he asked, smiling, but with a sneer in his voice. "What about you? Time to tell us about your freaky side."

"Who, me?" Erica said, blinking away her yawn and pushing hair away from her eyes.

"Come on, fess up."

"I'm totally tame," she said, placidly, without blushing or shrugging or shaking her head.

I lifted my glass to hide anything that might have shown on my face. And I congratulated myself for having hired her, giving her the opportunity to be as tame as she chose.

CR

So it's no wonder I was shocked the next time Harold brought me a CD and I opened it to find a new set with Erica—who again went by Daphne—in a sheer pink nightgown, hair in pigtails. There were the full breasts, the heart-shaped pubic patch, the thin lips that smiled demurely at guests in the hotel covered in pink gloss and touched by a pointed tongue. I was equally enraged and delighted. What was she doing it for, if not the money? Some part of me must have believed it was for me. From then on I gave up all the other girls, spent my nights only with Daphne. I made love to her on Harold's cream leather couch, on his prop bed, in his shower, from the front, from behind, from the side. We pleasured each other with our mouths, we played roles, we found new paths to ecstasy, and we were completely open with each other, with nothing to hide.

At work, on the other hand, I kept my distance. I went out of my way to avoid being alone with Erica. When she came to see me about her schedule for the coming week, I told her I couldn't think about it before an event, that she could leave a note with her availability on the banqueting desk, and I'd post the new schedule soon. I wasn't cold to her, just careful. I did everything I could to keep her from noticing how I looked at her with yearning and satiation, with a sense that we shared a secret, one we had to keep from the rest of the staff at all costs. I didn't ask anything about her life outside the hotel. I didn't want to know details about her family or friends or schooling, didn't want to learn about her interests. When I think about her now, I can say almost nothing about her personality. Was she sarcastic or sensitive or silly? I have no idea.

All I really remember is that she was quiet and deferential, addressing me formally though most of the staff used my first name, and that she was useless as a server. Even after a few weeks she remained slow and clumsy and took too many breaks. But I didn't scold her. Not even when the bartender who'd asked about her freaky side flirted with her, nor when she started going home with him at the end of a shift. Whatever they did together outside work was fine with me, because I still had her to myself as soon as I got home. Even when she and the bartender started dating seriously and she no longer appeared on the new CDs Harold gave me, I wasn't bothered. I had plenty of old sets to occupy me. They did so for months.

Then, one weekend in early spring, we were working a big wedding. The groomsmen and bridesmaids were already drunk by the time the reception started, and they kept drinking through the meal and the toasts and the dancing. I was checking out the buffet spread, deciding whether to bring out a new tray of glazed carrots, when a hand came down hard between my shoulder blades. And then a loud, sloppy voice. "It's my airbrusher!" It took only a moment to realize who was speaking. Auburn-haired Kaitlyn, the optometrist's receptionist, in a strapless green bridesmaid's dress, a new tattoo—a rainbow arching between two hearts, one red, one gold—just below her collarbone. "You made me look like a fucking goddess!"

I smiled at her, said a quiet hello, and then tried to continue going about my work, carrying the tray of carrots—still half full—toward the kitchen. But she followed, asking how long I'd worked at the hotel, saying she was surprised to realize I had a regular gig, too, but of course it's not like she made her living from those pictures, and really she mostly did it for fun anyway. "But you know I quit, right?" she asked. "That's why you haven't seen me for a while." She tossed back some chardonnay and waved her empty glass in front of me. "I couldn't do it anymore. Nothing against you. I appreciate the work you did. You're a pro. You made me gorgeous. And hey, the money was good, helped pay down my student loans." By now I was close to the kitchen door, but before I could push through, she took hold of my arm. "But that Harold. You know he's a total lech, right? He was always asking about my personal life, what was going on with my job, my family, giving advice and shit, like he's my fucking dad. Creepy fantasy stuff, I swear. Made my skin crawl to be in his basement after a while. Still makes me sick when I think about it. I hate imagining what he does with my pictures when I'm not there. Wish I could take them all back."

Her face was blotchy, her mascara smeared in the corner of one eye, but her voice was more controlled, lower now, and steady. I had the feeling she knew exactly what I did with her pictures at night, knew about my ever-expanding hard drive. I hadn't looked at her sets for months, but I remembered the way the trench coat draped over a thigh as she stuck out one leg, how the tall heel flexed her calf muscle. I could see the shade of her toenail polish and the shadow cast by the fedora over her left cheek. I should have offered some support, said I was sorry that Harold had made her uncomfortable. But instead I muttered, "No one forced you to show your pussy to the whole world." And without waiting for her reaction, I yanked my arm free, kicked open the door, and hurried behind it.

And then there was a crash near the dishwashing station, a cry of surprise, the sound of shattering plates. When I got there, a tray of dirties was down, shards spread across the floor, that ugly hotel uniform down among them, and still livid thinking about Kaitlyn and Harold, and the accusations I couldn't quite process, I shouted, before I could stop myself, "Damn it, Daphne. Can't you be more careful?"

Her face was pale when she looked up at me. The French braid stretched the skin tight over her cheekbones. Splotches of mashed potatoes dotted her skirt, and the smell of sirloin turned my stomach. She crossed an arm over her chest, another over her crotch.

"Erica, I mean," I said, quieter, trying to find a neutral expression, though my face was on fire. A sudden chill cut through the lower half of my body, as if I'd whipped off my trousers outside on a frosty morning. "Go ahead and keep clearing," I said. "I'll mop this up." I turned away as she stood and kept my back to her until I heard the door swing shut.

ॐ

The hotel business was a good fit for me for a number of years, before I eventually went back to school, pursued new passions, met my wife, became a counselor—drug and alcohol addiction, mostly—and set my life on a different trajectory. The work kept me active and moving all day, even after I transitioned into management, with a private office and a big desk and a staff of fifty. I didn't miss sitting in a cubicle, staring at a computer screen all day. My visual sensibility found plenty of outlets, from hiring florists and interior designers to approving sales brochures and website pages. I often brought in professional photographers to shoot our banquet rooms for promotional purposes, and I worked closely with them on lighting and perspective.

Not Harold Kantor, though. The day after that big wedding, when I accidentally outed myself to Erica—who moved on soon after—I wiped my hard drive. I wish I could say I was relieved the instant I hit return and scrubbed all those bodies from my life, but the truth is, it was excruciating. I felt it physically. A burning in my throat, pain in my guts. I immediately regretted it, wanted to take it back, and I could have, too. I still had all of Harold's original CDs, along with the backups I'd burned, in several shoeboxes in my closet. But I forced myself to carry them out to my car. I drove to Harold's neighborhood, which had come up even more since I'd first visited. Most of the houses on his street had been restored, and Harold's, too, had recently been repainted, a rotting pillar on the front porch replaced. It took a good minute after I rang the bell before he appeared, and I worried I'd caught him in the middle of a shoot, and that the sight of another disrobed woman would obliterate my resolve.

But when he opened the door, his shoulders relaxed, and he let out a long breath. "Glad it's just you," he said. "I heard the bell and wondered if I'd scheduled another shoot and forgot to write it down. Happened last week. I wasn't ready at all."

It was the first time I'd seen him out of his regular work outfit, the nice jeans and button-down. Today he wore old gray utility pants, a long-sleeve t-shirt with shredded cuffs. "I just came to drop these off," I said, holding out the boxes. "Been meaning to give them back."

"You don't have to," he said.

"I'm done with them."

"If you wanted to keep them," he said, looking down at his feet, and then letting his eyes slowly rise to meet mine, "it would be okay. You know, you've earned them."

"They've been taking up too much space in my closet."

"Sure, okay. I'll have more for you soon anyway." He took the boxes from me, balancing them precariously against his belly. Once again I hoped to feel relief, but instead I just wanted to snatch them back. "Come on in. I'll show you what I'm working on."

"I don't want any more," I said. "Pictures, I mean."

"Just to work on," he said. "You know, touch up. Like always."

"I'm done with them," I said again. "I mean, I'm too busy at work. Did I tell you I got a promotion?"

He was already on his way down to the basement, and I followed. The couch's leather was no longer fresh and looked dingy without any lights set up. He put the boxes on the floor beside it. I tried not to look at them, but I kept glancing over. The desire to run over and grab them made me shake, or at least I imagined it did, and I gripped my hands together behind my back. I was sure Harold could have seen my distress if he looked at me. But he kept his face angled away. There was a catch in his voice when he spoke again.

"That's too bad," he said. "But congratulations. I mean, it's good news for you, I'm sure. Better than slave wages. Though with your talents, you could have had a serious freelance career. No bosses, set your own hours. Pretty nice life."

"It doesn't suit me," I said. "I like security too much. And being around people."

"I get it," he said. "It won't be easy to replace you. Not many people with your skills. People I can count on to be, you know…" I thought he was going to say "discreet," which made me picture Erica down on the floor of the hotel kitchen, trying to cover herself from my view. But after thinking a moment, he continued. "Consistent. Especially not on short notice. Got a big batch coming up. Sure you can't do one more? Give me time to find someone new?"

"I can't," I said, my voice thin and desperate. "I need to stop."

"Yeah. Okay. I appreciate all you've done. I'll send you the last check soon. But hey, before you go," he said, sounding hopeful again, buoyant if brittle, "come take a look at what I'm doing. My real stuff. Not many people I know have an eye like yours."

He led me into the darkroom, where the smell of chemicals assaulted me and made me cough. It took a minute for my eyes to adjust to the safe lights so I could see the prints he had drying on a clothesline. More black and white outdoor shots, similar to the previous set of landscapes with ruins, only on a miniature scale. Close-ups this time, mostly of garbage left in the woods or abandoned in open fields. A scummy water bottle floating in a puddle, a magazine rotting in a pile of wet leaves, a chewed-up tennis ball balanced between bulging tree roots. He'd used the same technique as in some of the nudes, blurring out the background, so the central object seemed to float above the surface, popping out of the natural elements surrounding it. But here it just felt like a gimmick, and I didn't see the point. "They're interesting," I said, and tried to sound sincere when I told him I was sure a gallery would want to show them.

He turned his sad gaze on me, and I knew he wanted me to say something more. But my eyes stung from the chemicals, and all I could think was how impossible it must be to create something meaningful when whatever was in your head would always be so much clearer and more honest and better made. So I just thanked him for all the work he'd given me, wished him luck, and shook his hand. Then, to hide my shame, I hurried out of the basement, away from those photographs no one would ever give more than a passing glance, taking the stairs two at a time.

Lucky

Shortly after he turned seventeen and got his driver's license, which wasn't quite a year after he received his green card, Alexander Grinfeld drove his mother's car down a steep embankment into Shale Brook. He was more angry than drunk, though he'd downed most of a six-pack at a party in the woods, and when he reached the sharp bend halfway down Lenape Road, he turned too late, jumped the curb, and lost control of the wheel. The car—a Volkswagen Rabbit, nearly ten years old when his mother bought it—skidded over ferns, loose dirt, and exposed granite. On the way his head smacked the steering wheel, and by the time the Rabbit came to a stop, on its side in the water, he was unconscious. Here the brook was three feet deep. It was late spring, the water still warm from a long day's sunshine. His legs were submerged, along with much of his head. The current brushed back his bristly hair. It covered his ears, as well as his mouth, but left his nose alone. Another inch, the paramedics who fished him out later told his family, and he would have been gone. "Good thing you're not a mouth breather," his little sister Katya said.

When he woke in the hospital, with a massive headache and blurred vision, his anger had mostly dissipated, replaced by embarrassment. He apologized to his mother before she could finish crying and scold him, and later to his father, too, who berated him anyway, in Russian, a language Alex had been trying his hardest to forget. Wasn't life difficult enough without him trying to kill himself? Was this why they brought him across the ocean, to give him the freedom to smash everything they'd built? Didn't he think his mother had enough to worry about?

She did, Alex agreed: a year after they emigrated, his father left her for another refugee, a Cambodian who worked in his lab. But what did that have to do with Alex nearly cracking his skull and filling his lungs with silty water? If his father was so worried about his mother, he shouldn't have slept with other women. He wanted to say so, but it hurt too much to open his mouth, so instead he just glared at the stocky little man in glasses, balding and paunchy, who'd nevertheless managed to make a new life in this stupid country, while leaving Alex to fend for himself. By the time his father pushed through the privacy curtain separating his half of the hospital room from that of a boy recovering from hernia surgery, he was enraged all over again. If he were behind the wheel now, he'd run over anything in his way.

❧

Still, the shame returned every time a nurse told him how lucky he was to be alive. Or worse, when his ex-girlfriend visited, dropping off a card signed by two dozen classmates who'd never spoken a word to him. Her name was Jodi Lazzarini. To think of her as an ex somehow comforted him, made him feel as if their three and a half weeks together had meant something more than his eventual humiliation. The sight of her still gave him a little thrill, as if her appearance were a secret meant only for him—her wide lips and long eyelashes, black hair teased upward into a tumbling wave above a forehead dotted with cover-up that didn't quite match the tone of her skin. He wanted to believe she'd worn the peach-colored tank top for his benefit, as well as the short denim skirt, but he knew this was probably one of the two afternoons a week she waited tables at a café in Lakewood. She'd once told him she loved his accent, but now she was seeing a boy who'd recently moved north from Atlanta. She hugged him, said she'd been so worried when she'd heard about the accident. Her cheek brushed his, her bare shoulder pressed against his aching chin. When she began to pull away, he tried to keep her close, but she twisted her body free and said she'd see him again soon.

Only after she left did he wonder what, exactly, she'd heard. That a pair of assholes had taunted him, called him a Commie spy, even though the Berlin Wall had come down a year earlier? That all he'd been able to do was run away, and he hadn't even managed that without ending up in a ditch?

What ashamed him most was that he'd let their idiotic words get to him. And he knew why: because up to that moment, the night had been one of the best since he'd arrived in this stupid town, where people spent months giggling at his clothes and his haircut and his funny gargled way of saying words they'd known their whole lives and which he'd just learned. After two and a half years, he could finally forget he hadn't watched the same movies or played the same arcade games as these spoiled suburban kids—you've never seen *E.T.*? they'd asked just a month after he'd left Minsk; you don't know what *Pac-Man* is?—and instead just laugh and drink watery beer and smoke tasteless cigarettes around a bonfire, where a girl other than Jodi—blonde and long-waisted—smiled at him when he replied to someone's question with, "Vhatever you vant, man."

There were people around him he considered friends, or might one day, who put an arm around his back and said, "We're gonna have the best senior year ever," like something out of a movie he had seen since arriving, and for a moment he didn't have to resent them for having ridiculed his backwards childhood, when *they* were the backwards ones, living in a town full of ugly ranch houses and artificial lakes, most never having set foot in New York City, though it was only a forty-minute drive away. Even behind the Iron Curtain, Minsk had been a thousand times more sophisticated than Union Knoll, New Jersey. But tonight he didn't have to think about his classmates' narrow-mindedness, because here at the end of a gravel road, on wooded land owned by the state mental hospital but largely neglected, they were all equally tipsy and giddy, anticipating the imminent summer break and watching sparks from a bonfire swirl against a backdrop of dark trees and then fizzing out against a darker sky.

That is, until two boys he recognized from gym class but whose names he couldn't remember—there were several who looked nearly identical, with gelled spiky hair and gold chains and puffy shirts, and names like Billy and Tony and Jimmy—stumbled to where he sat on a mossy log and swayed in front of him. "Hey, Vladimir," one said, and the other replied, "No, it's Dmitri. Can't you tell a Vladimir from a Dmitri?" And then the first: "I can't tell any of these Commies apart."

It was just ignorance, he knew. But it infuriated him all the same, in part because he had a perfectly good American name—he never let his mother call him Sasha in public—and in part because his middle name *was* Dmitri, and what the hell was wrong with that? These morons didn't know the first thing about Communism, didn't know what it was like to live in a place where store shelves would suddenly go bare, where his father couldn't get a promotion because he was a Jew, and couldn't get a visa to leave for the same reason, not until Gorbachev saw the end coming and opened the gates. Yet they called him a spy, said he was here to steal secrets from Picatinny Arsenal, where the army apparently built classified weapons a few miles down Route 46. And he might have ignored them, except that they got in his face and poked his chest, and between their stupid spiky heads he spotted the blonde girl—she had a mulish chin and piggy nose, he realized now—laughing with her eyes squinted nearly shut. He elbowed past them, tossed his half-empty beer can onto the bonfire, where it hissed behind him, and spun the Rabbit's tires on gravel before peeling away.

He tore up Crescent Ridge, over the top of the knoll, and down toward Lenape Lake, cursing those Tonys and Jimmys and Billys, wishing he could have stayed in Minsk and starved with his actual friends. Or at least that his family could have settled in Brighton Beach or Sheepshead Bay with the rest of the refuseniks who'd finally been let loose, including his grandfather and aunt and cousins, real city neighborhoods full of people who sounded like him. But there were no jobs in New York, his father said, except driving a cab like all the other immigrants. He was a trained chemist, and here, at least, he could work in his chosen profession, even if not up to his ability or level of experience: he was a lab tech for the manufacturing department of one of the big pharmaceutical firms on Route 10. His mother, too, was a chemist, with a doctorate, and she'd done better for herself, hired to run a pair of labs as a quality assurance manager at the same firm, where she now had to bump into her former husband and his new girlfriend in the cafeteria before coming home from work to argue with Katya, who, at fifteen, had recently filled a drawer of the bathroom cabinet with multiple forms of birth control: pills and condoms and those weird little sponges that looked like they belonged on the ends of headphones.

It was all so idiotic and absurd, and when he saw the sharp curve in the road ahead, first he pumped the gas, thinking, fuck all these morons, before realizing what he'd done and jamming the brake. By then he knew he'd roll the Rabbit if he cut it too hard, so he took the turn as gradually as he could and heard the front passenger tire pop as it went over the curb. Something hard scraped the chassis, and as he bumped down the embankment he thought, Alex, you fucking moron, and experienced a surge of sadness mixed with an odd relief before the grille impaled the soft creek bed and his chin hit the wheel, cracking a molar, and then a blissful dreamless nothing as the water rose around him.

CR

So he almost died. Big deal. But he didn't, did he? He was still here, still stuck with his accent and funny middle name, still surrounded by morons.

These, he thought, were bigger deals: The car was totaled. His mother would have to ride the bus to work until she could afford a new one. Katya now had an excuse to catch a lift to school with the boyfriend whose sperm she was fending off with such diligence. And Alex? He'd walk the three miles each way, on winding roads with no sidewalks, where Jimmys and Billys and Tonys would grind past him in T-Birds and Camaros, shout slurs about the KGB, and hurl mustard-filled sandwiches at his second-hand denim jacket. Or maybe he'd drop out and move to Brighton Beach, wait tables or work in a warehouse, or maybe squat with junkies in an abandoned building and fill his veins with morphine. Except that he'd already taken his SATs and scored high enough on the math portion to get recruitment letters from half a dozen colleges, including a full tuition waiver at Rutgers, if he wanted to stay in this stupid state and put up with Tonys and Billys and Jimmys for another four years.

For now, though, his head hurt too much for him to return to school, and his vision stayed blurry enough that he had a hard time focusing on the TV in his mother's cramped apartment, the one she rented after his father invited his girlfriend to live with him in the ugly little ranch house whose down payment had been raised by members of a local synagogue they attended only once. The complex was sprawling but shabby, with more space for parking than for living, and walls so flimsy he could hear trucks accelerating up the interstate on-ramp three blocks away. You're lucky, everyone told him, to come out of a wreck like that with nothing more than a concussion and a dislocated shoulder. But the doctor said he couldn't read for two weeks, much less wrestle with calculus problems, which meant he'd miss his final exams and have to make them up sometime over the summer, when he was supposed to be working as an assistant in one of his mother's labs, dissolving pills in vats of acid and pipetting drops onto coated plates to test their shelf life. What would he do for those two weeks, if he couldn't even watch TV? After two days, the shameful highlight was listening to Katya and her boyfriend through the paper-thin sheetrock that separated their bedrooms and then giving her cover when she lied to their tired mother after work, saying she'd been alone with Alex, doing homework, all afternoon.

Otherwise, he spent his time lying on the sofa, listening to music to drown out the traffic, and thinking about the not-quite-a-month he'd dated Jodi—they went to three movies and made out in the Rabbit after each—who told him when she broke things off that one day he'd make a great boyfriend but that he wasn't quite ready yet. Ready for what? He'd never asked, and she didn't say. But he thought it might have to do with the one time she stuck her hand down his pants only to jerk back when he instantly made a sticky mess in her palm. All he wanted was for that moment to last, but it would forever be over as soon as it happened. He tried to slow it in his imagination while listening to Katya and her boyfriend, or while alone in the apartment, with his own hand inside his briefs.

That's where it was when, one morning a week after the accident, a quick loud knock sounded on the front door. Before it flung open—why hadn't he locked it? but then, who ever came here?—he managed to get his jeans closed and haul himself upright, wrenching his hurt shoulder and sparking a flare of pain in his head, just behind his left eye. He half expected Jodi to walk in, not to give him another chance, but to tell him he still wasn't ready, no matter how many times he tried to last longer. Instead, it was his grandfather, small and stooped, in a gray tweed blazer and matching hat. His father's father, whom he called Grandpa Benya. Since they'd left Minsk, Alex had never seen him outside of Brooklyn, usually in his Aunt Raina's crowded apartment smelling of onions, occasionally in his own small studio a few noisy blocks from the beach. "How did you get here?" he asked in English, to which his grandfather replied—in Russian, as he expected—"You think I don't know how to ride a train?"

"The station's two miles away."

"You think I don't know how to catch a cab?"

He suspected this line of question and answer could go on all morning, so he said nothing, just settled himself against the couch cushions and adjusted his sling. His grandfather looked around for somewhere to hang his hat, and finding none, cleared a spot for it on the square dinette table, which was smothered in unopened mail and empty coffee cups. Then he disappeared into the tiny kitchen, where Alex couldn't see him, though his smell lingered, a mixture of old sweat and industrial detergent—the smell of the Soviet Union, Alex thought, an odor that would never wash off no matter how many years he lived here. Then came the sound of running water, the click of a gas burner, the crinkling of plastic wrappers. After a few minutes, his grandfather returned with a teapot, a pair of cups, a plate full of the caramel cubes he'd come to love since moving to the States. They replaced the toffee he'd eaten in Minsk, which had ruined his teeth, making his rare smiles exuberant flashes of silver.

"You think I don't want to see my grandson when he's hurt? After he's nearly cracked his head open and spilled out his only useful organ?"

"I could use the company," Alex said. He gave up on English now, returning to the cadences that still felt more natural despite his attempts to excise them. "I've been bored out of my mind."

"I'm cheap entertainment," his grandfather said, setting the teapot on the table and pouring steaming liquid into both cups. The caramels he must have brought with him, since Alex's mother didn't keep any sweets in the kitchen. Now that she was single, she was trying to lose weight but had no time or patience for exercise. "But unfortunately you get what you pay for."

A quick flash of those silver teeth, and then they were hidden behind thick bristly lips. He pulled a chair away from the table and set it so Alex had to twist to face him. He tried to do so, in any case, but it hurt his head too much, so instead he settled back against the cushions again and looked at the old man from the corners of his eyes. The sight of him was familiar enough: sixty-six and widowed, round-shouldered and big-eared, bald except for a semi-circular band of white hair stretching from one ear to the other around the back of a fleshy head. He'd been a quiet presence in Alex's childhood, a glum figure in a corner armchair, reading newspapers with such concentration and close scrutiny that half an hour would pass without his turning a page. In Minsk he'd worked as an engineer, designing chemical storage tanks, but here he lived on the pittance scraped together by the organization that sponsored his emigration. Alex had never considered whether or not his grandfather paid any attention to what he did with his life.

"I didn't do it on purpose, if that's what you think," he said. "I wasn't trying to off myself."

"An accident, I understand," his grandfather said. "You accidentally drank a lot of beer. And accidentally drove like a speed racer on a twisty road."

"You don't know what I'm dealing with."

"That's true. No one knows what's in someone else's mind. Not unless he tells you."

"They took my license," Alex said. "I won't be able to drive again for a year."

"A great tragedy," his grandfather said. "And maybe a relief for your mother."

"You don't understand how these people treat me. The things they say about me. As if they knew the first fucking thing about Communists—"

"Have one of these," his grandfather said, leaning forward and holding out the plate of caramels. "They're almost as good as Kis-Kis. And without the paper that sticks."

"I can't. I've got a new crown on the tooth I broke. It'll pull off."

His grandfather took two of the brown cubes, tucked one inside each cheek. "They're cruel to you, these little Nazis," he said, his voice now garbled by the candies.

"Not Nazis," Alex said. "Guidos. That's what other kids at school call them. They're Italian, or pretending to be. They want to be the Godfather."

"Your godfather never hurt anyone."

"*The* Godfather," Alex said.

"Do you remember Boris? Your father's best friend from when they were little boys. Very loyal. Never would have left his wife and kids, even if he moved to a crazy new country where no one else cares about family."

"From the movie," Alex said. "Mafia."

His grandfather made a slurping sound, sucking the caramel saliva from between his teeth with such salacious pleasure as to make Alex queasy. "Whoever they are. They call you names."

"In front of everyone."

"And this makes you drive off a cliff."

"It wasn't a cliff. Just a steep hill. And I didn't do it on purpose."

"I understand."

"And Dad already yelled at me. So you don't have to tell me how badly I messed everything up."

"A man who leaves his family shouldn't have much room to criticize others."

"Tell him that."

"Do you think he listens to me?" His grandfather reached for another caramel but before picking it up seemed to reconsider and pulled his hand back. "What I'm telling you is, I understand. It's hard. You come to this new country, you just want to fit in and have friends like a normal boy, and these little ... what? Godfathers? They make your life miserable."

"Exactly," Alex said.

"The truth is, we should have come a long time ago," his grandfather said. "The Grinfelds, I mean. Long before you were born. Before I was born, even. When the grandparents and great-grandparents of those little godfathers came. But then of course I wouldn't have met your grandmother, and we wouldn't have had your disappointment of a father, and you wouldn't be here."

"Worth the trade-off," Alex said, with a bitterness he didn't entirely believe.

"Maybe," his grandfather said, more seriously than Alex expected. He twisted too late to see if the word was accompanied by another flash of silver smile. The movement hurt his shoulder, and he winced, but by then his grandfather had glanced up at the ceiling and didn't notice. "I used to resent them for staying. My grandfather and his siblings, and my father, too. They all had the chance. But they weren't adventurous people. No imagination. They were observant, obedient. They went to shul every week, davened three times a day. Did you know they were beer brewers? They owned the second-largest brewery in Slutsk. Supplied two regiments of the Czar's army. And never drank a drop."

"I'm making up for it," Alex said, and now his grandfather not only smiled but let out a brief and surprising laugh, high in pitch and breathy, and finished with a cough.

"Maybe they should have had a few," he said when he recovered. "Maybe it would have made them reckless enough to jump on a ship like so many of their neighbors, who worried about pogroms. But my family wasn't going anywhere. Sure, there was always the possibility of pogroms, but they'd never happened in Slutsk. Why give up everything they'd built for some imagined fate? They stayed. After the revolution, when the town switched hands between Red and White three times, they stayed. And when the Soviets finally took over for good and confiscated all the brewery's proceeds for the state, used the shul to store grain from the collective farms? They stayed then, too. They davened in basements, behind the brewing tanks. They accepted this new way of living the same as the old. I was born a year later."

This was the most his grandfather had ever said to him in one sitting, the most, in fact, Alex had ever heard the old man speak to anyone. Combined with his blurry vision the speech disoriented him further, made him wonder if he were imagining all of this—if he were still out cold in the Rabbit, maybe, hanging in the seatbelt, the water rising up past his nose after all. But even stranger than the flood of words was the silence that suddenly followed, a silence filled with the gruff whistling of strained breath through hairy nostrils. To erase it, Alex said, "They should have got out while they could."

His grandfather took another moment to answer. "Maybe you're right about that, Sasha. Even if it means you and I wouldn't be here." The heavy breath again, a slurp of tea. "Because of course things got worse."

"My head hurts," Alex said, returning to English, which now seemed more difficult for his mouth to form than the language he'd avoided speaking for the past two years. He worried the concussion was leaching away all he'd learned since he'd left home. "I need to rest now."

But if his grandfather understood the words, he didn't listen to them. "Do you want to know what happened to me during the war?"

This made Alex sit up despite the pain. He glanced at his grandfather to see if something had shifted in his expression. But he'd snuck another pair of caramels without Alex noticing, and his cheeks pooched out again, giving him a comical look rather than the somber one Alex expected. "Dad told me," he said. "You got evacuated. Spent four years in the Caucasus."

"Your father's … Let's just say he's got limited capacity. I might not have told him everything."

Hearing this gave Alex some satisfaction, though it also made him uneasy. What capacity did he have that his father didn't? "I do want to know," he said. "But not now. My head—"

"It's true I ended up in Sochi," his grandfather said. "Eventually. And yes, some kids were evacuated before the invasion. About a hundred or so. But I wasn't one of them."

⁛

What he remembered afterward was mostly the pain, and the way his grandfather ignored it, even as Alex begged him to stop. But once the old man started his story, no amount of pleading would cut it short. The details themselves penetrated Alex's mind as part of the throbbing behind his eye, upending what he thought he knew. His father had told him what had happened in Slutsk, the Grinfeld's home for two and a half centuries—a place in which Alex had never once set foot, though it was only an hour's drive from Minsk. The Germans entered the town on the morning of October 27, 1941. They pulled Jews out of their houses, rounded them up in the street, shot them at close range. Four thousand people in two days, including Alex's great-grandparents and two great-aunts. The rest were fenced off in a ghetto, which was later burned to the ground, those who didn't perish in the fire shot as they ran from the flames.

But his grandfather was supposed to have been hundreds of miles away, in relative safety with his youngest sister and two older cousins, though separated from the rest of his family. That he'd stayed behind wasn't just news—it erased an entire history and replaced it with a new one Alex couldn't yet accommodate in his rattled brain. How was it possible that he'd known this man for seventeen years and never once suspected?

His grandfather had been seventeen then, too. He woke to gunshots. His older sisters were screaming. Before he could find them, soldiers had entered the house, yanking them by the collars of their night clothes through the hall and out the front door. He didn't know what was happening, and it all went so quickly he felt as if he were still asleep, dreaming a terrible dream. But he also knew this was no dream he'd ever wake from. Outside, cold, barefoot in pajamas, he stood in a tight pack of people, maybe fifty, maybe a hundred, all huddled together in the center of the street. His father pressed against him on one side, one of his sisters on the other. He didn't know where his mother was. He couldn't see anything but the backs and heads of people on either side. And then the shots started, so much noise he couldn't even hear the screams, and the people in front of him started falling.

"Then my father did," he said. "And then I did."

By this time Alex's head pounded so hard he had to close his eyes. He didn't understand what his grandfather was saying, or else he believed he was inventing an alternate life to the one he'd actually lived. Because here he was, nearly fifty years later, talking around the bulge of melting caramels. How could any of what he said be true, unless Alex were listening to a ghost, or a figment of his imagination?

"I didn't realize I'd been shot at first," his grandfather said. "I didn't know what had happened." He was on his back, a cloud of smoke drifting over him. And only after a few seconds did he feel any pain. Then there was only pain, and before he lost consciousness, he had enough time to think that he would soon be dead.

"I need to sleep now," Alex said, sweating and nauseated, as if his entire body were rejecting the story, would vomit it out if forced to swallow any more. "The doctor said I need to keep from overdoing it."

But his grandfather kept on. As it turned out, the bullet passed right through him. Missed all his vital organs. And somehow left enough blood in him to keep his heart pumping. But he didn't know it as he blacked out. Nor did the soldiers who placed him in a truck piled with other bodies. Nor the ones who drove him across the river, or the ones who dropped him into a hole and covered him with the rich soil of a recently ploughed field.

"Grandpa," Alex whispered. "You're hurting me."

He wasn't the only person buried alive, his grandfather went on without pause. This he found out only later. There was a letter, well-known among historians of the period. Wilhelm Kube, the German civilian administrator in Belorussia, wrote to Himmler, head of the S.S., complaining about the actions of the military police in Slutsk. It was too chaotic, he said. It would turn the local populace against them. In particular, he was horrified to learn that wounded people had crawled out of their shallow graves, only to be shot a second time.

Alex could no longer respond. He could only focus on his breathing to keep from throwing up. He kept seeing the curve of Lenape Road looming ahead of him, growing closer, his hands unable to turn the wheel. His grandfather's voice would never stop, he thought, would keep drilling into the space between his ears, pushing his brain forward against the front of his skull, bruising it further until nothing of use was left.

"I wouldn't learn any of that for years," the voice went on. "I thought no one but me had woken in the dark that way." At first he believed he was indeed dead, and that death was this blackness all around him, and the pressure against his back and legs, and the stickiness on his neck, and the dirt in his mouth. And only slowly did it dawn on him where he was. That what he felt against his chest was the weight of other bodies, three or four layers of them. His neighbors, maybe his family. He had to shove limbs out of his way, and leaking torsos, and heads whose faces he couldn't see. He pushed and clawed and climbed until a finger broke through the surface, and then an arm, and then his mouth. It was nighttime. He heard voices near the river, saw lights in the distance. As quietly as he could, he spit out dirt and blood and slid on his belly to the edge of the field, beyond which a dark line of trees stood out against a sky too bright with stars.

"I get it," Alex said, though by now he didn't believe his grandfather was trying to teach him anything. The words were meant to punish him, to make him suffer. But to stop them he said, "You're telling me I'm lucky to be alive. That I should be grateful and quit doing stupid things. I get it."

"I didn't feel lucky," his grandfather said. "I was alone in the woods. Alone in the world. My whole family gone. Right then I wished the bullet had finished me. I still do, sometimes."

℘

Because Alex was sure his grandfather wouldn't stop until he made blood leak from his ears, the abrupt silence came as a shock, as unnerving as the speech it followed. He let his eyes open a crack. The plate of caramels on the coffee table was empty. His cup of tea, untouched, still let off a thin wisp of steam. His grandfather leaned back in the chair, with his legs crossed, cheeks bulging. It took Alex a moment to realize what had stopped him: the door opening again, quietly this time, without a knock first. There, beneath the ugly oblong light fixture—not so different from the one in their Minsk apartment—stepped Katya and her boyfriend, a lanky freckled kid with a helmet of brown curls and a big Adam's apple, laughing and whispering, hands around each other's waists. It wasn't even lunchtime, so they must have cut out of study hall. They were used to Alex being home and hardly even acknowledged him. They didn't glance at him now, and only after a moment did Katya—short, wide-hipped, and busty like their mother, wearing blue eyeshadow and a high ponytail—notice their grandfather. She pulled up quickly, tugged at the hem of her shirt, but kept her arm around the boyfriend as she asked, "What are you doing here?"

"You think I don't care about my grandson who nearly split open his skull?"

The boyfriend, not understanding a word, smiled and blinked, and kept his free arm crossed over his crotch. "This is Justin," Katya said. "Justin, Grandpa Benya."

"Justin," their grandfather said, making it sound like "Justine." He pushed himself up from the chair and shook the boy's hand. Then he went on in English: "I hope you know my granddaughter is, how do you say, very tough. Tougher than you. She will, let us see ... she will crush your heart."

He laughed his high breathy laugh, and Katya laughed with him. Justin kept smiling but looked stricken, his lips frozen above a weak chin. What made him ready to be a boyfriend when Alex wasn't? Was it just because Katya had fewer expectations than Jodi? It didn't seem fair, but he couldn't think about it now. If he didn't sleep soon, he'd end up with brain-damage for sure, and then he might really throw himself from a cliff. He rolled off the couch and stumbled to his bedroom without another word to his grandfather. He slept then, for how long he wasn't sure, without any dreams he could remember, but woke to the sound of his sister's voice through the thin wall beside his bed. Not ecstatic this time, nor even sweetly post-coital, but solemn and sincere. "He's totally broken," she said, and Alex assumed she was talking about him. He wanted to protest—I'm getting better, I can keep myself under control from now on—but she continued: "A Holocaust survivor, you know? You wouldn't believe what he went through."

"What, like gas chambers and shit?" Justin asked. Alex didn't know how his sister could put up with that nasal, dim-witted voice.

"You think he'd be here if he was in a gas chamber?"

"I mean, I don't know."

"They shot him. Thought he was dead and buried him alive."

"Jesus."

"I guess, sort of like that. He crawled out of the grave. But not so much a miracle, just an accident."

"No wonder he was so, I don't know—"

"I'm the only one he's told," Katya said, a little quieter, but no less difficult for Alex to hear. Her accent was milder than his, though they'd been here the same amount of time. Everything had been easier for her, he thought—because she was younger, because she was a girl? He wanted to blame it on anything other than some failure in himself, something he didn't have to try to fix. "He never told his own kids," Katya continued. "They think he got evacuated before all the shit started. But on the plane over? You know, when we first moved here? I sat next to him. I was crying because we were leaving all my friends. I knew I was supposed to be grateful. We were finally getting out. But I was scared. And maybe I wouldn't shut up or something, and he asked me if I wanted to know how he escaped. I thought he was trying to comfort me. But then, I don't know. It was weird. Like he wanted to torture me for being sad. Told me the whole story. Every fucking detail.

Even when I asked him to stop. You wouldn't believe it. There were bodies on top of him. Bleeding all over his hair, into his mouth. He had to climb through them to get out. I don't want to think about it now. Gives me nightmares. I didn't stop crying the whole trip. By the time we landed, I was so tired I didn't care about anything. Just wanted to get on with my life."

"Your family's so fucked up," Justin said. "I thought it was just your brother. And your dad. But it's all of you."

"Maybe," Katya said. "But I'm the tough one, remember? I'm gonna crush your heart? First I'm gonna do something else."

Then her voice dropped off, replaced by the now-familiar sounds of smacking lips and slurping tongues. But Alex no longer wanted to hear them. He buried his sore head under his pillow. When that wasn't enough, he pulled the sheet over, too, and then the blanket that was too warm for the season, and several dirty shirts from the pile of laundry in his closet. But the sounds seeped through anyway, and no matter which way he turned his face, his breath kept carrying the smell of his sweat into his nose.

The Next Ten

Ted Fessler hadn't spoken to Angela Cohn in nearly a decade. In their late twenties, they'd enjoyed—and then suffered through—a brief and volatile romance that had ended badly, with regretful words Ted had yet to forgive himself for saying. This was when they both lived in Seattle, working for an environmental non-profit, Ted writing grants, Angie directing public relations and marketing. Not long after they split, Angie quit the job and moved away—to Colorado, then New Mexico—and only occasionally did word of her make its way to Ted through mutual friends. He heard when she got married, when she got divorced, when her mother died suddenly from an aggressive tumor and she had to return home to a suburb of Detroit to look after her father. He bought a card then, wrote a note expressing condolences, but when it was addressed, stamped, and ready to go, he reconsidered and slipped it into the recycling bin.

During the year or two after their break-up, his feelings about Angie were complicated and intense, and he often worked through them in therapy sessions. He resented her for the pain she'd caused, berated himself for his own behavior, but also treasured their time together, during which, he thought, he'd been more vigorously alive than at any point before or after. He played over their early dates, their long nights of drinking at a Ballard bar followed by wild lovemaking in his tiny studio, their quarrels and moments of tenderness. He agonized over the memories, sometimes wishing he could erase them, other times fearing they'd begun to slip away despite his efforts to hold them close.

Eventually, however, these feelings faded. He changed jobs several times, met his wife Claire, moved to Portland, and started a family. He decided that fraught emotions were a waste of time. Relationships didn't have to be so difficult. His marriage and children made him far happier than he'd ever been with Angie. He came to think of their time together as a youthful experiment, necessary but fleeting. He expected never to see her again.

And yet here she was, in the fourth row of chairs in the medium-sized conference room of a downtown hotel, where Ted was addressing a group of executive directors and development staff. He'd done well for himself over the past decade, rising up the ranks of non-profit management until being hired by a large foundation as a senior grants officer, doling out project funds and working with organizations to help them achieve financial stability. Today he was giving a talk on the strategic planning process, and he was a third of the way through before he spotted Angie, in a black sweater that matched her black hair, which she'd cut shorter since he'd last seen her, a wedge bob that ended in points on either side of her face. From the front of the room, she seemed otherwise unchanged, the angular jaw and deep-set eyes, the nose that tilted slightly to the left, the long slim fingers twirling a pen above a knee in black tights. The sudden recognition startled him so completely that he lost the thread of his talk, and he had to glance down at his notes, clear his throat, and quickly apologize, before he recovered and carried on.

For her part, Angie didn't seem terribly surprised to see him, though of course his name had been on the program for months. When he glanced at her again, holding off until he'd gotten several paragraphs farther into the talk, re-grounded and confident, she gave a little smile, lips closed, shy and sheepish. There was no anger in her expression, no hurt, and it almost threw him again, but he managed to keep a steady pace and finish without another stumble. Applause followed, louder than he thought he deserved, but he checked to see what Angie made of it, the respect his job garnered, the attention and admiration of the eighty professionals in the room, most of them women. But she was looking away then, toward something in her lap he couldn't see. For another twenty minutes he fielded questions, many of them inane, but he answered with magnanimity, as if each were equally significant. When it was finally over, there came more applause, but hastily this time, as the attendees packed briefcases and tote bags. It was the end of the work day for many, a chance to catch a bus twenty minutes earlier than usual, and most hurried out of the room. But a small number lingered, came up to thank him for his talk and ask if they might follow up via email, overly solicitous people hoping for his largesse. He shook hands, accepted compliments, made small talk, felt his face grow sore from smiling.

Angie waited off to the side until everyone had finished talking to him before approaching. When she got close he expected to see more changes—lines around her eyes and mouth, gray roots at the part in her hair—but if anything she looked better than when he'd last seen her, skin free of the acne that had still plagued her at twenty-eight, the set of her jaw less severe, eyes calmer. She'd grown up, yes, just as he had, and before she reached him she threw open her arms for a hug. He stepped into it, breathed in the scent that was both familiar and new—the same citrus shampoo minus cigarette smoke—gave a quick squeeze, and quickly let go.

"It's so good to see you," she said, which was what you were supposed to say in a situation like this, though he didn't think *good* was the right word. Odd, confusing, exciting, terrifying. Any of those would have made more sense. "You look great," she said. "Healthy. Happy."

Unlike Angie, Ted had clearly aged in the last ten years. Work and family had taken a toll on his body. His hair had receded at the temples and begun to gray above the ears, his belly had pooched out, his shoulders, once firm, had softened, threatening at times to go flabby. He wondered if she would have recognized him if they'd passed on the street instead of here, where his name appeared so prominently on the hotel sign-board. The thought of her walking by without noticing him, as if he were a stranger, momentarily filled him with an old resentment—as if she'd been untouched by their fights, and by their love, too, freed from the burden of their time together the instant she'd walked away, moving seamlessly on with her life, while he'd suffered years of bitterness, cycling through several failed attempts to replace her before realizing it wasn't possible, and instead marrying a woman who made him feel comfortable and accepted, if not fiery and love-mad.

But of course Angie had suffered, too, he knew that, even if it hadn't been over him. Her divorce must have been painful, the loss of her mother even more so. He mentioned the latter now—saying how sorry he was when he'd heard, how he'd thought about reaching out but didn't want to cause her more turmoil when she was already dealing with so much—and while he spoke, she nodded and smiled a fragile smile, her cheeks flattening in the way he remembered when she was holding back tears, her nose wrinkling slightly. "It was hard," she said. "The hardest thing I've ever gone through."

And again the resentment bubbled up, the jealousy, even as he knew how ridiculous it was to be jealous of a dead mother. Ridiculous, too, for their break-up to be the hardest thing *he'd* ever gone through. He hadn't lost any parents or close friends, hadn't suffered major illness or financial trouble. Any of the difficult things he might face were still in his future. Raising children was a different kind of challenge, too wrapped up with joy to compare. Tragedy was one more thing Angie had over him. But he made himself ask after her father, and as she told him about his struggles, both physical and mental—he had the early stages of Parkinson's, and his wife's death sent him into a devastating depression—Ted found himself growing over-heated in his blazer and tie, the empty conference room seeming too large now with just the two of them present, and yet still somehow claustrophobic, not enough space to breathe. "I got him settled into an assisted living facility before I moved back out here," she said. "It was a tough choice, but my brother's nearby and can look after him, and I just missed the Northwest so much, I couldn't stay."

Ted gestured at the pitted ceiling panels. "Do you want to go up to the bar?" he asked. "Grab a glass of wine and catch up?"

"How about a coffee," she said, not in a cutting way, though he felt chastised all the same, as if it were inappropriate of him to suggest a drink. A drink was what he needed, a stronger one than wine, but he agreed to coffee and led the way out of the conference room, down the bland corridor, fawn walls and hazel carpet. Stairs winded him more easily than he wanted to show, but the thought of being in a small elevator with her intensified the constriction in his chest, and he worried she'd find it strange to ride up just one floor. So he tried to breathe steadily as he took each step, exaggerating a limp on his left side and telling her he'd hurt his knee playing tennis. He had hurt his knee, though he didn't know how—he hadn't played tennis in years. On the way up, she commiserated, telling him about a hamstring injury that had slowed her down a while ago, and what a relief it had been to finally get back to the gym and yoga class.

The coffee stand was right in the middle of the lobby, with a few tables off to one side, open and exposed. The bar, tucked around the corner from registration, would have been more private, and perhaps more intimate. When he glanced at the clerks behind the registration desk, thoughts came into his mind unbidden, almost against his will: whether the hotel might have any open rooms, whether he could somehow pay for one with the foundation's credit card and avoid being questioned by the bookkeeper who oversaw expense accounts. The idea was absurd, and he immediately dismissed it, chalking it up to how little sex he and Claire had these days. They were too exhausted after work, and on weekends they watched movies in the evening to relax. He often fell asleep before she came to bed and awoke aroused, but before he could do anything about it the kids came charging in, demanding breakfast and attention. It may have been a month since the last time they'd fulfilled the erotic intentions they often expressed—"I wish we had time for quick romp," Claire would say on her way out to catch her bus, and he'd reply, "Let's find time for one soon"—without making the effort to carry them out.

With Angie, there had been sex at all times of day, and in every conceivable spot in his Ballard studio or the Capitol Hill apartment she shared with two other women: on couches and armchairs; bent over sinks and counters; once, when her roommates were out, against the railing of her tiny balcony overlooking East Harrison Street. Much of it had been drunken and sloppy but always exhilarating. Now her movements across the lobby struck him with their familiarity, those short hard steps, head thrust forward, arms hardly swinging at her sides. It was strange to know so much about her despite all the years they'd been living their separate lives. He knew what sort of underwear she had on—black cotton thong—and could picture her reaching behind to unhook a matching bra. He could still hear the way her breath caught in her chest just before the aggrieved groan of orgasm. He didn't want to know what she remembered about him from those days when he was still just a development assistant struggling to pay rent on a pitiful salary. His worn boxer shorts, shredded around the elastic waistband? His grunts and near whimpers?

She insisted on buying his coffee, though he tried to talk her out of it, flashing his purchasing card before she nudged his hand away. As they waited by the counter, he asked what organization she was working for—he hadn't seen her name on any staff lists, but then he worked with so many non-profits now, there were nearly two hundred in the metro area, so it wouldn't surprise him if he'd simply overlooked it. He said this with conviction, though he didn't believe it for a moment. He'd never have passed over the name Angela Cohn, not without double-checking to make sure he'd read it right. He wondered if she'd married again and taken a new husband's name, though that didn't sound like Angie. He couldn't even imagine her hyphenating last names into an equitable combination, as Claire had done for the sake of the kids. In either case, she wasn't wearing any rings.

"I'm not in the sector anymore," she said. "I just saw you were talking and decided … I thought it would be a good way to reconnect." Then came the sheepish smile again, though this time he thought he detected a hint of slyness in it, and once more he glanced at the registration desk. This time he pictured a card key slipping into the dark slot of an electronic lock, a little green light flashing followed by the whir of a bolt sliding back. "I don't even live in Portland," she said. "I'm back in Seattle. But I looked you up and saw the event listing and decided to take the train down."

This was far more direct an admission than he'd expected. An "accidental" meeting he could have imagined easily enough—that is, he could have imagined arranging for one himself, if he'd known she was back in this part of the country—but then Angie had always been bolder than most people he knew. After they'd been working together a couple of months, flirting tentatively while maintaining a careful façade of indifference, she'd slipped into his cubicle one afternoon, handed him a square of paper with her phone number, and said, seriously, with a hint of irritation, that he should probably take her out for a drink after work before she lost interest and looked for someone else.

Still, having her seek him out after all this time was more than he could have hoped for, though now it satisfied a longing he hadn't been aware of harboring. "I'm glad you did," he said. "I've thought about you—"

Before he could finish the sentence, their coffees arrived, and Angie made her way to a seat near the windows that rose floor to ceiling and faced the rush hour traffic on Broadway. So many people in their cars could turn and see him sitting across from a woman he'd bedded more times than he could count, who'd taken a three-hour train ride to see him. From outside, they would just look like business associates, in their careful work attire, and maybe no one would suspect this attractive black-haired woman would have ever had any interest in the prematurely balding man across from her, though perhaps some might recognize in his relaxed and confident posture a degree of professional stature and its allure. He sat back in the stiff leather chair and pulled down his tie knot to unbutton his tight shirt collar. His mocha he sipped with a delectable sense of hiding a secret, one he was oddly desperate to share with anyone he could. He wanted to shout it out to strangers in the lobby, narrate his and Angie's entire history for everyone to hear.

Angie placed her drink carefully on the block of granite that served as a table, though it was awkwardly low, a better height for a footrest. A foamy heart floated in the center of her mug. She crossed her legs so the tights, opaque around her ankles, stretched to translucent across a thigh. "I heard you got married," she said.

"That's right," he said. "An amazing woman."

"And kids?"

"Two of them. Emma's four. Owen's two."

"A tiny Ted. That's adorable."

"He has his mother's personality."

"I always knew you'd make a good dad."

If she asked to see pictures, that would be too much. He'd refuse, though he had dozens on his phone—both kids strawberry blondes like their mother, round-faced, with her sturdy Nordic features. "And you? Any children?" he asked, though he knew the answer.

"Not yet," she said. "It may be too late now. I know that. But I wasn't ready before."

"You've got time," he said. Up close he couldn't see any gray in her roots, though maybe the lines around her smile had deepened, and the slightest bit of extra flesh hung below her jaw.

"I wasn't ready for a lot of things. For a long time. But I'm trying to make up for it now. That's why I came down to see you."

He felt himself flush with anticipation, and even as he determined to go forward with whatever she proposed, he couldn't believe how prepared he was to let raw desire carry him wherever it might lead, as it had so many years ago. Had it been lurking inside him all this time, just waiting for the right moment to wreck everything in his life? Had he really cared so little about the things he'd claimed to value, job and family, security and comfort, his marriage vows and the well-being of his children? "I've been ready all along," he said, as calmly as he could manage.

"Here goes, then," she said, and closed her eyes lightly, showing him violet-shadowed lids. "I'm sorry for all the ways I hurt you."

"You don't have to be sorry," he said, automatically, waiting for what would follow.

"But I am."

"It wasn't just you. I did plenty wrong."

The words came out before he'd thought them through, before he'd really considered that what she was saying wasn't preamble to her intended subject but her actual purpose. Why take the train three hours just to say she was sorry for things that had happened ten years earlier?

"I was the one responsible for it," she said. "You just reacted."

He agreed with her, had always believed this to be the case and at times had wanted, badly, for someone to affirm it. His therapist hadn't been willing; instead, she'd told him to focus on his own behavior instead of Angie's. Back then he'd thought she was helping him heal, though in retrospect, he wondered if instead she'd exacerbated the pain, making him dig at the wound until it festered. Now he put on that magnanimous tone once again, the one that served him so well in his job. "We were both at fault."

She uncrossed her legs and threw back her head, bangs flipping backward. This, too, was a gesture he recognized, a hint of the anger that would flash out of nowhere, always catching him off-guard. "Goddamn it, Ted. I'm trying to apologize. I want to make amends."

"Amends?"

"For the harm I caused when I was drinking."

"Wait a minute," he said.

"On your own," she went on, "you're basically a solid, stable guy. If I hadn't been an alcoholic … I know I brought out the worst in you. And I'm sorry for it."

"You weren't an alcoholic," he said.

"I didn't know it then. Or at least I wasn't ready to admit it. I hit rock bottom after my mom died. It's been a long road back. Sober a whole year as of April six."

"So this is just part of—"

"I know I can't change what happened," she said in a voice that sounded rehearsed. "But maybe it helps to hear that I wish I could."

A twelve-step program. He couldn't believe it. Here, too, she had something over him. When they were together, he also drank a lot, far more than he did now. More, even, than he did during his darkest days following their break-up. But he'd never had a real problem. Anything he'd done or said was his, not the alcohol's. "What is this, Step Six?"

"Nine," she said. "And I'm working on Ten, too. Personal inventory. Admitting mistakes as they happen."

"I never figured you for a giving-yourself-to-Jesus type," he said, with more rancor than he'd intended.

"It's a non-denominational program," she said, her smile tight now, the edge of one tooth peeking over her bottom lip, another sign of the old anger that used to come raging out when he least expected it, that could suddenly cut him with insults about his clothing choice or cleaning habits, that could make him feel as impotent as a neutered cat unless he responded in kind. He didn't believe for a moment that being sober was enough to tamp it down for good. "But it's true," she said. "I have accepted a higher power. It's been crucial. I started going to services again. First time since my bat mitzvah. And now I'm back in school to become a counselor. Help other people who've gone through the same thing."

"It must feel good," he said. "All this forgiveness from God."

He tilted his drink high, drained the last dregs, and noticed only then that she still hadn't taken a sip of hers. The foam was gone now, just a flat beige surface even with the lip of the mug. She slumped back in her seat. "Actually, it feels fucking awful." The careful tone had dropped from her voice, and she spoke naturally now, for the first time, he thought, all afternoon. "I hate having to look back at that period of my life."

"We had some good times," he said, and now all he wanted was for her to agree, to share a small yearning for those rowdy nights they'd spent in Ballard, clothes strewn everywhere, bodies tangled, even if they'd never try to recapture them.

"All I see is chaos."

So she'd take the memories from him, too, distort them for her own bullshit self-actualization. "It's all behind anyway," he said. "I'm fine. You don't have to ask for my forgiveness."

"I don't need you to forgive me. I just want you to know you didn't deserve how I treated you. And the way you reacted to it … you can give yourself a break."

She held his gaze then, for too long, it seemed, until he glanced away. The cars on Broadway had stopped dead, no one moving an inch. Claire would have made it home by now and spelled the nanny, and she'd expect him within the hour, though he always left open the possibility he'd come home late, never giving an exact time—he'd have to see how things went, he said in the morning, his meetings might go long. At least a couple of afternoons a week he stopped off for a beer with co-workers before crossing the river, drawing out the time Claire and the kids waited for him, savoring their anticipation. His favorite part of the day was the moment he stepped in the back door, when he felt their need for him most acutely, Claire relieved to take half an hour on her social media sites before sitting down to dinner, the kids desperate for the games he'd play with them, tickling and wrestling and horse rides.

"Really," Angie said now, with a kindness that was worse than anger, her face as open and vulnerable as he'd ever seen it, the way he'd seen it only once before. "You can put it on me."

He wanted to. He always had. Because he still couldn't believe he'd been the person who'd wished misery on her, shouting down the hallway as she fled his apartment for the last time, "I hope you get cancer. I hope you get hit by a bus. I hope someone rapes you and cuts your fucking throat." How could those be the words she'd heard as she hurried out of his life, the words she heard every time she thought of him for the ten years after? Worse, though, was the pleasure he'd taken in saying them, the relief, as if he'd wished he'd said them every day. He saw himself standing in his open doorway, hands cupped around his mouth, calling loudly enough to ensure the neighbors would hear. And as she pushed through the fire door and ran down the stairs, he reveled in the echo of his voice from the plaster walls and ceiling, as if he'd finally come into his own.

"I'm glad you're better," he said. "And as far as I'm concerned, the past can stay the past."

She nodded with disappointment. Whatever she'd wanted from him, she hadn't gotten it, and now she seemed to let it go. She returned to congratulating him on his successes at work, on his family, her tone lighter and more distant. He asked how long she was staying in town, stopping just shy of asking if she wanted to see his house, meet his wife and kids. It was an appealing thought, though whether it was to show off his family to her, or to show her off to his family—look, I once slept with this beauty—he didn't know. "Just down for the afternoon," she said. "My train back leaves at seven."

No time for a hotel key. Nor even for a meal. She stood before he did, grabbed his empty coffee mug along with her full one, and brought them to the counter. Then she hugged him again, quickly, and said she wanted only the best for him, she hoped for it often. He saw the same tight-lipped smile, the same arch of eyebrow that had long haunted his memory, and when she turned, the same easy sway of hips. Maybe the last had widened a bit, but as she walked away from him, he felt as if she'd run down that Ballard hallway only moments before, while in the interim he'd aged ten years. He supposed he should have wanted her to be youthful still, letting loose that nearly silent laugh that made her squint and rock to the side, a sign that his words hadn't drained all the joy from her, that his curse hadn't landed a fatal blow.

And yet, as he watched her cross the lobby, what he really wanted for her was a decade of graying and sagging, of looking backward into pain or forward into the void. Before leaving the hotel, he went to the bar, ordered a beer, a basket of onion rings. And as he ate them, he imagined seeing her in another ten years, this time perhaps passing on a cold, crowded sidewalk. She'd finally look haggard and lonely, he hoped: those hips fallen to fat, the lines around her mouth cut into ugly grooves, her best days clearly behind her. Maybe then, he'd wish her well.

Babenhausen, 1947

By the time he arrives, stealing has become more habit than necessity. Not so at Budzyn, where he nicked tools from the airplane factory and sold them to Ukrainian guards for an extra bowl of soup and half a pound of bread. The additional food kept him strong enough to live out those final months, fevered but still able to work, until being transferred to the main camp at Majdanek days before the Russians appeared. And from them he stole socks and cigarettes and a pocketwatch he still carries in his coat, which he stole from an American civilian on the train to Frankfurt.

Clumsy as a boy, and awkward, with big feet and ears that stuck straight out from the sides of his head, he has since learned deftness and caution. If he is good at anything besides thievery, he has not discovered what. He was seventeen when Minsk fell, which, if he understands the dates correctly, will make him twenty-three late this year. People tell him he looks older, even now that he shaves regularly, his hair grown back to a length he can comb, his cheeks no longer hollow. Only recently has he been willing to answer any question about his origins, or at least to answer honestly. He once had a stolen name, too, taken from a dead Polish machinist at the airplane factory, but now, whenever anyone asks, he forces himself to use the one he was given at birth: Semion Gurevitch.

Except the Semion he remembers, a mediocre student who enjoyed reading philosophy but struggled in mathematics, who planned, grudgingly, to follow his father into the textile business, is not the same one who huddles into his stolen coat, hat pulled low on his head, so no one is likely to remember him as he slips down the camp's central lane, its gravel and dirt dusted with snow. It feels strange still to walk freely, without fear of being shot, especially as Babenhausen differs little in appearance from Budzyn. Rows of barracks, guard stations, a muddy field, barbed wire still being removed. He hurries past the newer housing units with tin roofs, occupied by families, to the former stables where single DPs like him sleep on bunks stacked three high. If he's caught, he won't be shot, but he doesn't know what will happen, so he ducks around the side of the women's dormitory, presses himself against rough stones, and waits until he's sure no one has followed.

Before entering, he checks the pocketwatch. It's just past eleven o'clock, a gray morning with moist air that chills the freshly shaven skin of his neck. Most residents are occupied with a visit from a distinguished guest Semion has never heard of, come to sell them dreams of a new life in Palestine. He caught a glimpse of an old man with wild white hair, too fleshy to trust. What does he want with Palestine anyway, a place he knows only from books his grandfather made him study in the year leading to his thirteenth birthday. It has a sea nearby, that much he remembers, but he has never learned to swim. Nor does he care for the sound of Hebrew, which some devout camp residents chant after meals. Above all, he can't imagine living anywhere without tin-roofed barracks and soldiers patrolling after dark.

When no one has passed for nearly five minutes, he eases open the tall wooden door just enough to slide through. The stench of hide and droppings and old straw fill his nose, though no horses have stood here for years; before the Jewish refugees arrived, the camp housed German prisoners held by the Americans, and before that, Soviets kept by the Germans. Others hate the smell, but Semion doesn't mind. It's preferable to the stink of the latrines beside his block in Budzyn, where guards drowned prisoners caught trying to escape, head-first in putrid water.

His eyes adjust slowly to the dimness, taking in clotheslines strung across the open space between bunks and wall, draped with dresses, blouses, cotton undergarments he shouldn't see. So instead he scans for items left behind. He doesn't know what he's looking for, or rather, he's looking for anything that propels him forward. He just needs something to grab and tuck into his pocket, to finger as he waits for his meals, or as he lies awake in his bunk deep into the night. Last week he found a silk handkerchief, the week before a pair of reading glasses. Eventually he sold these things, too, for a pouch of tobacco, a crumpled green bill. That it's wrong to take from those who have so little, he tries not contemplate, because what other choice does he have? Sneaking into soldiers' quarters would risk too much. Though the Americans are here to protect them, he hesitates to cross anyone with a rifle in reach.

Also, he suspects, a number of the refugees, those who managed to evacuate from Minsk and Kiev ahead of the invasion, who spent the last five years in relative comfort and safety, some in the Caucasus, others as far east as Kazakhstan, have held onto valuable items from their old lives: necklaces and rings, silver forks and menorahs, gold coins. So he eases open metal footlockers at the end of each nearby bunk, runs his hand beneath wool skirts and more soft underthings, loose threads tickling his knuckles. In the first he finds a hand mirror, a simple one with a wooden frame, too small to show his whole face, which, in any case, he has no desire to see. He drops the mirror into his pocket. In the second locker he comes up with nothing.

The third's hinges creak when he opens it. He pauses a moment, listens, hears nothing. At the bottom he feels a small box, with a velvet cover. The texture alone, reminding him of the shop in Minsk, a corner where his father kept bolts of his best fabric, releases a strange ripple of relief, as if this is what he's been searching for all along, and he pockets the box without opening it. He'll save it until he has enough light to examine it properly, and until then he'll luxuriate in expectation and possibility. But the excitement makes him careless, and he closes the locker too fast. This time the hinges squawk, the lid clatters. And the sound is followed by a voice, from the dormitory's far end. "You can stop now." It's husky and tired but clearly that of a young woman. She has spoken in Yiddish, and when he doesn't answer, she tries again in Russian. "You don't have to do it any longer."

He understands both languages but stays quiet, crouching beside the locker. His fingers are still wrapped around the velvet box inside his coat.

"Work so hard, that is," the woman says, sticking now with Russian. He can't see her past a wall of clothes hanging from the nearest line. "You can rest now, a little."

He stands slowly. There's too much space between his head and the high roof, no nearby supports to hide him. If he moves, she might catch a glimpse of his face, or maybe just his silhouette, but enough to identify him to the soldiers who police the camp. He pulls the cap lower on his forehead.

"I'm resting now," the woman says. "I can't get up to talk. And calling out strains my voice. You may as well come closer."

He knows he should run, take his chance that she won't see. But her voice, low and gently hoarse, complements the velvet against his fingers. He pushes through the hanging clothes, lets one of the cotton garments—one meant to be snug against skin—brush over his face. She is in the second tier from the end, in the middle bunk. Her outline comes clear first, small lump of head surrounded by black hair not yet grown past her ears, jut of feet beneath a blanket, and between them a huge mound of belly overtopping both.

"It feels good to rest," she says, her lips wide and dry beneath deep-set eyes, dark as her heavy brows. "To prepare for whatever's next."

He assumes she's referring to the coming child, though the way she inflects the word *next* suggests something as yet unknown. He thinks he should ask how soon the baby will arrive, but instead, in a voice surprisingly clear given how little he's used it, he says, "The father?"

She shrugs, passes a slender hand in front of her face as if to brush away the thought. "I have to sleep now. And you should leave before the others return." Her eyes close, but then, as if remembering something important, she forces them back open. "But since you've made the effort. That is, if you've found something worthwhile."

He fishes the mirror out of one pocket and then, reluctantly, the velvet box from the other. She reaches out the same slender hand. This time he sees, past her wrist, dark marks that reveal the place she has been, one even worse than Budzyn. The mirror leaves his fingers, hovers over her face. The reflection of dark irises flash at him, and then wood and glass slide under the blanket, disappear beside that impossibly round belly.

"Save the other," she says. "For next time."

He stuffs the velvet box back into his coat, turns, and hurries out into the cold. From the open field where the fleshy old man peddles dreams of a new life by a green sea rise faint applause. In a dirty crust of old snow, he spies something that might be made of metal. Perhaps a shell casing, perhaps a tarnished coin. He leaves it for someone else to find. Above him, clouds hurry past on a breeze he can't feel.

Coming Clean

1. Identification

My freshman year of college had been something of a disaster. I'd spent the fall pining for a girl who never responded to my hesitant advances and did poorly in all of my classes. To make up for it, I devoted the spring to studying in the library, and most of the friends I'd made drifted away from me. The one time I went out drinking with kids in my dorm, I made a fool of myself, puking on a crowded sidewalk in front of a late-night restaurant.

Over the summer, I determined to make everyone forget the person I'd been. I swiped my brother's expired New Jersey driver's license and carefully doctored it to make it look current. I grew my hair out to match the picture on front, taken when my brother was nineteen. Now twenty-three, he'd recently had to cut his short for a job as a computer programmer at a Dallas telecom company. I didn't see what good it did being old enough to buy booze legally when you had to get up at six every morning, sit in traffic for an hour and then in a cubicle for another nine. I was glad to be nineteen, though I hoped I looked twenty-three. When I put on my glasses and checked myself in the mirror, I thought, sure, I can pull it off, especially when I held my chin at an angle to make my neck look thicker than it really was. In the picture, my brother sported a few sparse hairs on his upper lip and chin. I quit shaving for a week and managed to grow a faint shadow all the way across my cheeks.

As soon as I got to school for the start of sophomore year, I showed the I.D. to almost everyone I met. No one could tell the photo wasn't of me. I was quite pleased with myself and eager to use it. It wasn't long before people started handing me cash and putting in orders. Sparkly-eyed girls came up to me, opened their purses, and squeezed my arm as they whispered their thanks. Kids I hardly knew flashed looks of admiration, even envy. My dorm suite-mates became protective, guarding me from frat types who'd try to bully me into buying for them first. Take a number or get out of line, they'd say. For a month my answering machine filled up every day while I was in class.

The changes were so swift and striking I began to believe I really could erase the previous year. Why shouldn't everyone come to see this new version of me as the only one who'd ever existed? So far it had all gone better than I could have imagined. When one of the frat guys asked, while handing over a twenty for a gallon of rum, "Aren't you the kid who blew chunks in front of Time-Out?" my suite-mates jumped in and said, "Order canceled." Their loyalty or amnesia or self-interest paid off. Any change left over from other people's purchases I claimed as a surcharge and put into a collective pot, which quickly grew large enough to fund weekend binges for all of us.

∞

By mid-October, I'd used the I.D. ten or twelve times, at nearly as many stores. Not a single clerk questioned its authenticity. It probably helped that I was from out of state and no one knew where to find the expiration date on a New Jersey license. Still, it didn't take long for me to get cocky. One evening I paraded through the nearby Harris Teeter with nine cases of Busch Light stacked on a cart and took my time rolling up to the check-out. There were at least six slots open, several without lines, but one of the cashiers was the girl whose interest I'd failed to attract a year earlier. I'd known she worked there before coming in but feigned surprise. I hadn't seen her yet this semester and decided I'd take the opportunity to say hello, give her a glimpse of my new long-haired maturity, impress her with the amount of beer I was buying.

I'd met her at Hillel, whose events I'd attended regularly when I thought I had a chance with her, then sporadically for the rest of the year. She was a quiet, studious girl, pretty in a round-faced unobtrusive way that normally didn't do much for me. But she had a breathy laugh I liked, and a habit of writing indecipherable notes on her hands that made her seem mysterious. She wore oversized jeans and tight-fitting t-shirts and button-downs. To Shabbat potlucks she brought undercooked chicken or burnt lasagna and then spent the dinner alternately apologizing or complaining about the oven in her dorm. Above all, I thought I recognized in her some of the loneliness I'd experienced when I first arrived on campus, a sense of being out of step with everything around me.

Now I wanted her to see what sort of change was possible—for her own sake, sure, but also to confirm that my transformation was real, that I could get away with abandoning a fumbling, self-conscious timidity in favor of this newly confident persona, bold and daring and widely sought-after. Mostly, I suppose, I wanted to show off.

She greeted me warmly, happier to see me than I'd expected, and I wondered if I'd misread her deflections last year, if my advances had been more welcome than I'd imagined. If she was surprised by the change in my appearance, she didn't let on. As she rang up the beer, we exchanged a few words about our summers and classes, and she asked if I was planning to go to some upcoming Hillel events, a lecture on Holocaust memorials, an outing to a comedy club. "Comedy sounds good," I said, and before I could change my mind, added, "I like hearing you laugh."

I was proud of myself for saying it. It was more evidence that I'd grown since she'd last seen me, even if her only response was to slide the next case of beer over the scanner. There were words written in blue ink between her thumb and forefinger, too tiny for me to read. I had my wallet out, the I.D. right there behind a plastic window. I wanted so badly for her to see it, to see what I'd done. But she didn't ask for it. Maybe the illusion was so successful she didn't need any proof of my new identity. More likely she hadn't known me well enough to guess that I was anything other than what she saw in front of her.

In either case, she just read the total amount from the register, took my cash, handed back change and a receipt. I invited her to stop by my suite when she was finished working: my friends and I had better things to drink than this swill—I was just buying it as a favor to someone—and she was welcome to swing by any time. She smiled and thanked me and said she had a lot of studying to do, but maybe, she'd see. And then she turned to the next customer.

I left the store so distracted I couldn't find my car, heading up the wrong aisle before realizing my mistake and circling back. That she hadn't sparked to my invitation was a letdown, yes, but even more it unnerved me. I was suddenly sure I hadn't pulled off anything. In her eyes I was just as fumbling and lost as I'd ever been, no matter how many cases of beer I wheeled across the parking lot. I was tempted to open one of them right there, chug can after can and obliterate all memories of freshman year and Hillel and girls who didn't return my interest. But my suite-mates were waiting for me, and the frat guys who'd paid for the Busch Light, so instead I popped my trunk and started to load the cases in.

But before I finished, someone called out behind me. I didn't catch the words, but the voice was deep and threatening, and I whirled to see a big man, bald, wearing a long leather trench coat and sunglasses, though it was dusk, the parking lot's lamps just coming on. When he reached into the coat, I flinched and threw up my hands. But instead of a gun, he pulled out a badge. State police. Alcohol law enforcement. "How old are you?" he asked.

I was too startled to lie. Or else I knew he wouldn't believe me if I did. And when he asked if I had a fake I.D., I told the truth about that, too, and handed it over. Once I started I couldn't stop. I kept telling the truth even though I should have known better. "I took it from my older brother without him knowing," I said. "I had it in the store, but I didn't use it. No one asked for it."

CR

Later I told myself it was self-preservation that made me say it. I knew I would have been in far more trouble if I had used the I.D. Police station. Court. Community service. A fine to keep it off my permanent record. But none of those things actually entered my mind at the time. I wasn't thinking about consequences of any sort, only of the cop's clipped voice as he asked the questions and wrote out a ticket for underage possession, and then his practiced cold stare as he watched me transfer the beer from my car to his unmarked cruiser. After I finished, his firm hand between my shoulder blades led me back inside.

Only then did it occur to me what was happening. I tried to take it back, say I'd lied about not using the I.D. Cite me for whatever you want, I told him. But he didn't listen. He walked me across the front of the store, called the manager over, made me point to the clerk who'd sold me the beer.

She was ringing up someone else, and remembering the look she gave after my invitation, the quick dismissive flip of hair, I thought, just briefly, this is what she gets. But then she must have caught movement in her periphery, because she turned, and as soon as she spotted me standing with her manager, she started crying. She wiped her eyes and finished bagging the customer's groceries before coming over to us. The manager led us to a small windowless office, the space mostly taken up with a metal desk and file cabinets, bulletin boards scattered with pushpins and safety notices. There wasn't room for all four of us, so the manager said, "I'll leave you to it," ducked out, and closed the door.

The girl's arms were crossed, hands tucked under elbows, the scribbled words on them hidden. Her round, pretty, bland face was red and puffy. But the cop made her answer his questions. "Did you sell this gentleman alcohol? Did you ask to see identification?" He still had his sunglasses on. I hated him and his silly leather trench coat, the costume of a hustler in a '70s crime show. I tried to catch the girl's gaze, give a signal that it was okay for her to lie. But she kept her eyes focused on the floor, nodded, then shook her head. "Say it out loud," the cop told her. "Yes or no. Did you check his I.D.?"

This time instead of answering, she unfolded her arms. One hand reached up to the collar of her shirt and undid the top button. It was hot in the little office, and I guessed she was feeling faint. But then she unhooked the next button down and the next. She kept going. Neither the cop nor I said anything. I glanced over at him, and even with the sunglasses covering most of his face I could see he was puzzled, maybe alarmed. When I turned back to the girl, she was looking straight at me. She kept unbuttoning buttons until there were none left. The shirt, white cotton, hung open to reveal a simple bra, also white, mildly curved and lightly padded to keep the nipples from showing. Below it were a few light moles. The opening of her navel was more vertical than horizontal. I thought she was trying to show me something about herself, something I'd overlooked, but I had no idea what. I raised a hand to touch her, but the cop grabbed my wrist and forced it down.

"Put it back on," he said.

She had all but two buttons refastened when she whispered, "I didn't check his I.D."

I wondered if she said it to protect me or because she, too, thought she couldn't get away with lying. I hoped it wasn't because she simply believed in telling the truth. As soon as she spoke, the cop backhanded my shoulder and said, "Get lost." I opened the door to the office, and there was the manager, waiting to come in. Before leaving I glanced back at the girl to make sure she was all the way dressed. She wasn't gazing at me anymore, and she was no longer crying, though her face was still red. She looked tired. She'd misaligned the buttons, so the shirt hung crookedly at the neck.

I hurried out of the store and drove back to campus. To the frat guys I said I'd gotten busted, that all their beer had been confiscated. I didn't mention the girl. They got angry, demanded their money back, and my suite-mates, no longer loyal now that the I.D. was gone, refused to stand up for me or let me borrow from our collective pot. Instead I wrote a check and hoped it wouldn't bounce.

♋

I avoided the Harris Teeter after that, instead driving across town to get my groceries. I stopped going to Hillel. I didn't want to know if the girl had lost her job, if she'd had to drop out of school, if I'd destroyed her life. I kept growing out my hair until it was down to my shoulders, and then my beard, too, which, after another year, year and a half, filled all the way in. I wore an army surplus jacket and work boots everywhere I went. None of the kids who'd known me freshman year recognized me when I passed. I took to studying hard again, but only the subjects that interested me. I did well in some classes, poorly in others. I spent much of my time reading in the library smoking lounge or in the corner booth of a basement bar. My I.D. was legitimate by then, but I used it only for myself.

And that's when I saw her again, walking out of a building I never frequented—a chemistry building, maybe, or physics. Baggy jeans, white shirt buttoned to her throat. Round face pink despite a cold breeze, backpack heavy with books. She didn't look any different, and somehow this was worse than anything I'd imagined.

She was heading straight toward me. But I doubted she'd recognize me, and I could have easily let her pass. Except now I wanted to stop her, reveal myself. And then what? Beg forgiveness? Assure her I hadn't meant to get her in trouble, that it had all been an accident? That aside from one moment of bitterness, I'd never wished her harm? That the version of me she'd seen in the Harris Teeter hadn't been the real one, the person I'd become since? Mostly I wanted to know that she, too, had been altered by what had happened, that I'd had some impact on her after all.

She marched steadily along the brick path. I held my ground. This was my chance, I thought, though I guessed whatever I had to say wouldn't matter much to her. She was close enough for me to see that her hands were free of ink, almost close enough for me to speak. Back then I still remembered her name, though it has since escaped me. It was right at the front of my thoughts, ready to form on my lips. I could feel it trembling there, along with the relief that would follow its release.

But then, where the path forked in front of us, she turned aside. I didn't know if she was following the route she'd already had in mind, or if she'd spied me after all. To be safe, I shuffled forward with my head down, in case everyone could see through my disguise.

2. The Mirror

Tom and Kathleen lived across the hall from my former co-worker Rick, a composer of electronic music, on the fourth floor of a downtown Portland apartment building whose boiler conked out every few weeks. Rick befriended them after knocking on their door to ask if they had a blanket to spare. His lips were blue. This would have been late November or early December of 1999. They invited him in, gave him tea, buried him in sweaters, and left another message for the landlord, threatening to call the cops if he didn't fix the heat soon. It was an empty threat. Tom, a recovering heroin addict, never would have voluntarily spoken with the police.

Rick and I had worked together over the summer as temps at a furniture and appliance warehouse near the Hawthorne Bridge, taking inventory and filling orders. I'd since gotten a permanent job, but Rick stayed on with the agency. He worked one or two weeks a month and devoted the rest of his time to music. His recordings baffled me—they all sounded like the same haphazard hums and clicks, with hardly any beat—but he never asked for my opinion. He'd play a track for me only after I asked several times, and when it ended and I took off the headphones, he'd read my expression and say, "It's really for people who know what they're listening to." If not the music, I admired his dedication and self-sufficiency. We were the same age—twenty-six—but I was nowhere close to trusting my own vision with such unwavering confidence.

Because he didn't have a car and it was cheaper for me to ride the bus to my job than pay for parking, I often let him borrow mine. On my way to work I'd leave the car outside his building and drop off the key. One morning, as I was closing Rick's door, Tom and Kathleen stepped out of theirs. They introduced themselves and exchanged sly smiles. We chatted briefly and agreed that the four of us should go out for drinks one evening soon.

Only later did I realize they'd assumed Rick and I were a couple, or at least that we'd hooked up for the night. It was a reasonable enough mistake. The building was close to the cluster of gay nightclubs on Stark Street, and there were pride flags hanging in several of its windows. "Have you two been together long?" Kathleen asked when we went out together that weekend, to a smoky windowless bar around the corner. Rick was less than thrilled. He pushed his chair away from mine and kept protesting even after Kathleen apologized for the misunderstanding. The next time we went out, he brought an ex-girlfriend to the bar with us, a small pushy naturopath who dominated the conversation. She kept trying to convince Tom, who'd been in N.A. for almost a decade, that there were Chinese herbal remedies for narcotic addiction, far more effective than Western approaches. "It makes sense, right?" she said. "The Chinese have been dealing with opium a lot longer than we have."

By the end of the night none of us could stand her—except for Rick, who, clearly still smitten, kept buying her drinks and asking if she wanted him to walk her to a taxi. After that, Tom, Kathleen, and I started going out together on our own.

182 | SCOTT NADELSON

CR

I also told them I wasn't gay, but unlike Rick, I didn't insist. Nor did I mind when they didn't believe me. It made me more interesting, I thought, and also made it easier for me to be in close proximity to Kathleen, a stunning woman of twenty-four, with long eyelashes and piles of curly auburn hair pinned to the top of her head. She didn't seem to notice how I gawked at her, how I let my arm brush against hers at every opportunity. She'd lay her head against my shoulder, prop her feet on Tom's lap, and say, "I've never been so comfortable. Two husbands are definitely better than one." Or else she'd point out men in the bar and raise an eyebrow, trying to gauge my taste.

Tom didn't notice, either, or else he didn't care. He was slender, smooth-faced, and boyish, but he had at least five years on me and far more experience. He'd lived on the street for a year in his late teens, spent some time in jail in his early twenties, watched a friend overdose and die. But he'd come through it all with a poise I envied and a gorgeous young wife who obviously adored him. Though his criminal record should have made it hard for him to get a decent job, he'd charmed his way into managing a small film and video production studio, despite having no previous experience in either film or management. But he knew how to connect with people and get them excited about projects in which they otherwise would have had no interest. The studio made most of its money on commercials, but they also did music videos for up-and-coming Northwest bands and the occasional independent feature. Tom's role was to bring together writers, directors, cinematographers, and editors, and get them all to work for less than their going rate. At the bar he'd tell me about some movie he was trying to get made—a comedy about Bigfoot hunters in the forest near Mount Hood—and though the plot was beyond absurd, his enthusiasm was contagious, and before I quite knew what was happening, I'd agreed to take a look at the script and find places to tighten the dialogue, which, he had to admit, was the slightest bit slack.

Tom's charm derived from his ability to make you feel as if you were the center of every conversation. He'd involve you in whatever scheme he was cooking up as if you'd already signed on, and he made it sound crucial to have you on board. As soon as he heard I'd graduated from a writing program, he started telling people about the new wordsmith he'd found to rejuvenate all the studio's scripts. It didn't matter that I'd never written screenplays—or read any—or that I was working as an administrative assistant for a solar power company and wouldn't publish anything for another five years. His belief in my abilities was genuine. After I fiddled with a page or two of the Bigfoot movie—slack was an understatement; it was juvenile at best and largely incomprehensible—he told Kathleen I'd finally made the characters sound real and nailed the comic timing. He never mentioned any pay, but it was enough to be called a wordsmith and to hear him praise my ear for dialogue. He invited me to tour the studio, an even smaller operation than I'd imagined, in a suite of rooms on the fifth floor of a shabby concrete building that housed an evangelical church for street kids in its lobby. There were a couple of cramped offices, an editing room with three stations, a sound booth, and a room for shooting green screens. Tom introduced me to the handful of other employees as the newest member of the team. "We can get rid of what's his name," he said. "The freelancer. He charges too much."

All this before he'd read anything I'd actually written. It was Kathleen who asked to see one of my stories. She made the request quietly, with hesitant anticipation, as if she were afraid to hope for too much. I put her off at first, pretending to forget until she asked a second time. Then I spent a feverish night revising a story based on my older brother's experience as an amateur bodybuilder and handed it to her, casually, as if an afterthought, the next time we went out for drinks. "I'm not sure it's finished yet," I said, letting my knuckles brush against her bare arm as they dropped. "Let me know if you see any spots that need more work."

"I can't wait," she said, and gave me that sly smile I'd caught the first time I met her. "I hope it's juicy."

For the rest of the evening I kept sneaking glances at the little stack of paper on the table, the words I'd worked so hard to arrange, and winced when Tom put his beer glass on top. But when we got up to leave, Kathleen hugged it to her chest and said again she couldn't wait to read it—if she hadn't been drinking she'd start it tonight, but she wanted to come to it with fresh eyes, so she'd probably wait until morning. We'd taken to kissing each other on the cheek whenever we parted, and this time I lingered with my lips against her skin and breathed in the fragrance of her shampoo, strong even with all the smoke around us. Tom patted me hard on the back and asked why I didn't kiss him, too.

"I don't want to get excited," I said.

We all laughed, and on the street I watched the two of them head back to their apartment, Tom's arm over Kathleen's shoulders, Kathleen's arm around Tom's back. I need to stop, I told myself, and swore I'd quit lusting after married women, that I'd find healthier outlets for my desires. But first I'd wait to hear what she thought of my story.

ॐ

"Fucking love it," Tom said a few days later, when I dropped by the studio during my lunch hour to deliver a few more pages of the edited script. Kathleen had passed the story on to him, he'd started reading it over his breakfast, he got so into it he couldn't stop until he'd finished, and he showed up an hour late to work. "It's a movie waiting to be made," he said. He'd already put in calls to a few directors he'd been wanting to work with, and he'd pitch it as soon as he heard back.

I'd never thought of the story as cinematic, and I couldn't quite imagine it on screen, especially as it revolved around a painful episode from my childhood, when I'd betrayed my brother to impress a friend. But as usual, Tom's enthusiasm infected me, and I soon found myself talking through details of how the film might be shot, what sort of aesthetic it might have, what might work for its opening scene. "I can take a crack at a script," I said. "Might need some time off to do it right. It would be easier if I had an advance so I could quit my job."

"We'll wait and see if someone bites," Tom said. "No reason to put in the work first. Plus, they might want to hire a professional. Of course, we'll make sure you get final say."

It was the first time my own eagerness had gotten ahead of Tom's, and I was left embarrassed and deflated, staring at the green screen, before which sat an empty drum kit and a pair of microphones. Some local band would play their jaunty power-pop in front of it, I guessed, and later an editor would make it look as if they'd been rocking in front of a massive stadium crowd.

"Did Kathleen like it?" I asked.

"Of course she did. She passed it on to me, didn't she? It's fucking brilliant."

಄

But Kathleen didn't mention the story the next time I saw her. Instead she told me about a man she was sure I'd fall for, a physician's assistant at her dermatologist's office. "He's cute and funny, and he likes books. A little bit feminine but not prissy. That's what you're into, I can tell, even though you aren't very forthcoming."

We were in her apartment this time, and we were alone. It was a Friday evening, and Tom was meeting a client for happy hour. He'd catch up with us for a late dinner, but first just the two of us would go out for cocktails. We'd made the arrangements by phone a few days earlier. Not at that dump around the corner, Kathleen had said, but somewhere classy. It would be exciting. Like a date. "I haven't been on one of those for three years," she said. "But this is so much better. I won't have to get all nervous and wonder if I'll get lucky at the end of it."

Now she was standing at the mirror, pinning up her hair. She'd just come out of the shower and wore a long terrycloth robe. The apartment was a small studio, the bed at one end, a couple of armchairs and a side table a few feet away, no door to separate us. I was woozy with the sight of her ankles beneath the fabric, with the steam carrying her scent from the bathroom. "He was in a relationship for a long time," she said. "But now he's single again and ready to get out and meet people. I told him about you, and he seemed intrigued. I'd be happy to set you up."

"Let me think about it," I said.

"It would be good for you," she said. "You haven't been out with anyone since I've known you. Unless you're holding back on me."

"I'm not. I mean, there's someone I'm interested in, but … It's complicated."

"He's involved with someone else."

"Yes."

"You're better off starting fresh," she said. "Someone without baggage."

"Like Tom?"

I expected her to laugh, but she didn't. Her face in the mirror was hard and lovely, big eyes focused back on themselves. "Some baggage is worth it. But you know when it is." She disappeared into the closet, came out with a black dress on a hanger. She laid out a bra and a pair of underwear, also black, on the end of the bed. "Cover your eyes," she said.

I did. But then I heard the robe drop to the floor.

I'd seen naked bodies before then, and I've seen more since. Why one should have the permanent effect of making me simultaneously dizzy and aroused and nostalgic I can't quite say. I don't really believe some bodies are more perfect than others, though Kathleen's was certainly fit and shapely and nicely proportioned. In the end it was just made up of the usual parts: collarbones, breasts, navel, hips, a triangle of hair visible in the mirror, round buttocks soon covered in black lace. I caught all these things in flickers, sometimes blurry, sometimes obscured by lashes, as I let my eyes flutter behind my barely separated fingers. Rather than shame, in the moment I experienced only gratitude. I felt as if I were being given a gift, not by Kathleen but by some unseen hand of cosmic grace or irony, the same one that had led me to lend Rick my car and walk out of his apartment early in the morning, the one that convinced Kathleen I was attracted to other men. I would never have admitted to believing in such a force at the time, or in any power other than my own blundering will, but with Kathleen's body flashing through my fingers like old film footage played too slowly, I was quite sure I had no will other than that which kept me from crying out in celebration. By the time she said, "Okay, all done," I'd broken into a full sweat beneath my clothes. The backs of my thighs were especially slick against my jeans, fresh dark ones, the nicest I owned. "Ready?" she asked, slipping her feet into leather mules.

If she noticed a change in me, she didn't say anything. But her expression had stiffened, and I was sure she knew exactly what had happened. My ruse was finally exposed. Still, she linked arms with me as we left the apartment, said again that she was excited to go out somewhere nice; Tom liked dive bars, but she occasionally wanted to be in a place with windows and stemmed glasses. And there in the hallway we came face to face with Rick, who was returning with a bag of groceries. He and I hadn't spent time together for weeks by then, though I still let him borrow my car whenever he needed it. The look he gave me was either astonished or disgusted, and instinctively I reached up to touch my flushed cheeks. He was probably just surprised to see me with Kathleen, to discover that I'd kept up a friendship with his neighbors separate from him. But in that moment I had no doubt he believed I'd just fucked another man's wife. And I felt as if I had, too, only without her knowing. By then shame had arrived, my flush deepened, and my damp thighs prickled against the rough fabric of my jeans.

"Has Tom had a chance to listen to the tracks yet?" Rick asked.

"I'm sure he'll love them," Kathleen said.

"If not, I've got ideas for a few more that might fit." In the four months I'd known him, I'd never once heard Rick worry whether or not someone liked his music. But now his voice was full of doubt, his brows dipping toward his nose. He bobbled his key and nearly dropped the groceries. "Just tell him to let me know."

"I'll bring the car on Monday," I said, but Rick disappeared into his apartment without answering.

CR

At the cocktail lounge, a long, high-ceilinged room connected to a French restaurant, with lots of polished wood and brass and servers in bow-ties, Kathleen and I talked less easily than before, and I was careful not to let any part of me touch her. She didn't say anything more about the cute physician's assistant or ask about the person I fancied. She didn't point out men at the bar and ask what I thought. I put down a Scotch more quickly than I meant to and then kept tipping the empty glass to my lips. After the first couple of sips from her drink, Kathleen started telling me about Tom, how fragile he'd been when they'd first met, how long it took to get him to trust her. I could tell she was trying to reset our friendship, return us to solid footing, because she was a gracious and tolerant person, I guessed, accommodating to the flaws of those she cared about. But I'd deceived her from the start, and now I'd used that deception to cross another line. I didn't know if we could ever go back.

Even now, she told me, Tom would sometimes slip into long angry silences punctuated by sudden outbursts, and when he did, there was almost nothing she could do to pull him out. She just had to sit by and let him work through it. His anger was directed inward—who could understand what it was like to carry around so much guilt, having watched a friend die and knowing it could just as easily have been him—but sometimes it made him lash out at her. "Don't worry," she said, languidly, in no apparent hurry to ease my concern. "It's not physical. Nothing even close. He just starts picking at me. Makes fun of me for being young, for not knowing things. For not having seen the movies he likes. For not rinsing the sink after I brush my teeth. Anything."

"That's crazy," I said. "You're amazing. Doesn't he know how lucky he is?"

"You're sweet."

"I mean it."

"I know. And he does. It's just hard for him to believe he deserves it."

I tried to be outraged but couldn't quite manage it. I kept thinking she was talking about someone other than Tom. This sounded nothing like the guy I knew, and though I prided myself on understanding there were always more sides to a person than what you could see on the surface, I still couldn't layer this new image over the one to which I'd grown accustomed. And as if to prove that the two were incompatible, he showed up then smiling his infectious smile, said, "The two most beautiful people I know," kissed me on top of the head and Kathleen on the lips. I wanted to hate him for treating her badly, but I couldn't. So I told myself I didn't believe her. But that wasn't true, either. I believed her, but I didn't care. I still thought she was just as lucky as he was, to have such a charming husband despite his baggage, to live with someone who could lift the heaviest mood the second he walked into a room.

In any case, I didn't think she was seeking sympathy. She'd divulged her private life to me because I'd finally come clean with her, though not directly. That's what I guessed. And now all the awkwardness between us evaporated. We ordered food and wine, ate and laughed, and Tom told us about the studio's newest project, a commercial for an internet provider, featuring a claymation dog. It would be their first animated spot, and they had to find an animator, quick. He'd told the client they could start shooting in a week and a half. Did I know any animators who'd work pro-bono? Any connections at the local art colleges?

Only after we'd finished our entrées and were debating whether or not to order dessert did I work up the courage to ask if he'd heard back from directors about my story. Any interest? The same shaky uncertainty I'd heard in Rick's voice trembled through mine. I wondered if Tom knew how much power he had over us with all his optimism and zeal.

"They all love it," he said, too quickly, his voice strained. The enthusiasm was no longer natural, the effort to sustain it draining. I didn't know if he was keeping it up for my sake or for his own. "But stories about kids," he said. "Tough sell. There aren't enough good young actors to pull most of them off."

I tried not to show disappointment, but my attempt at lightheartedness was labored and brittle. "I'm not surprised. I think it works better on the page anyway."

"Fucking brilliant," Tom said, with relief, a sweep of his arm waving away all doubt.

"It's well written," Kathleen said, "but I wish you would have put more of yourself into it."

"It's autobiographical," I said.

"Sure. But you leave out so much. I mean, you were thirteen, you must have had feelings… You and your friend wrestling… It's intimate, but there's no hint of any attraction. Why keep it all repressed?"

I didn't say anything then. I was too amazed to find she still believed the fiction she'd invented for me—and in which, of course, I'd willingly participated. It was far more convincing than anything I'd ever written. Tom took my silence for insult and cut Kathleen a fierce look of judgment I knew she'd have to answer for later, when they were alone. Now it made her apologize, but I told her no, she was right, I hadn't revealed enough. I'd try to get more out in the next draft.

"Did you tell him about Liam at your dermatologist's?" Tom asked, smiling big again, anxious to change the subject.

"He's not interested. Too smitten with a boy who's already taken." Kathleen flicked my sleeve with a finger and gave me a look of pity or disdain. A thick strand of auburn hair had fallen out of its pin and lay across her cheek.

"Worked for you," he said. "Did she tell you I was married when we met? Wasn't much competition, though. My first wife used to hit me. Plus, she was in prison."

Out on the street, I hugged them both, and we talked about getting together again soon. They stood holding hands, facing me, this time reluctant, it seemed, to walk away. Their look was a little desperate, as if they needed me more than I understood—to keep them from fighting, maybe, or to remind them how fortunate they were to have found each other. Perhaps it was easier for them to believe they'd been wise to follow their impulses when comparing themselves to me, who seemed incapable of making bold choices or letting passion propel him.

I wanted to offer whatever comfort or assurance I could. But I knew I'd never be able to glance at Kathleen without seeing her naked in front of the mirror, slipping one leg and then the other into lace underwear. I wouldn't be able to talk to Tom without wondering if he might one day land me a movie deal. And they wouldn't be able to look at me without seeing a young gay man yearning for a boy who didn't exist. I hopped on a bus, rode across the river, and never met them again.

3. Collision

Late one night, when I was driving home from a party in Southeast Portland, a bicycle appeared out of nowhere and swerved in front of my car. I spotted it in my periphery just before it crossed my path and braked hard, or thought I did, though when I came to a stop I was in the middle of the intersection, and the bike was behind me and to the left, one wheel bent and spinning. Its owner was on his back a few feet away, a black helmet beside him. If I'd felt the thud of impact, I couldn't remember it afterward. But my chin ached where it must have hit the steering wheel, blood seeped from my lower lip, and in my ears rang the sound of breaking glass. From one of my headlights, I guessed, though as my vision cleared I could see that both still sent out their beams, lighting up the steady drizzle in front of the car's grille and the wet pavement beyond. The sound I imagined, in any case, was far more calamitous than the shattering of something as small as bulb or casing. As I sat there watching drops pass through the light, too stunned to move, I kept picturing a rock puncturing a plate glass window, a fantastic rain of glittering shards.

When I finally turned back to him, the cyclist had rolled onto his side. I was surprised to discover he was alive but even more to think I'd expected him not to be, to know that in those moments of confusion I really believed I might have killed someone. A huge sob of relief belched out of my throat. And then I was quiet again, listening to the swish of windshield wipers and the hum of a cassette that had reached the end of its last track on one side but hadn't yet flipped. The cyclist rolled onto his stomach, pushed up to hands and knees. What I'd taken for a helmet I now saw was a backpack, partly full but not stuffed, with a white patch or flag sewn above the zipper of a smaller, secondary pocket. Still on his knees, he slung the pack over one shoulder and slipped the other arm through the loose strap.

Only then did I put the car into park. I waited until he was on his feet before opening my door and getting out. He was a young guy, maybe twenty-two, with patchy stubble and a messy hairstyle either fashionable or indifferent or both. His jeans were ripped at one knee, and so was the elbow of his sweatshirt, but whether those things had just happened or pre-dated the accident, I didn't know. I had plenty of ripped jeans in my closet, though the pair I was wearing now were relatively fresh, as was my shirt, an ironed gray button-down I left untucked. This was my party outfit, not too casual, not too dressy, or so I hoped, though all the people at the party I'd just left had been either dressier or more casual, the men in t-shirts or old plaids, the women in halter-top dresses and wedge heels. The cyclist would have fit in well at the party, certainly better than I had. At thirty-one, I'd been the oldest person there.

He hadn't yet turned to face me. Instead, he stared off in the direction of Belmont Street, a block to the north. In profile, his features were blunt and undistinguished, small nose, thin lips, flat chin. Only his eyebrows stood out, darker than his hair and odd-looking at the base of his high forehead. Those, and a dark streak that might have been blood or maybe just dirt between his cheek and ear, extending forward from his sideburn. Concussion, I thought. He needed to get to a hospital.

But what I said was, "You're not hurt too bad." I meant it as a question, but it came out sounding like a plea, or maybe a command. "You should wear a helmet," I went on, and though I knew there was no point in scolding him after I'd already hit him with my car, added, "You don't have any lights. How was I supposed to see you?" He didn't respond, just rubbed his eyes with his fingers and adjusted the backpack straps so they were tighter on his shoulders. Then he reached down for the bike, lifted it by one handle, rolled it back and forth. The rear wheel wobbled, and one of the spokes caught on the chain.

"I'll pitch in to have it fixed," I called, and fished my wallet out of a pocket. This time he did answer, or at least his mouth moved. But I couldn't hear what he said, because behind me my car was still running, and the cassette had flipped over. John Lee Hooker. The guitar licks and growling vocals swallowed his words. All I found in my wallet, in any case, were three dollar bills, a pair of crumpled receipts, a pink post-it note with a phone number written in pencil, no name. Behind my credit card was a spare check, but I had no idea how much it cost to fix a bike. "If you give me your number, I'll get the money to you by the end of the month," I called. "After I get paid." Then I touched my lip and added, "I might need some dental work. My face hit the wheel pretty hard."

The bike was an old cruiser-style Schwinn, an original from the '60s by the look of it, with a red frame and red hand-grips, the seat updated to a black gel saddle with fresh chrome springs. It looked heavy as the cyclist rolled it away from me, bent tire scraping the fender. Across Yamhill Street, he passed a two-story brick building with a storefront I'd never noticed before, though I'd passed it dozens of times. "Digital Solutions," its sign read. "Computer Repair and Services." The computers in the window were all at least five years old, bulky monitors and dusty towers with slots for floppy disks, many with missing side panels or gaps through which you could see to the circuit boards underneath. None of which inspired much confidence in the repair skills of the proprietors. Who'd take a machine there?

I asked the cyclist as much, and this time when he answered I did hear him, despite John Lee and my rumbling engine. "Could have happened to anyone," he said. His tone wasn't absolving but awestruck, as if he'd hit upon something profound and terrible. The rain had flattened his hair, and his face was white. He was likely in shock, I thought, though it was early spring in Oregon, drizzling every day for months, and a lot of people were sickly pale. Since I'd never seen him before, I had no way to tell if he looked different than usual. I knew I should offer to drive him to the hospital, but I didn't know how I'd get his bike into my car, a small Toyota already more than a decade old, with no roof rack or ropes to tie down the trunk. Plus, I didn't want to drive more than the half dozen blocks to my apartment. I'd been drinking at the party, not excessively, but not prudently, either: four, maybe five glasses of wine over the course of as many hours.

I played the drive over in my mind: purposely taking side streets to avoid other cars, keeping carefully under the speed limit, coming to a full stop at intersections, only occasionally letting my thoughts drift back to the party, to the woman who'd invited me there, who'd kissed me in a hallway and then disappeared. I didn't know her well. We'd been introduced by a mutual friend who knew I'd been depressed for months following an ugly breakup, had gone out for coffee and then a drink. She was sleepy-eyed but vivacious, with a gap between her front teeth and a slightly crooked nose, and twenty minutes after I'd parted from her I could still hear the gravelly sound of her voice in my ear.

I'd spent much of the party trying not to crowd her. We talked for a few minutes when I arrived, then several more times as we passed through the kitchen refilling our glasses, each encounter with a sharper edge of flirtation. But mostly I gave her space to talk to her friends, pretending I could enjoy myself at a party where I knew no one but her, where I was at least five years older than everyone in the room. I hung out on the back deck, leaning against the railing and trying to peer into the windows of a house across a high fence, or stood at the back of a crowd in the basement, watching a parade of scruffy bands set up their gear, play three or four ear-blistering songs, and then pack up indifferently, with cool, detached expressions, as if they were high on a stage above cheering fans.

My feigned independence paid off. When the young woman found me in the upstairs hallway, waiting to use the bathroom, she placed a hand on my chest and said, "I've hardly seen you all night. I was afraid you left. But you didn't. You're right here." And then she pulled my face down to hers. Her mouth tasted like vodka and strawberry gum. "But now you need to pee," she said. "I won't stop you." When I came out of the bathroom, she was no longer in the hallway, and the party was clearing out. I searched for her in every room that wasn't locked but found only a few people smoking or talking or passed out on a pile of coats. The host, who'd played bass in one of the bands, asked if I was the guy from the record label. He'd heard I was coming. Had I caught the set? What did I think? "I'll be in touch," I said.

I spent the car ride imagining what might have happened if the young woman had let me drive her home, or even better, if she'd agreed to come home with me. I envisioned the moment we'd get to my door, key snapping the deadbolt, my hand on her back easing her forward. Would I turn on the light or lead her through the dark space I knew so well? Would we sit together on the couch, have another drink, or head straight to my bed? I tried not to picture anything more. Just let me have that kiss again, I thought, and everything else could wait.

While driving I hadn't even felt tipsy, though now the reflection of street lights on puddles blurred my vision, and blood pumped hard in my ears. "Make sure you get a light," I called as the cyclist reached Belmont Street. He walked unsteadily, but I could see no visible limp. We'd both gotten so lucky, I thought and wanted him to acknowledge it, too. But he just bolted across the street, the mangled back wheel of the Schwinn bouncing and skidding across the pavement. I half-expected another car to charge out of the darkness and knock him down once more, and I held my breath until he made it safely to the other side. Then he turned east and kept running, and soon disappeared behind a building on the corner.

I was shaking when I got back into the car. The clock on the dashboard read nearly two a.m., but since I hadn't changed it when daylight savings began a week earlier, it was actually close to three. The cassette was still playing the first song on its B-side, the boogie guitar driving hard. I couldn't have stood in the rain for more than a minute and a half, but it had soaked through the shoulders of my shirt, and I felt it dripping down my back. Even though I was in the middle of the intersection, I didn't want to move, not yet, so I sat there until the song finished. Then I drove the last stretch even more slowly, stopping for a full five seconds at each intersection before rolling through without touching the gas. I parked two blocks shy of my place, in the attic of an old Victorian duplex, and walked the rest of the way.

When I got inside, I called the number in my wallet, which belonged to the young woman who'd kissed me at the party. If she answered, I would have told her about the accident. And if I did, maybe I wouldn't still be thinking about it now. But instead I got her voicemail and left a rambling message: just wanted to make sure she got home okay, wanted to thank her for inviting me to the party, I'd had a great time, saw some not terrible bands, but of course the highlight was getting to see her, and especially the moment we shared outside the bathroom, I was reminding her in case it was all fuzzy tomorrow, and maybe we could get together for a drink again soon, or dinner, I was a pretty decent cook, I'd make something for her if she wanted to come by my place some evening in the near future.

She didn't call me back, not that night, not the next day. After a week or two I stopped expecting to hear from her, stopped imagining a second kiss or a visit to my bed. It didn't occur to me to wonder where she went after I stepped into the bathroom or to worry that something had happened to her on the way home. Instead I assumed my message had shattered any illusion of nonchalance I'd hoped to project at the party, that it had scared her off. Her silence knocked me back into the hole out of which I'd been trying, half-heartedly, to climb, and I stayed there, depressed and single, for another two years before meeting the woman I'd later marry. Then I moved on to what would become the next phase of my life, though now I think it feels that way only in retrospect. While I was living it, it just seemed a part of the same phase, one day giving over to the next, with a variety of changing circumstances—new house, new job, new baby—and nine or so years passed before I saw the young woman again. It was on an airplane to New York. My wife and daughter and I were making our annual pilgrimage to look at artwork and visit friends, and while I stood in the back of the plane waiting to use the bathroom, someone said my name.

There she was, in the flight attendants' work space, rocking an infant. She was still lively and attractive, though whatever had drawn me to her those years ago felt distant and shallow, no longer worthy of my attention. And I could read similar thoughts in her expression. Now that she understood what it meant to love a child, why would she have wasted a moment with something as fleeting and insubstantial as a kiss with me? We spoke pleasantly enough, caught each other up on our work, exchanged thoughts about parenthood. She didn't refer to the party or the phone call she never returned, only said, "I always hoped I'd run into you again when my life wasn't such a mess. But that never happened. The second part, I mean." She laughed and touched the baby on the head, just below the spot where her knitted cap stopped short of her temple. Then she lowered her voice. "I'm running away from her father. I used to love him, but now … I don't know, the smell of him makes me gag."

Before I could respond, the bathroom door opened, and it was my turn to go inside. I worried that she'd be gone when I came out. Anything could happen while the door was closed, I thought, and then found myself recalling the moment before I knew the cyclist was still alive, before I put the car into park. If he hadn't gotten up, would I have driven away? I couldn't have said for sure. Nine years later I still had moments of imagining it, easing my foot off the brake, rolling the rest of the way through the intersection and then the six blocks to my apartment. The possibility seemed as alive now, the plane jiggling thirty-thousand feet above the Rocky Mountains, as it had in the moment I lingered in the car, foot on the brake. Spared the choice at the time, I was stuck with both scenarios, sometimes staying, sometimes fleeing, one version never more or less plausible than the other.

This time when I came out of the bathroom, the young woman was still there, rocking her child. "Come up and meet my family," I said, and told her our row number. She and my wife exchanged hellos, my daughter waggled fingers for the baby, the woman and I said it was great to see each other and that we should stay in touch, though I knew we wouldn't and suspected she did, too. What might have happened if she'd returned my call all those years ago was like a taut wire between us, alive and buzzing with electricity no matter how far apart we stretched. I wasn't sorry for the way my life had played out since then, not for a second. So why did I still need to hang onto those other lives, the ones I'd lived only in my imagination? She made her way to her seat, bouncing her baby, and we flew on to New York with different memories of a night nine years earlier, with pasts that would follow us or fade but which, in either case, we could never change.

A Minor Blues

Frank would always shoot while we were rehearsing in the studio. He was never in the way. You weren't aware that he was taking pictures—they were never posed shots. He pretty much stayed in the background, but there was an underlying strength to his presence, as if he didn't really need to say any more than he did.
—Herbie Hancock

It's late summer, 1957. Van Gelder hasn't yet opened his famous studio in Englewood Cliffs, nor has he given up his day job as an optometrist in Teaneck. For now he still records at his parents' house in Hackensack, and that's where Francis Wolff drives two or three evenings a month with his old friend Alfred Lion—over the impossible span of the George Washington Bridge, from which he can see all the way down the wind-rippled Hudson to the tip of the island where he arrived eighteen years ago. Eighteen years since he escaped what would have been his certain death. L'chaim. He owes his life to Alfred, who got him on the last boat out of Hamburg before the Gestapo began checking papers and pulling Jews off gangplanks. He would thank him again now, except as he drives, Alfred talks about a session Frank missed a few weeks ago, the interplay between the alto and a young guitar player, just brilliant, Alfred says in German, wait until you hear the recording, it really swings.

Frank feels particularly grateful tonight, though also shaken, having just returned from his first trip back to Berlin since the war, to visit his only surviving relatives, a pair of cousins he hardly knew growing up, one five years older than he, the other six years his junior. They'd been among a crowd of children at holiday meals, and their parents' names were ones his father regularly mentioned. But if he'd ever had a full-fledged conversation with either, he could no longer remember it. They were near-strangers when they met in a café near the Tiergarten, though the bond they shared, that of being the last of their kind, made them tearful when they embraced, their words tender and intimate as those between old friends. Neither cousin could give Frank news of what happened to his parents after he'd left, nor his sister, but they did fill him in on the fate of several aunts and uncles and other cousins who'd been closer to him in age. All perished, of course, but the details of where they'd last been seen, when they'd been arrested, which trains they'd been herded into, all seemed crucial to hear now, when he was in danger of forgetting them altogether, as if they'd never actually been present in his life.

Above all, his time in Berlin made him miss Alfred, who has become his true family since he emigrated, the person who now knows him best in the entire world. Along with his life, he owes Alfred his livelihood, his purpose. Though he'd worked as a commercial photographer for a decade, when he arrived in New York, all the magazines and advertisers turned him away. The only job he could find was as an assistant in a Midtown portrait studio, developing another photographer's mediocre shots of grim families who couldn't afford anything better, their carefully oiled hair reflecting too much light. By then Alfred had already started the record label, and there was never any question as to whether he'd bring Frank on as a partner, though Frank had no experience producing music, nor any funds to invest. Nor did he have Alfred's big personality, his ability to talk at length to anyone he met, unashamed of his accent, his history, his ancestry. But he shared Alfred's passion for jazz, ever since they first encountered it together at sixteen years old, when Sam Wooding's orchestra played in Potsdamer Platz. He preferred to work behind the scenes in any case, writing contracts and keeping track of finances, or behind his camera, the Rolleiflex he once used to shoot

German models and actresses, one of the few items he carried with him across the ocean.

For fifteen years he and Alfred kept their day jobs, running the label in the evenings and on weekends, but they have finally begun to earn enough from record sales to pay themselves modest salaries and devote themselves full-time to jazz. Now the only photographs Frank takes are during rehearsal sessions in Van Gelder's living room, shots of musicians Alfred uses on the covers of records to keep their design costs down. He is proud of these images, though his favorites often aren't the ones Alfred chooses. His friend prefers shots suggesting action and ecstasy, the ones that make you imagine sound surging from frozen instruments. But Frank is most partial to the moments between the songs, when a horn player cleans his mouth piece, or a drummer wipes sweat from his brow. In these he feels he has revealed the players at their most honest and vulnerable, and even more, that he has managed to commune with them, though his shyness otherwise prevents him from exchanging more than a few words.

ဆ

Tonight, six musicians are crammed into the tight space, all in their early twenties, except for the saxophone player, who is not quite thirty-one. In his stiff suit and black tie, hair beginning to recede at the temples, Frank at fifty feels both old in their presence and also rejuvenated, as if their youth lets off a steam that smooths his slackening skin. They laugh and call out to Alfred, who addresses each of them by name: Donald, John, Sonny, Curtis, Art, Paul. In turn, they say to each other, It's the Lion and the Wolf. Watch out, the Lion and the Wolf are here, gonna tear you apart.

Frank, too, should know their names—he has written all their contracts—but in person he always finds himself flummoxed when searching for them in his mind, and rather than risk mixing them up, he has quit trying to keep them straight during recording sessions. He will put faces and names together again when he prints his negatives and cuts their checks.

For now, he wants only to study those faces on their own terms, consider angles and lighting and reflection. One of the great challenges of his career has been adapting to photographing dark skin, of which he saw so little in Germany, especially after jazz was banned in 1933 and American musicians stopped passing through Berlin. The task here is made more difficult by the dim light fixtures in the Van Gelders' living room, the backdrop of ugly horizontal blinds and a cheap floor lamp. With instruments and microphones filling the tight space, there is no room for studio lights, which would make the place too hot in any case. So he has adjusted to using a hand-held flash, which he raises above his head with his right hand while snapping the Rolleiflex with his left.

The musicians have to put up with him flashing in their faces as they play, and as a result some of his best images show them with eyes closed, as if they are deep in contemplation, when in truth they are just blinking away the blaze of light. He jokes with them that he is doing an impression of the Statue of Liberty, holding a torch high to light the way to freedom, and most of them are good-natured about the intrusion, especially because they like having their portraits on the front of their records. It has become a signature of his and Alfred's label, as much as the tone produced by Van Gelder's engineering, an unintended benefit of their need to do everything on the cheap. Since giving up their other jobs, they have had to work sixteen hours a day to keep in business, doing almost everything themselves. But while using Frank's photos was at first a way to save money, word has gotten out among the musicians: the Germans can't pay as much as Columbia, but they include rehearsal time in the contract, and if you're the session leader, you get your face on the album cover.

All the players tonight are used to him, except for the saxophone player, who, shy like Frank, turns to the side when the camera comes close. Once the rehearsal starts, however, he quickly loses himself in the massive sound coming out of his horn and ignores the flash and click. The rest have done sessions here before and seem entirely comfortable, especially the baby-faced pianist, who has been a regular in the Van Gelders' living room, playing on more than a dozen records for the label over the past three years. Though he's usually a sideman, tonight he's the session leader, composer of most of the tunes, which are jaunty like him but also bounce with a wistfulness that comes from his generous use of minor keys. The other musicians defer to him, even the saxophone player who's a good five years older and scheduled to lead his own session in just a couple of weeks. The fluidity of roles in modern jazz has always appealed to Frank—whatever hierarchy exists is temporary and pragmatic, necessary only for decisions about repertoire and arrangement. Once the music starts, such divisions disappear, and all the musicians enter into conversation, giving space to each other no matter who's in charge.

It's the same with him and Alfred: now that rehearsals have begun, Alfred moves out of the way, leaning against the wall, snapping fingers out of synch, and listening only to make sure the music has sufficient swing. That's his single criterion. No matter how innovative or avant-garde, as long as a tune makes him want to move his hips, he's happy to press it into vinyl. Frank, meanwhile, steps up with his camera and flash, unable to keep his feet in brown derbys from shuffling into a little dance as he bends and snaps, preferring low angles to give his subjects sufficient stature. He wants to make them as mythic as they have become in his mind, these passionate young men who have grown up in ghettos like the ones his relatives suffered in Europe, though the American version is less overtly circumscribed, liquidated more gradually with poverty and neglect rather than trains and gas chambers. His biggest regret on returning to Berlin was not having used his camera to document what was still there when he had the chance. An entire culture obliterated in a matter of a few years, and now nothing remains. He will not let the same thing happen to these evenings, which feel equally fragile and fleeting. The photographs may serve a practical purpose, but privately—this he hasn't even discussed with Alfred—he has come to see them as something far more important, an attempt to preserve a world that might vanish at any moment.

And he thinks that's what the young pianist and his fellow musicians are doing, too, why they work so hard to record their music, even though they make more money performing live at nightclubs. They are twenty-two, twenty-five, twenty-seven years old, but already they can imagine a moment when they are no longer here. And it's easy to understand why, when so many of their friends and family members have succumbed to hardships. The stakes are high when the tape rolls, and the mood then becomes more serious, which is why Frank chooses to shoot during rehearsal time instead. Now the musicians play joyfully and laugh between songs, with nothing driving them but love for what they are doing, for the sounds they make together, while for Frank the stakes are at their highest, when only he knows he is snapping the shutter to keep oblivion at bay.

༉

When the rehearsal comes to an end, they are all sweating, Frank included, and they take a break so Van Gelder—nearly the same age as the saxophone player but seeming to come from an earlier generation, or a different universe, with his bow tie and thick glasses and double-chin—can set up his microphones, which he does with an obsessive precision, warning everyone multiple times not to move a single cable once he has set things in place, not even to touch it. Frank wanders to the kitchen for a glass of water, and there he finds Van Gelder's mother, a small stout woman not much older than he is, who, with her husband, has run a clothing shop in Passaic for the past thirty years. What she thinks of her son inviting groups of colored musicians into her home every week he doesn't know. She has always been polite and distant, bringing out a bowl of nuts or crackers for them to snack on and otherwise staying out of the way.

During one of their first encounters, however, she made sure to let Frank know that she is also Jewish—born a Cohen, in fact—though she married outside the faith. Now she asks about his trip to Berlin, says that she could never have brought herself to go back; her family left Poland before she was born, and she doesn't know how many relatives stayed behind. She is just trying to focus on the future, to keep the store in business, to make sure she and her husband can leave Rudy enough that he'll be comfortable, no matter what he decides to do with his life. She knows he loves music far more than eyeglasses, and if that's how he wants to make his living, who is she to say he shouldn't? Much of what she hears coming from the living room makes no sense to her, it jangles her brain, but tonight's session she enjoyed, she says, it has rhythm and melody and not too many high-pitched squawks.

This is the most she's ever said to him at one time, and she speaks without giving him a chance to answer. But she hands him a glass of water without his having to ask, and for that he's grateful. Though the sweat is beginning to turn cold under his shirt, his throat is dry. It's better, Mrs. Van Gelder says, to look ahead rather than behind. It isn't too late, she adds, glancing down at her hands, to start a new family. Not for a man, it isn't.

I have a family, he says. I have Alfred. He thanks her for the water and excuses himself.

❧

Two of the musicians, the drummer and the trombonist, stand outside the water closet, whispering to each other as Frank makes his way down the hall. They look solemn and concerned, each in turn pressing an ear to the heavy paneled door and trying the knob. Should we break it? asks the trombonist, tall and bulky but big-eyed and nervous-looking in a too-tight striped shirt, and the drummer holds up a hand to quiet him. Then comes a soft groan, followed by what sounds like the snapping shut of an instrument case. Both men let out a heavy breath, though they still look uneasy as the toilet flushes and the lock clicks. The door opens to reveal the baby-faced pianist, appearing even younger now, just a little boy blinking in the dim light and smiling a blissful, dreamy smile. His hands are empty, but one sleeve of his shirt is unbuttoned. He stumbles over the threshold, and the trombonist takes him under his long arm, steadies him, asks, you ready for this?

I can play in my sleep, the pianist says. It looks as if he might have to do so: his eyes droop, his head sags to one side. The drummer, shorter, with a dense mustache and a calm expression both wise and weary, takes his other side, and the two of them walk the pianist through the kitchen, as Mrs. Van Gelder looks on through thick glasses that match her son's, sipping carefully at a cup of tea.

Alfred has expressed his concern about the pianist, as well as about others—that they might overdose before a session, or even worse, during one—but what are they to do? Write into their contract that using narcotics is forbidden? Frank worries, too, but what he hasn't said is this: how can Alfred expect them to do otherwise? This is the difference between them, the reason Alfred has a wife and children while Frank has decidedly avoided any new ties. Alfred left Berlin in 1933 and didn't witness the worst of what would come; his optimism is genuine but naïve, Frank thinks, and as much as his friend loves these musicians, as much as he admires them, he can't see how deep their pain runs. Nor, for that matter, can Frank, who sat across from his cousins in the Tiergarten café unable to picture what had happened to them after he'd stepped on the boat in Hamburg, even with the details they offered—the horror of their experience pushed beyond the reach of his imagination, and all he could do was apologize to them for having run away.

When he returns to the living room, Van Gelder has finished setting up. He and Alfred consult about the volume of the snare drum as the musicians prepare, the saxophonist wiping the neck of his horn with a cloth, the bass player tuning a string. They chat and joke, but more somberly now, and the pianist sits silently on his bench, listening to the others, or maybe only to his thoughts. Frank glances at Alfred to see if he has noticed anything wrong, but his friend just bounces on his heels and smiles in anticipation. Would it serve any purpose to upset him? Frank decides then: he will keep what he witnessed outside the bathroom to himself.

Van Gelder disappears into the control room, which was once his childhood bedroom, all the furniture replaced with sound equipment he refuses to show anyone else how to use. Frank has just another moment before it's time for him to get out of the way, but before he does, he grabs his camera and flash once more. Crouching, he focuses on the pianist across the plane of his instrument, his face framed by its propped lid.

In the view are the exposed guts of the piano, and behind the pianist's head a cymbal and the dark space of an open door. The young man glances to the side, as if contemplating a note only he can hear, and in his expression is something Frank saw in the expressions of his Berlin cousins. It's a haunted look, both resigned and restless, possessed, he thinks, only by those who have confronted death, or rather, those who have stepped as closely as possible without crossing to its other side. Afterward they carry the weight of what they've seen, a burden they can never set down. It's a terrible thing to bear, but also oddly beautiful and necessary, and he suspects they wouldn't trade it away if given the chance, despite the suffering it brings them. His cousins couldn't articulate such contradiction, but the pianist can, through his minor keys. And as if confirming it, his hand rises over the top of the piano, a short pencil gripped between two fingers, scratching something onto his score. Perhaps Frank can express it, too, or at least this photograph can, the camera able to see what he, who escaped his cousins' fate, never will.

It's not the kind of shot Alfred prefers, but it will be the right one for the album cover. Frank will insist on it.

He raises the flash high over his head, releases the shutter, and turns the crank to advance the film.

Among Thorns

The dizzy spells likely started soon after his army service ended. But Ilan spent most of that year drunk, so at first they were hard to distinguish from the regular spins he experienced after leaving a bar or waking naked in a strange man's bed, first in Cyprus, then in Turkey, and finally in Spain. He often forgot to eat, and many mornings he threw up whatever he'd gotten down the night before. By the time he made it home to Haifa, a few weeks past his twenty-second birthday, he'd lost nearly twenty pounds. His ribs showed through his shirts. Veins appeared close to the surface of his skin, forking down his forearms, over his temples, across his bony chest.

His mother tried to stuff him back to health, but even after he'd begun to fill out again, color returning to his face, the dizziness remained. He quit drinking, mostly—except for an occasional binge with friends in his university classes—and still he'd experience the strange tumbling sensation, not sideways like a drunken spin, but more of a forward roll, as if someone had pushed him hard from behind. It happened two or three times a week, always when he wasn't expecting it: during a biology lecture; while drinking coffee with a new boyfriend, whom he hadn't told how many men he'd slept with the previous year; in the shower, where he had to lean against the tiles to keep from falling.

He didn't say anything to his parents, and if they noticed something was wrong, they didn't let on. His mother was just relieved to see him eating, and his father, worried about finances and the retirement he'd been counting on since the day he'd started working, spent most of their time together offering advice about careers. "Do something you love," he said, "or else you'll just wish your life away." The boyfriend was too smitten and sex-blind to recognize anything beyond his own pleasure.

Ilan avoided their family doctor and instead found one at the university health clinic. While waiting in the examination room, he stared down the slope of Mount Carmel onto the city where he'd spent his first eighteen years, and beyond it to the sea he'd crossed the week after he'd ceased being a soldier. He imagined himself on his way back to Cyprus, back to the obliterating bliss of those first months abroad. But then he felt another roll coming on and lowered himself carefully to the edge of the exam table. Along the paths outside, fit young people hurried to classes without stumbling or falling. What had happened to him? When he'd reported for service, his body had been perfect. He'd been approved for a combat unit after his first physical. After two years, he'd come out more muscled and more tan. His only visible wound was a bad nick he gave himself while shaving with a straight razor he used only to show off to others in his squad.

The doctor was an American in his early thirties but already balding and paunchy, the type who'd been enamored with Israel since he was a boy but who'd waited to make Aliyah until he was too old for conscription. "Where did you serve?" he asked, in stilted Hebrew, as he looked over the numbers the nurse had written down, temperature and heart rate and blood pressure. What business was it of his? But Ilan answered anyway, "First Ofrit. Then Hebron."

The doctor didn't ask any more. Instead, he talked about diet and exercise, said he thought it was probably low blood sugar, that the nurse would take a sample and send it off to the lab. "You need to get on top of it early," he said, in English now. "Diabetes isn't something you want to live with for sixty years."

Sixty years sounded impossibly long, too long for anyone, but Ilan thanked the doctor and watched his blood filling tiny vials the nurse held at the end of a rubber tube. When the results came back negative—

for hypoglycemia, as well as STDs—and the dizzy spells persisted, the doctor suggested more tests. He tried not to show any concern, but Ilan could see it in his small, watery eyes, the set of his girlish lips. He'd been smart to avoid army service, Ilan thought. The other boys would have pinched his pudgy belly blue, wrapped him in blankets and abandoned him in the Negev in the middle of the night. Keeping his head down in the States until now was best for everyone.

"What sort of tests?" Ilan asked.

ଔ

A week later, he rode a bus to the port, alone, and from there walked to Rambam Hospital. It was a morning he didn't have class, and he'd told his parents he was going to interview for a part-time job at a café. "Give it two days," his father had said, "and if you don't enjoy it, quit on the spot." To the boyfriend, whose flat he usually visited for lunch and a fuck, he said he needed to put in some extra time in the lab, had to finish a report. The boyfriend was petulant on the phone, a whining child, and Ilan decided as he passed through the front doors of the imaging center, the smell of the sea strong until overtaken by disinfectant, that he was finished with this one, he'd sleep with someone new the first chance he got, whatever the tests revealed.

The doctor had decided on a PET scan rather than an MRI, and the acronym made him picture a small dog, a friendly one who'd follow him wherever he went. "My little PET," he joked with the nurse who gave him a paper gown to wear before injecting him with a radioactive liquid that would highlight any unusual activity in his organs. The technician was tall and clownish in scrubs, with long eyelashes and a high smooth forehead, and Ilan tried to flirt with him as he readied the machine. "I bet this is how you get the get the girls," he said, the paper gown hardly reaching the top of his thighs. "Or maybe boys? Once you find out they have only six months to live, then you pounce."

The technician laughed, but briefly, maybe coldly, and Ilan wondered if he wore a kippah underneath the surgical cap. He was sick of this uptight country full of fanatics. If he got better, he'd leave again, and this time he'd stay away for good. But as soon as he thought so, he felt a pang for the boyfriend's firm body and soft tongue, for the hour he could lose himself in friction and sweat and panting breath. By then he was on his own in the room, and the PET was buzzing, more like a giant locust than a little dog. The test lasted longer than he expected, longer than he cared for, but he'd gotten used to waiting during his two years in the army, waiting in barracks, waiting at guard stations, waiting in position above a street in Hebron, where nothing happened for hours at a time.

And when it was over, there was only more waiting. The technician betrayed nothing on his face as he turned off the machine, gave no sign that Ilan should worry or relax, though he did let his eyes drift across Ilan's thighs as he sat up, the paper gown hitching toward his waist. Ilan put both hands over his crotch. "We'll get the results to your doctor this afternoon," the technician said, his back turned, body shapeless beneath sagging scrubs.

☙

The next day he stopped at the boyfriend's flat at lunchtime, stripped him down before he'd even kissed him, and then lay in his arms longer than he meant to, skipping a lecture and a lab. The boyfriend was asleep when he finally got up, sitting on the edge of the bed and feeling that forward roll. Even when he put his head between his knees, it kept going, as if he were a gymnast whirling around a greased horizontal bar.

He found a bottle of vodka in the boyfriend's kitchen, mixed a tumbler with grapefruit juice before heading to his last class of the day. His professor lectured about the interaction of viruses in cells, the way human DNA had been altered by diseases that had disappeared from the planet thousands of years ago. Ilan pictured the radioactive liquid moving through his body, an electric green streak passing from brain to heart to lungs to liver to kidneys, and finally streaming out his cock into the toilet. He wanted to imagine it flushing out whatever made him tumble so insistently, giving him back control over his senses.

But even after he drank three liters of water and pissed himself dry, there it was, the nudge on the spine he couldn't feel, the resulting force he couldn't resist.

Cઆ

He waited two full weeks after the test before going back to the American doctor, canceling one appointment at the last minute and rescheduling twice. By then he'd broken up with the boyfriend and taken him back, their sex fiercer and more distracting for a few days before returning to routine. He was a lovely boy with strong shoulders and hairy chest, who liked to talk about history and the World Cup, and that Ilan felt nothing for him but lust he blamed on the dizziness or its source, whatever was emptying him out from the inside.

This time as soon as the nurse finished taking his stats, he lay down on the exam table, the sanitary paper crinkling beneath him, and closed his eyes. He kept them that way as the door opened and closed, rubber soles squeaking toward him, then the tap of a pen on a clipboard, the smell of strong medicinal soap. Before the doctor could speak, Ilan said in English, "It's psychological, I know. It's obvious. Probably has been to you all along. I should go to a therapist."

He didn't give the doctor a chance to respond. Instead, he kept talking, slowly but without pause, telling the American what he suspected he'd been curious about since Ilan's first visit: the tedious months in Hebron, maintaining position for six hours a day on the roof of a building across the street from the settler compound they were meant to protect, even though most of the boys in his unit hated those settlers who caused everyone so much trouble, far more than the Arab residents who'd spit in the street after the soldiers passed. He wasn't political, he told the doctor. Yes, his grandparents had been refugees, part of the great pioneer generation, but that was all so long ago, how could it mean anything to him now? He just wanted to do his duty and then live his life, go to school, earn a living, maybe have a family.

That was what he wanted for the residents of Hebron, too, who looked at him with hatred and terror when he patrolled the streets. Up on the rooftop he could pretend they were the people he was protecting, and not those Kahanists with their thick beards and smug piety and scornful way of speaking to the soldiers who kept them alive, especially those without head coverings, or worse, the female military police in trousers and hair too short to pull back into a bun. And if they knew what Ilan was, how he spent his free nights, and with whom? They would have despised him, cursed him, cast him out. He was no Jew to them, but they benefited from his silhouette against the sky above their compound, rifle resting across his knee. It gave them the right to harass residents returning from the casbah, or so they must have believed. He was clearly visible when several teenage boys surrounded a pair of women, one carrying an infant, and knocked their sacks of vegetables to the ground. The women ran away, and the boys shouted after them, tossed stones at their backs, and not once did they glance up to see what Ilan thought.

It made him so angry, knowing he gave them cover, and knowing, too, that they took his presence for granted. One of the stones hit the woman carrying the infant, right between the shoulder blades. She stumbled, recovered, kept running. Ilan raised his scope only so he could get a better look at the boys, recognize their faces in order to confront them next time he spotted them while on patrol, or else report them to the police who handled settler violence. He had his safety on; his hand was nowhere near the trigger. But he stared at those boys' faces, with their first wisps of beard, their pimpled noses, and felt all his weariness and boredom and disdain rushing through the scope. Eleven months of guarding these boys with whom he shared nothing but a common ancestry in a Europe he'd never visited. He could have shot them as easily as any of the terrorists he was meant to look out for. The desire to punish them rose up so strongly in him that he experienced it as a sudden thirst, so overwhelming he found his tongue stuck to the roof of his mouth, his nostrils itchy, parched air scorching his throat, and maybe a part of him believed he really was getting ready to shoot them, or was shooting them already, because when he heard the footsteps of the soldier coming to relieve him, the crunch of ancient stones beneath heavy boots, he started, lost his balance, nearly toppled off the roof into the street.

And of course that's what he was still feeling, he told the doctor, his eyes remaining closed. It was obvious, wasn't it? Just the horror of imagining what he was capable of, picturing himself pulling the trigger and watching as each boy flopped on hard ground. And no matter how much he drank or how many men he slept with, he wouldn't shake the dizziness, because it was just in his head, right? Because it would be too absurd a coincidence, too perfect an irony, if there were really something wrong with him, if soon after he'd felt himself tumbling from the dusty building in Hebron, a mutation in his cells made him relive that tumbling over and over again. That sounded too much like divine retribution, but he didn't believe in divinity, and anyway, wouldn't such reprisal seem too severe even for someone who did?

"I'll go to the counseling clinic as soon as I leave here," he said. "Maybe you can refer me to someone good."

And only then did he open his lids and take in the soft feminine features of the American doctor, the shiny bald head and little eyes blinking behind narrow lenses, plump hands raising the clipboard with the results of his test, pale lips parting to tell him what they said.

The Downs

Waking up is the hardest part of his day. The pain begins in his back, rises to his shoulders, then his neck, and settles in his jaw, which took so many blows in his fighting days he's surprised it still works at all. It's his favorite instrument, far preferable to his fists, and he uses it all day now as innkeeper and publican of the Admiral Nelson, which he purchased with winnings from his last purse, eighty guineas for a comeback bout against his old friend and frequent second Harry Lee. Now he blinks eyes open with difficulty and pulls himself from the straw mattress in the storeroom behind the Nelson's bar, which means he drank too much last night to walk the quarter-mile down Whitechapel Road to his home on Petticoat Lane. Esther will be up already, with the children who still live at home, and she will tell them that their dad works hard, that an innkeeper's job is an important one, and therefore they shouldn't expect to see him most nights. He stretches, runs in place, throws a few punches at the air, breathes hard. He is no less heavy than in his prime, but at fifty-five his body isn't as solid as it once was, his stomach developing a gentle bulge, skin sagging beneath his arms. Dressed, he remains small and swarthy, with a lively bounce to his step, chest thrust out, head back to give each person he encounters a passing glance of scrutiny and appraisal.

He is the pugilist Daniel Mendoza, in the late spring of 1820. Fourteen years have passed since his last fight, four since he published his second book, memoirs of his life from childhood through his initial retirement. The money he earned from its meager sales he has long since spent. His first book, on the art of boxing, still brings in small royalties every year, but not enough to bother mentioning to Esther, who would encourage him to save it against future debt. But future debt doesn't concern him. It's the present that makes him drink enough in the evening so that he might forget he owes twenty guineas to a bank in Surrey and another twenty-five to a theatre owner in Covent Garden. The former was for a loan to start a wine import business that never made it past the planning stages, the latter an advance to turn his memoirs into a drama for the stage. But every time he tried to turn his life into a script, he quickly lost interest—not because his life hadn't been dramatic, but because he couldn't bear the thought of words he'd spoken thirty years ago spilling from the mouth of a young actor who'd never set foot inside a ring.

The Admiral Nelson on its own brings in enough income to sustain itself and feed his family. But if he hopes to avoid another stint in prison—debt has already landed him there twice, six months in Carlisle, another six at the King's Bench here in London—he'll have to find another way of making money. All his previous attempts have failed: giving boxing demonstrations from Edinburgh to Cardiff, opening an academy for aspiring pugilists, hiring himself out to the same theatre owner to help suppress mobs rioting against higher ticket prices. Publican is the job that suits him best, as it gives him the opportunity to chat all day with his Whitechapel neighbors, many of whom still ask him how things are up in Windsor, though thirty years have passed since he defeated Bill Warr for the championship of all England and his former patron—then Prince of Wales, now King George IV—invited him to visit the castle. They consider him a hero still, representative of East End peddlers and laborers, defender of London's Jews, and among each other refer to him as *our Dan*. If a fight breaks out here, all he has to do is square into his famous defensive stance and say calmly, Outside gentlemen, unless you'd like to pay for a lesson, and fists quickly drop and loosen.

This morning the inn is quiet. In the six rooms above, he has only two overnight guests, one a traveling textile merchant, the other a young woman who gives him a percentage of her earnings when she brings customers here; when alone, he lets her stay for free. Her name is Eliza, the twenty-year-old daughter of a glass-cutter Mendoza knows from school days, when he learned enough Hebrew to read along with hymns. He rarely attends services now, though during his wealthy years he gave large annual donations to the Bevis Marks Synagogue, where he was bar mitzvahed and married. Now in exchange for his generosity on her quiet nights, Eliza has offered *her* services, but while he often enjoys the company of women other than his wife—which is part of what keeps him in debt—out of respect for her father and the moral teachings of their childhood, he has thus far declined.

She is already waiting in the pub when he comes out from behind the bar. A fire burns in the stove, a cup of tea steams on her table. Took you long enough, she says. You might as well start employing me.

If he could afford to, he would, he tells her. If she wants to take over the kitchen, he'd happily fire the old cook, who complains about her swollen feet more hours than she works.

I'm better at other things than cooking, she says.

I don't want to hear about that.

Eliza laughs at his discomfort. She is a small plump girl with a sly dark face and over-large eyes, the same age as his oldest daughter Sophia, though her complexion is closer to that of his youngest, ten-year-old Mathilda. Mendoza has often worried that his daughters, too, will end up in Eliza's trade, which makes him even more desperate to pay off his debts and reclaim the fortune he so foolishly squandered. Not long ago, a neighbor spotting Sophia walking with a friend in Petticoat Lane called out, I see there are Jewish whores as well as Gentiles, which led to a scuffle, bruises, a bitten thumb, and a day in court. Mendoza had still been in the King's Bench then, or else there would have been broken bones, too.

Such an innocent fellow, Eliza says. Never gives a pretty girl so much as a glance. Is that right?

None whose families I know, he replies, and then asks why she is up so early. Didn't she have a gentleman last night?

He was gone by half-ten, she says.

Didn't want to pay the full hour?

Didn't want to pay at all.

Mendoza suggests he must have gotten cold feet, but when Eliza doesn't answer, asks, Afterward?

Then Eliza tells him: the gentleman had words about the cleanliness of a Jew's nethers, how they aren't worth a shilling. Then slapped her when she tried to keep him from leaving. She shows him the left side of her face, which he can see now is darker than the right, an unpleasant ruddiness marring its olive tone.

You should have called for me, Mendoza says, the old outrage lifting his chin and chest—the same that made him challenge a porter twice his size for insulting his employer, a tea dealer, when he was hardly more than a boy. He pummeled the porter into humiliating submission in a makeshift ring outside the dealer's premises. That was his first public fight. A week later he took his first prize, which was easier but somehow less satisfying, driven as it was by ambition rather than anger on behalf of his people. Now he says, I would have thrown him down the stairs.

I know you would have, Eliza says. But then you wouldn't have let me pay you in return.

Breaking his neck would have been payment enough.

I was in no shape to call anyone. And now I don't have a share for you.

Next time she sees his miserable face in Whitechapel, he tells her, she should let him know. He'd show the scoundrel what was dirty.

Friday nights are always worst, she says. All our fellows home with their families. Tonight will be better.

He hears the door to the street open, excuses himself, and hurries around the half-wall separating the pub from the entryway. It's too early for the cook, so he expects to see Esther, with Mathilda in tow, and wants to head her off before she spots him with Eliza. She wouldn't appreciate the glimpse of him alone with this girl in the empty pub, though in all their years of marriage she has never once questioned him about how he spends his nights. She has been loyal and supportive, bearing him eleven children as his fortunes rose and fell, and she has complained little, except to urge him to find a straightforward source of income to sustain the family. The sight of her always makes him feel guilty, as if he *had* just gone to bed with Eliza, erasing any pride he might otherwise take in his restraint. And the guilt in turn makes him resentful. When he steps around the divider, he is ready to accuse Esther of meddling in his affairs, pestering him when he's trying to get the inn ready for the busiest night of the week—other Jews may take Saturday off from work, but he can't afford to do so—and why doesn't she bring Mathilda to the Bevis Mark rather than dragging her into a pub on Shabbat morning?

But instead of Esther, he finds Joseph Caday, an old Whitechapel friend and regular patron of the Admiral Nelson, though never one to appear before noon. Joseph is twenty years younger than Mendoza, stout and beaky, with slumped shoulders and long arms. He was a student at Mendoza's short-lived boxing academy, and he fought several bouts with Mendoza as second, winning none. Yet he read Mendoza's boxing book, as well as his memoirs, and he knows his record better than Mendoza himself, naming dates and numbers of rounds that often slip his mind. What year was his first fight with Humphries? How long did it take for him to lose to Gentleman John Jackson? He no longer recalls, if he ever knew. Joseph can recite any such detail, though when he throws a punch he can never remember to defend his face. Now he says, Good news, Dan. I've got the answer to all your troubles.

Mendoza waits, but Joseph only grins a half-witted grin, wrings his hands together. Are you going to share it with me?

Joseph's grin suddenly wilts, his heavy brows drooping over his little pig's eyes. Perhaps you won't want to do it, he says.

I can't know until you say what it is.

Perhaps it's a bad idea.

Was he talking about a purse or a murder? Mendoza asks.

A return to the ring, Joseph tells him. Two former champions.

Jackson?

Oh, no, no. Jackson doesn't need the money. Tom Owen. Innkeeper in Hampshire now.

Who'd pay for two publicans? Mendoza asks.

For the most famous pugilist in English history? Joseph says. Then his grin returns, his hands rub together again, and he bounces on the toes of his filthy shoes. Forty guineas each. An extra ten for the winner.

Sounds like a lot of trouble for fifty guineas.

Did he know what Owen's been saying? Joseph asks. That no low-bred Jew could so much as tap his chin.

Before Mendoza can respond, Eliza steps around the dividing wall. She's buttoned into her jacket though the morning has warmed already, light revealing thousands of dust particles floating between floorboards and rafters. Morning, Mr. Caday, she says brightly, and Joseph blushes, looks down, bunches the hat in his hand.

Miss Eliza, he says. A good Shabbat to you.

Indeed, she says. My favorite day of the week. Especially after the sun goes down.

Not for me, Mendoza says. All the horses let out of the stable after being locked up all day.

Will you be back this evening? Eliza asks, still smiling up at Joseph, who won't meet her gaze.

Oh, he'd see, Joseph replies. Perhaps he'd stay home tonight.

Too bad, Eliza says. The company's been lacking of late.

Off to services then, Joseph? Mendoza asks, to give him escape.

That's right, Dan. On my way now.

Give my regards to all the folks.

Joseph steps toward the door, pauses. And will you join us soon? For that special … celebration I mentioned?

This time Joseph's grin is brittle and uncertain, and he peeks up with one eyebrow raised. Eliza glances at Mendoza, too, as if she knows he's about to make a momentous decision. Or is there any decision to be made? A pair of old innkeepers. Fifty guineas to the winner. Joseph's eager face. A cell at the King's Bench awaiting his return. He tries to call up the anger he should feel at Owen's insults, but the effort merely tires him.

Of course I will, he says. Wouldn't miss it for anything.

ᘍ

Because prizefighting is no longer tolerated in the city—following his coronation, the former Prince abandoned his passion for the ring— Joseph has arranged for the bout to take place in the middle of Banstead Downs, twenty miles south of the Thames, two weeks hence. July the fourth, the day before Mendoza's birthday. He will celebrate turning fifty-six by paying off his debts, freeing himself from the burdens that have weighed him down for years. And assuming he wins, he will have some additional funds left over to invest in improvements to the Admiral Nelson, or to spend however he sees fit. In order to nurture his anticipation, he makes an additional five-pound wager on his victory, with a shoemaker whose shop is adjacent to the inn, and then spends some time exercising in the room behind the pub. He gets winded more easily than he used to and has to pause after twenty push-ups to let the burning in his arms subside. But he remembers how to move his feet as if he were in the ring yesterday, how to parry imaginary fists hurling toward his face or abdomen, how to sneer just before delivering a blow to the ribs.

Mendoza has never fought Owen, though they have met on several occasions, and once participated together in a sparring exhibition to demonstrate the classic style of boxing at the Five Courts. The event netted them each ten guineas but wasn't enough to seed a friendship.

During his brief time as champion, Owen claimed in the newspapers that he could have easily beaten Mendoza in his prime, and John Jackson, too, though both had retired before he had the chance. Mendoza, never one to accept an insult without response, in turn said he could have knocked Owen across the English Channel, though his boots would have remained in London. Soon enough Owen lost to Jack Bartholomew, a lesser boxer whom Mendoza could have flattened, especially if he were ten years younger. But now whispers reach him that Owen has further besmirched his character, called him shifty, a filthy Jew thief who only won a bout when he played hurt and tricked other boxers into letting down their defenses. This time the words stir up embers of rage hot enough to spur him through another set of push-ups.

He doesn't tell Esther about the fight, nor any of his children, nor even any of his Whitechapel fans. He doesn't want anyone to try to dissuade him, not when he has begun to count on the money, has even committed several pounds to new linens for his guest rooms—thinking, as he purchases them, of Eliza on the nights she spends alone, and the comfort she might find in a new set of well-made sheets—and is determined to go through with the bout, even as he hears his wife's voice in his head: If you get hurt and can't work, what will we do then, Dan?

Yet soon enough word spreads that Mendoza the Jew will fight once more. Patrons of the pub come up and shake his hand, wish him luck, tell him to show the innkeeper from Hampshire how they do things in the East End. Mendoza Messiah, one friend calls him, and though he brushes off the remark, he finds himself talking loudly, carrying fresh casks of bitter on his shoulder for all to see, taking an extra glass for himself to keep his spirits up. One night he visits a reputable stew across the river in Southwark, where he has his choice of half a dozen young women. To make himself feel as if he is preparing for combat, he selects the largest of the group, wrestling with her for several hours and handing over to the proprietor nearly a full week's take of the Admiral Nelson.

During this time, he even attends services at the Bevis Mark one Saturday morning, not because of any religious feeling, or a need to pray for his safety or even his victory, but because he knows people there will look at him, whisper to each other about his upcoming return to the ring, wish him well without giving away to Esther that he will soon fight again. The stern cantor, whom he's known since he was a boy, shakes his hand, says it's good to see him, that he should consider letting someone else look after the Admiral Nelson on Friday nights so he can observe Shabbat in its full glory. He also meets Eliza's father, whom he hasn't seen in years, and in the glass cutter's worn, pitted face he glimpses a hint of the daughter's features, her prominent forehead, the sweet slyness of her grin, and he determines then that he will no longer take a share of her profits; so long as her customer pays for the room, she is free to do as she pleases.

Soon it seems that only his family remains in the dark. Joseph plods in and out of the pub all day, telling him who has placed bets on him most recently. He'll enrich the whole of Whitechapel, Joseph says, and as for himself, he's placed all his savings, seven quid, on his mentor.

You might hold a little back, Mendoza says. To be safe.

Against the horse's arse from Hampshire? Joseph asks. No need.

I'm not as young as I once was.

You'd beat him if you was a hundred.

And fourteen years is a long time away.

You'd beat him in your sleep. With one foot in the grave.

Beat who? Eliza asks, coming down the stairs late this morning, and still looking sleepy, with hair pinned up and dress buttoned to the throat. She had a customer the night before, a big, square-faced tradesman, handsome in his way, though mean-looking. Mendoza didn't like his face or his manner, and ten minutes after she'd led him upstairs, he followed and listened at the door. He always told her if a fellow got too rough, she should stomp down on her floorboards; no matter how loud it was in the pub, he'd hear it and come running. Now all he heard was a whimpering sound followed by Eliza's throaty laughter. The bloke stayed a full two hours and came down to the pub just before closing. His neck was red on one side as if it had been scuffed with a stiff brush, but his smile then made him less menacing, which only made Mendoza hate him more. He asked for a whisky, but Mendoza told him it was too late, he was finished serving for the night. When the fellow objected, he dropped into his defensive stance. He would have taken pleasure in knocking him to the floor and dragging him out to the street. But the bloke only laughed and said he'd taken all the punishment he could for one night. Then he left without another word.

Now Eliza walks behind the bar, pours herself tea as if she's the proprietor, sits and props her boots on a stool. Who're you going to beat? she asks again.

Any fool who treats my guests poorly, Mendoza says.

He's going to clean the Downs with him, Miss, Joseph says.

You're not still fighting, Eliza says, peering hard at Mendoza over her cup, with eyes squinted in a way that reminds him of Esther's look whenever he explains how he plans to pay off his debts. At your age?

Wouldn't dream of it.

He could have beat them all in his day, Miss, Joseph says. Did beat them all, practically. And him half the size of some.

Size isn't everything, Eliza says. I can attest to that.

Joseph's ears go red. Eliza blows steam from her tea, glances at Mendoza through long eyelashes, and slurps.

ଔ

It seems as if the entire East End has emptied into Banstead Downs, along with plenty of well-appointed fancy from Westminster and Chelsea. More than two hundred people are waiting in a foggy dip between a pair of chalk hills when he arrives, walking half a mile across the fields from where the carriage left him, Joseph tripping alongside, talking too fast about Owen's defensive style, the weakness he has on his left side, a tendency to drop his shoulder before releasing an uppercut. He sounds nervous, as if he were the one about to step into the range of coming blows, and to calm him, Mendoza asks him to repeat the ground rules to which Owen has agreed—Broughton's standard rules, with the addition of no grabbing or pulling hair. That was what allowed Jackson to beat him back in 1795. Some gentleman he was, regardless of the nickname. Four inches taller, nearly three stone heavier, and he resorted to shoving Mendoza into a corner, grabbing a tuft at the back of his head, and holding him firm while landing one blow after another with his left fist. Mendoza's second objected, and others agreed it was a foul, but the rules allowed it: when Broughton wrote them, he'd already taken to shaving his head to avoid a similar fate. The purse, at least, had been two hundred guineas each, a reasonable payment for such a travesty.

Now, in any case, he has less hair remaining on his head—less, in fact, than on his chest—and Owen is closer to his size, maybe an inch or two taller, half a stone heavier, a few years younger. He looks his age as he hands off his jacket to his second, who folds it carefully and lays it on the grass. Eyes sunken, hair beginning to gray. There's a stiff, lumbering quality to his movements, as if his bones have stuck together at the joints like candles heated, pressed end to end, and quickly cooled. But his jaw, too, works well enough, and so do his lungs when he calls out, loud enough for everyone in the crowd to hear: The stinking Jew thief is late. He should forfeit his purse.

Murmurs and a few loud cries follow. Owen gives Mendoza a wink—in ridicule, it seems, or maybe encouragement. The innkeeper from Hampshire is so afraid for his life, Mendoza shouts in turn, that he seeks to walk away before a blow has landed. Therefore, the forfeit is his.

More cries of objection, and then Joseph takes up the call: Those of you who want to see the great Mendoza, former champion of all

England, greatest boxer who has ever lived—any of you who want to see him fight, say so now! Loud cheers rise up, and Mendoza lifts both arms over his head. The fog has dispersed, but in its place comes a steady drizzle, making the skin on his shoulders tighten with cold. Who among you, Joseph goes on, is willing to sweeten the pot to see your champion fight? He sends his hat into the crowd, and Mendoza watches it bob from hand to hand, some dropping coins inside. Now Owen looks satisfied and has nothing else to say. He and Mendoza meet in the center of the grass square that has been marked off with posts and ropes, their seconds standing near.

It's a true honor, Mr. Mendoza, Owen whispers. I saw your second fight against Humphries. A work of beauty. I've read your book, too, and learned a great deal.

So all the taunts have been a show, meant to drum up interest in a fight between a pair of worn-out old men. Mendoza wants to hang onto his anger, even if it's feigned, but Owen's words sound genuine, and despite himself, he feels a measure of gratitude and respect. Joseph reads out the agreed-upon rules, mostly for the benefit of the audience, and then he and the seconds step out of the ring. Mendoza wonders if the next part, too, will be just a show. The truth is, he has always preferred the stage to the ring, saw his actual fights as a means to get people to pay him for exhibitions. He wants to think of this, too, as simply an exhibition, a friendly sparring, and it's easy to imagine it so as he approaches Owen, crouching low, fists raised before his face. He keeps his feet moving, though they don't move as fast as they once had, and at times he forgets which one is supposed to lead, which to stay back. He focuses on maintaining his equilibrium, as he advises in his book, while Owen stands with arms loose at his sides, his chin high, an easy target. A demonstration, then, no different than the dozens he used to give on his tours of Britain, during which he often used Joseph as a sparring partner to show audiences how to lay flat a man twice your size with cunning, skill, and tenacity.

But when he steps close to Owen now, the innkeeper from Hampshire throws a surprisingly quick left to his ribs that sends him reeling sideways, and nearly down on his backside. He recovers, but not before Owen follows with another left, this time catching a cheek, glancingly but enough to sting. So, not just a demonstration after all. He feels himself sweating already, heavily down his back though hidden by the rain, which falls harder now. His breath is thin. He manages to get his feet under him and stagger out of Owen's reach, and for the next few minutes he shuffles at a safe distance, focusing on dodging and parrying his opponent's jabs, the fists coming at him more quickly than he anticipates, looming suddenly out of the bright green hill opposite and lurching at his face.

Eventually he manages to land a solid right to Owen's chin, but it hardly moves the other man, whose head snaps forward again as if he's only been nudged. And then comes a rapid series of blows that has Mendoza crouching and ducking and tripping backward until he goes down on one knee, ending the round. After that he loses track of how many rounds pass, concentrating instead on keeping his balance, keeping Owen in view, though at times he loses sight of the innkeeper among the crowd. Now that his eyes are swelling shut, everything in front of him blurs, faces and clouds and the ground, and sometimes he hears Joseph shouting to him, telling him to get his arms up, to duck or jab or parry; his friend might have been reading to him from his own book of instruction, but when he swings he hits only air. During breaks following each fall, his bottle holder brings him water. He sips but tastes only blood. The crowd jeers, and someone shouts, Put the little Jew out of his misery. The rage he's counted on for so long is gone now, or else he can imagine it coming only from Esther: How will we live if you're in the ground?

He begins a new round—tenth? fifteenth?—still on his feet, and Owen has tired enough that he can get a fist through his defenses from time to time, feel the warm slick skin against his knuckles. But there's little strength behind his strikes, and he knows it's over. This is true defeat, without anyone grabbing his hair, the defeat of time and age and desperation, an idiotic defeat for a man who should know better, who needs money, yes, but even more needs the adoration of men like Joseph, the respect of those in the crowd who now cry for his blood, cry for him to be put in his place after all the years they've tolerated a little Jew laying their hulking brutes low. Finally now, a real Englishman will pound his dark face into oblivion. It doesn't matter that Mendoza was born in London, as was his father, grandfather, great-grandfather. He'll never be one of them. Enough is enough, England for Englishmen, even in lowly Whitechapel, and down he goes, the bright wet grass covering the chalk-white earth rushing at his face.

CR

He wakes in the carriage, head knocking against the wooden bench, the stench of horse strong in his nose, and beyond it, the smell of smoke. They are almost back to the city, then. The muffled humming sound in his right ear makes it hard to understand what Joseph is saying, so he doesn't bother listening, just watches through slit eyes as fields give way to scattered houses and then tightly packed groupings, the world eventually turning to brick. Joseph hands him his purse, a small stack of coins, fewer, he guesses, than the number of bruises on his body. Five quid will go the neighbor who bet against him, and five each to the theatre owner and the Surrey bank, just enough to keep him from being sent back to prison for the debts. And the rest? A man has to enjoy himself while he still breathes. He hands five to Joseph, whose wide blunt face looks hopeless, as if all his dreams have been mangled and left to rot in Banstead Downs. He asks if Mendoza wants to go to a tavern, or to one of the Southwark houses he favors, or perhaps even to his home, but Mendoza says no: the Admiral Nelson, he has to open the bar, customers will soon finish work and come in for a pint.

Only Eliza is there when he arrives, and she makes a fuss over him as he limps in, leaning against Joseph. She helps him onto the mattress in the back room, wipes his face with a wet cloth, and then holds it to his left eye, which must be the worse of the two, though he can feel only equal throbbing in both. She shoos Joseph out of the way, tells him to get the bar ready; any dolt can pour a beer, she says. Her breath smells of strong, bitter tea, and even her soft hands scrape at his tender skin. There are worse paths for his daughters, he thinks, than to be like her.

Why in hell would you want to go and fight again? she mutters, and then goes on without waiting for a reply. Better ways to prove you're still a man.

Does he want to prove anything now? He reaches up, grabs a fistful of flesh through the coarse cloth of her dress, but she slaps his hand away.

Now of all times? she asks. When all I'll do is hurt you worse than you're already hurt?

She pours water into his mouth, but most of it slides sideways, dribbling down his cheek and onto his neck. Above him, her face is no longer sly, just round and scared, nothing hard in it. And then it's gone, only wooden beams overhead, the one solid thing in his life. If he loses the Admiral Nelson, he'll have nothing, and he tries to sit up so he can do his job. But the pain ripples downward from his head and along his spine, flaring across his ribs, and he lies back again. He sleeps without realizing it, wakes to hear voices outside the door, the sound of pints against wood. Every so often Joseph returns to ask a question—how much change for two pints against a five-shilling note? we've run out of mince pies, should I tell the cook to make more?—and Eliza checks on him from time to time, forcing more water in him, replacing the cloth on his eye. Don't you have customers? he asks, but she only shrugs and answers, The night's young. There's no hurry.

And later he wakes to the sound of thumping overhead. So she has found a customer after all. The noise continues for another minute, then stops abruptly. A short while later comes a cry, raised voices, a smack of skin on skin, the sound so much worse, somehow, when it isn't against his own. This time he pulls himself upright despite the pain, swivels onto his feet. The left eye is fully closed now, and the right is blurry, but he makes his way by the light of a lantern into the pub, which is empty, mugs strewn everywhere, a sopping rag on the bar, chairs and stools askew. Even drunk he has never left the place in such a condition. But he can't clean it now. Another cry descends from above, this time clearly Eliza's voice, and it is followed again by the sound of a blow. He runs for the stairs but has to stop at the foot to catch his breath, wincing at the pressure of ribs against his lungs.

What good can he do her if he does make it up there? What good has he ever done her, or anyone else in his life—his wife, his children, his neighbors, his friends? He has brought them only false hope, worry, and disappointment. He pulls himself up, one step, a second, but before he makes it past the third, a door flies open above, slamming against the wall, and then a figure appears on the landing, a big dark burly shape, hurrying toward him. He squares himself to face it as it bounds down, but it doesn't stop, just shoves him aside as if he were no more than a bedsheet blocking the way. And only as his back hits the banister does he recognize Joseph's face, blood leaking from his nose, a bright red mark on his cheek. Nothing covers his huge body as it bolts toward the door, not a single strip of cloth, which makes Mendoza let out a laugh even though it brings more pain.

Then Eliza is on the stairs, in her long robe, cinched only with one hand at the throat, so that her plump white legs emerge from the slit below. She shouts after Joseph, No one gets seconds without asking! And Mendoza, useless and old, his body battered, his debts growing by the day, watches his friend run naked into the street.

Up Ahead

1. After the Flood

It was a hot evening in mid-summer, orange-pink light slanting hard through high basement windows. Dust floated across bright shafts and disappeared, including several big tufts Eileen had dislodged kicking boxes out of her way. But the pipes were opposite the windows, where the sunlight didn't reach. The stairs partially blocked the overhead bulb, casting shadows, and even with a flashlight she struggled to follow the lines of galvanized steel, splitting here and joining there, and then stubbing up to the sinks and toilets and bathtub, as well as to the bloody dishwasher filling her kitchen with water. The smell was musty and rank, and it made her picture caves from stories she'd heard in childhood, or those she'd read to her sons when they were small, the kind with trolls in them, or maybe it was ogres. What was the difference between a troll and an ogre? The boys would have known, but the older was at a wrestling camp four hundred miles away, and the younger, Jeremy, was sloshing barefoot across the flooded kitchen, calling down through the floor, "Mom! It's not off yet!"

She'd made the mistake of telling him to stay upstairs while she went down to look for the shut-off valve, to let her know when water finally stopped surging out of the loose hose the inspector had failed to notice, along with a dead burner on the stove and rotten boards beneath a planter on the front porch. Not that any of those things would have kept her from buying the place, or even prompted her to negotiate a lower price. The sellers, children of the previous owner, whom they'd recently shipped off to a nursing home, had refused to fix anything.

Nor would they work with a realtor. Eileen paid for the inspection herself, and still they said take it or leave it at every step of the process, guessing—correctly—that she already had her heart set on the house and wouldn't walk away.

But if she'd known about the broken hose, at least she wouldn't have loaded both racks with dishes and filled the dispenser with soap. She wouldn't have bothered cooking at all, instead taking Jeremy out for pizza as he'd requested. But it was their first night in the house, and she wanted to prove that their lives would soon get back to normal—at least some new version of normal, though maybe a little rougher than the one they'd been living before the divorce. Despite the broken burner, she managed to bake chicken legs and boil ears of corn. Nothing exciting, just normal. And now gushing water, and Jeremy calling out gleefully, "It's up to my ankles!"

There were other houses she could have bought with money from the settlement, houses in better shape, that didn't smell of dog and molasses. But the location sold her: on the west shore of Lenape Lake, with a view of two tiny wooded islands that gathered mist in the morning. A great place for the boys, she thought the first time she saw it, though it wasn't the boys she pictured then. She saw only herself, sipping a glass of wine as the sun set behind her, tracking the wake of mallards paddling around the closest of the islands. If she had to start over, she wanted to do so with style. And it didn't hurt that her ex-husband, Peter, a pharmaceutical salesman who liked to fish on weekends, would envy her for the proximity to water stocked with trout. She'd snap photographs of every rainbow Jeremy caught and encourage him to show the pictures to his father as often as possible.

What did it matter that it was a man-made lake in suburban New Jersey, just two miles from the traffic snarls of Route 10? With her head tilted at enough of an angle to keep the nearest neighbors out of view, she could imagine she'd moved to a secluded place in the country, a lakeside cabin like the ones she used to see in Peter's *Field & Stream*.

Or maybe she'd pretend she'd taken Jeremy to live at Walden, so they could commune with nature and explore their inner lives, though unlike Thoreau, whom she'd read in college, she had no intention of eventually surviving on vegetables alone. She'd always been a person with discerning tastes, if not grand ones, and she expected one day to live again in a manner that rose to her standards.

But she was also practical, flexible, accommodating to life's sudden swerves—or at least she wanted to be, given that she had little choice. The house was one of the oldest of the lakeshore homes, and one of the smallest. Most others like it—Craftsman cottages, single-story, with bathrooms off the kitchen—had been torn down to make way for ranches with open floor plans and throwback brick-fronted colonials. This one had been owned by the same family for ninety years and had suffered three generations of neglect. The roof sagged, the chimney leaked, and three pillars on the porch were badly bowed. An old yew hedge had overtaken most of the driveway, and the yard was a tangle of thistle and blackberry, with an ancient concord grape vine snaking through the underbrush and sending tendrils into the branches of a neighbor's maple.

What the place had in abundance was potential, and Eileen, optimistic by nature or necessity, could envision the outcome of efforts not yet undertaken. She could see the new kitchen she'd design, the furniture she'd buy, the garden she'd plant. There was so much to look forward to, and owning a house of her own—a house on a lake— provided a small bubble of pride to buoy her after all the humiliation she'd suffered. Without it, she knew, she'd likely drown.

The main obstacle, of course, was money. Payments from Peter gave her enough to live on, to feed and clothe the boys, but not to build. To make up the amount she fell short of the down payment, she'd borrowed a thousand dollars from her former father-in-law, who—out of guilt, she suspected—sent a check the week after the divorce was finalized. She hoped guilt would keep him from asking her to pay it back. Suddenly single after fifteen years of marriage, she had no career and hardly any savings. She was thirty-eight and hadn't worked since her second year out of nursing school—in 1970, just before giving birth to Kevin, her oldest—and though she'd recently managed to land a job as a receptionist at an orthodontist's office, the salary was a pittance. It would take decades to save up enough to do a real overhaul, years even to deal with surfaces. She wondered if her ex-father-in-law's guilt might extend to another three thousand; or, if guilt expired, whether pity might replace it and deepen his pockets.

These were the challenges she'd been reckoning with, while trying to balance her checkbook a few weeks before the move, in the bland, soulless apartment she'd rented after the separation. And that was when Kevin told her, casually, as if she wouldn't experience it as an elbow to the gut, that he'd move back in with Peter when he came home from camp. All his friends were in Chatwin, he said, and the high school had a better wrestling team. Of course he'd visit on weekends, when he didn't have matches out of town.

"It's no big deal, right?" he said, angling his eyes away. He'd recently turned fifteen, and dark fuzz grew on either side of his upper lip, though not yet below his nose. It made her think of the mustache Peter sported for most of their marriage. She'd never enjoyed the prickliness of it against her mouth, but it hadn't occurred to her to complain. And then, after falling in love with one of his clients, a purchaser at a hospital in Parsippany, he abruptly shaved it off. How different would her life have been if she'd known she could just ask for things she wanted?

"No big deal," she replied, blinking hard. "You do what you think is right." And then she turned to Jeremy, who flinched when he caught her expression, which she tried hard to keep neutral, though she could feel her lips pressed together uncomfortably, creases forming on her forehead. "You could stay with Dad, too, if you prefer."

He did his best not to hesitate, she could tell, but his mouth hung open a moment before he spoke. "I want to live by the lake."

And then, taking advantage of the moment, he asked, "Can we get a dog?"

She already wondered how to get the dog smell out of the house and had no intention of adding to it. But she answered, "Maybe after we get settled in. And get the place in shape." Jeremy winced—with disappointment and self-pity, she thought then. He was almost twelve and small for his age, pale and fragile-looking, with bushy hair and glasses. Unlike his brother, he was clumsy and useless at sports, struggled in school, didn't make friends easily. Now he held a hand over his belly as if she'd slugged him, and she found herself irritated by his helplessness, his constant need. She tried to ignore him, instead glancing at Kevin and feeling pathetic as she added, "Maybe you'll want to come over more often if there's a puppy around."

That night Jeremy's cries woke her from dreams she didn't remember but which left her feeling sorry for herself and put upon. Her first thought was, Does it always have to be about him? Then she heard vomiting, and when she stumbled into the boys' bedroom, she found Kevin holding his shivering brother, looking nearly adult in his pajama bottoms and no shirt, his chest and shoulders lumpy with muscle, the facial hair looking thicker in the dark. Jeremy pressed a hand to his side and cried out again, and she decided she was being punished unfairly, that she couldn't take any more. Not only had her husband left her for someone else, not only was her older son abandoning her just when she needed his help and protection, but now the younger was being taken from her, too.

It was a brief moment of despair, one that had passed by the time they made it to the emergency room, where a doctor said, "appendix"—a word that sounded mystical and oddly comforting in the frenzy of the moment—and assured her they'd remove it before it caused any harm. By then the feeling embarrassed her, and she told herself that all her choices from that point on would be about the boys, that she wouldn't make another selfish decision in her life. The house, of course, was already hers. It was too late to change her mind about that.

CR

Now Jeremy's cries weren't agonized so much as celebratory, perhaps even vindictive. "The water's still coming! It's gonna fill the whole house!" She knew it was still coming, because it had seeped into the linoleum's cracks and rained through the boards beneath. It splattered her head, rolled down her back. The flashlight's beam was weak, and when she shook it, it grew only weaker. Ogres sounded bigger than trolls, though both, she supposed, would gnaw your bones happily enough if you wandered into their cave. Still, she would have preferred either to the spiders whose webs she kept walking into and wiping from her face. She ran a hand down each of the pipes, trying to find something that felt like a valve, but her skin just slipped over smooth metal. At least the water dripping over her face would hide any tears, if they came, though right now she mostly felt like laughing. Hysterical laughter, perhaps, but pleasurable all the same. Drops rolled into her underwear, and she let out a squeal.

"You okay?" Jeremy called.

"Just losing it, that's all."

The door swung open, and with it came a wave, splashing across the landing and cascading down the stairs. "Can't you find it?"

"Sure I can. Just thought I'd let it run a while longer. Give the walls a good wash."

"Did you check by the water heater?"

"Of course I did," she said, and then traced the pipes in the opposite direction from the one she'd been following, until she came to a plywood panel behind which sat the water heater she'd never seen. The inspector had checked it; his report noted corrosion near the inlet shank. She didn't know what a shank was, or how to tell inlet from outlet, but she managed to unhook the plywood and find the place where pipes met tank. There were valves here, a pair of them she couldn't twist. She shook the flashlight, trained its dim beam on the little chrome wheels, saw rust caking the threads behind them. The giddiness that sparked her laughter had dissipated, and now she thought she really would start crying. All her effort these past months, all her reassurances, and this was the closest she could come to normal. Why even bother?

"That's the grossest thing I've ever seen."

Jeremy's voice, just behind her, more delighted than disgusted. She hadn't heard him approach, and she started at the sound. The flashlight beam passed over a hump on the floor, just beyond the edge of the aluminum drain pan. When it passed back, it picked up empty eye sockets, pointed skinless snout, bared teeth, a few bits of leathery hide sticking to ribs. Dragon, she thought, or dinosaur, though Jeremy provided the right word: opossum. Wounded, most likely, by the previous owner's dog before crawling in here to die. Nothing to do with trolls or ogres, though still it seemed ancient to her, or otherworldly, with its long stiff tail, an arrow pointing to the spot where the pipe jutted out of the concrete wall. And there, just above the first joint, a flat piece of metal, three inches long. Lever, not wheel. She pulled it, and it moved without resistance from vertical to horizontal. The pipe shuddered, and the gushing sound abruptly stopped, though water continued to roll over the stairs and dribble through the floor.

Jeremy reached down and grabbed the end of the opossum's tail between finger and thumb, lifted it, dangled it in front of her. Under his shirt, the ragged red appendix scar was still tender, the stitches out just over a week, but his eyes were huge behind his glasses, his smile wide and as lopsided as the hair he hadn't brushed after waking up this morning. She couldn't remember the last time he looked this happy. And once again she told herself that the change would be good for him, a chance to start fresh and become a different boy from the one who suffered at school in Chatwin, who often came home with bruises on his arms, where other boys took turns punching him to see how much he could take.

Shouldn't she know better? Earlier in the day, while the movers unloaded the truck, she'd taken him to the little mucky beach at the south end of the lake, where he swam with his shirt on to hide his scar. Then, with her encouragement, he approached a pair of boys fishing near the boat ramp. She stayed close enough to hear him catch their attention with a joke, a raunchy one Kevin must have taught him. It involved oral sex, menstruation, and pizza, and its punch line mostly confused her. But she was impressed by his boldness as he spat it out— "Needs more sauce"—and filled with pride as one of the boys cackled and pounded a fist into the ground. The other, lanky and freckled, with a swoop of dark hair over his eyes, smirked and asked his name. This would be the right boy for him to befriend, she thought, a good-looking and confident type, athletic and popular. Like Kevin, and like Peter, too, both of whom had betrayed her, or at least let her down. But Jeremy answered too fast, mumbling, and the boy who'd laughed, buck-toothed and sneering, with a bubble of sandy hair, shouted, "Germy Moss! Don't go near the Germy Moss, or you'll get the shits!" The lanky boy smirked again, and Jeremy retreated across the silt.

♋

Now, once more, the resilience or stubbornness of hope surprised her. Every time she thought she'd doused it and put it out for good, she found it smoldering again and ready to flare up with the merest puff of possibility. And yet thinking about what might come distracted her from what was right in front of her. When Jeremy turned to head for the stairs, she noticed he was still barefoot, leaving a track of puddles across dusty cement. "There are nails down here," she said. "And who knows what else. You have to wear shoes."

"I've had a tetanus shot."

The opossum's empty eyes glared at her upside down, its mouth hanging open, teeth surprisingly white in the gloom. "What are you going to do with that thing?"

"It's hideous," he said. "I want it in my room."

"You've got to clean it first. It might be diseased."

"It's been dead forever."

"Outside. In a bucket. With bleach, or something."

He was already on his way up, arm held straight out from the chest, the opossum swinging with each step. The sound of his feet sloshing again sent her after him in a hurry to survey the deluge. The water was three inches deep near the dishwasher and covered the refrigerator's lower grille. Still, it was a relief to be out of the dimness, into the kitchen which filled with soft light at the end of the day, just as she'd imagined it would on her first visit, though that had been in the morning. She pulled sopping boxes off the floor and set them on the counter, where they tore and spilled utensils onto stained laminate. The pool was shallower near the stove and the entrance to the dining room, which meant the house wasn't level, not even close. Either the foundation had sunk, or the frame had slipped off of it. One more thing the inspector had failed to note in his report, though now it was a small blessing. Water poured out the back door Jeremy had left open, down the concrete steps into what passed for lawn, a few patches of crab grass sprinkled between knee-high weeds, the ground so dry and cracked it quickly soaked up every bit that spilled.

Jeremy had abandoned the carcass near the spigot—they had neither hose nor bucket yet—and gone back to blowing up the rubber raft he'd been trying to inflate when she first shrieked at the sight of water spurting over her sandals. His face went red with each huff, cheeks pooching, eyes screwing up behind his glasses. It was still warm out, the sun a few fingers above the hills to the west, and her wet shirt felt pleasantly cool against her back and arms. The opossum no longer looked exotic to her, or even particularly gruesome, just a sad dead thing not even alluring to flies.

"You're not supposed to exert so much," she called. "Your incision."

"I'm not blowing with my stomach."

"You need to take it easy."

"Shouldn't you, I don't know, mop the floor or something?"

"Might as well let it drain first," she said. "And dry out a bit. I left the windows open."

He bent over the raft again, again went red, and this time held a hand over the scar. "I guess you can take a turn."

She put the plastic tube between her lips and blew, but nothing happened, except that dizzying lights flashed in her periphery. The raft remained mostly flaccid on the ground.

"You've got to squeeze and blow at the same time," Jeremy said, slapping mosquitoes away from his ankles. She heard the water streaming out the back door and thought that something was draining out of her, too, taking with it the panic she experienced in the basement, which was a reprise of the one she experienced on the way to the emergency room—both eruptions of an anxiety she'd been tamping down all year, since she first moved the boys out of the house she'd shared for a decade with a husband now planning his second wedding. It seeped out of her fingers and through the ends of her wet bangs, steamed from her skin in the dense humid air, heaved from her mouth into the tube she squeezed as her son had instructed. Her worries had largely come to fruition, nothing but chaos followed by her frantic attempts to reign it in, and yet here they still were, mostly whole and soothed by a light breeze that hardly stirred the seeds of a nearby dandelion.

There was a hiss this time as her breath passed into the raft, and the rubber stirred. But it left her just as winded, and after two more puffs, she paused and looked out over the lake, still enough to reflect trees on the far bank, though nearer the glare made her squint. She wished she had her sunglasses but had no idea where they were in the jumble of boxes and suitcases the movers had stacked along the walls and in the basement. Still, gazing in this direction, she once more found herself believing that living in such a beautiful spot was worth all the trouble, that it would eventually be good for Jeremy, who'd happily hole up reading comic books if nothing compelling pulled him outside.

When she turned back to the raft, though, she caught sight of the partially collapsed dock sticking ten feet into the muddy shallows, and then Jeremy's skinny legs all but disappearing in the tall weeds. He bent down again to slap away swarming bugs. The whole yard hummed with them, and she thought she could feel the vibration through her squishy sandals. With the windows and doors open, they were probably filling the house, too, and she wondered if mildew was preferable to mosquito bites.

"We probably have some bug spray," she said.

"Where is it?"

"In one of the boxes. Who knows which one."

He stayed where he was, and she blew three more big breaths into the plastic tube. There were flashes in her periphery again, less like stars than darting silver minnows. The rubber grew full, if not taut, and she blinked the fish away. "Good enough," she said, and carried the raft to the water's edge. But when both she and Jeremy climbed in, it sank so its hull barely topped the surface. Jeremy paddled with his hands, and they drifted only a few feet before her end started to submerge. She hopped out, into waist-deep water, mud squelching between her toes.

"Can we get a real boat?" he asked.

She wanted to promise him something. That life would get easier, that he wouldn't always have to struggle so much, that the past year would one day seem far away, maybe even benign. Or if nothing else, at least that things wouldn't get any worse. But all she could manage was the same mild optimism she offered herself, one that wouldn't die but wouldn't flourish, either, a crimped and anemic hope she only half-believed, or believed only half the time. "Maybe you can meet some other boys who have one."

He didn't answer. Dusk slowly thickened as the sun slipped behind trees. With it came a weariness she knew she'd soon give in to, but for now she bit away a burgeoning yawn. Jeremy turned wide circles in the raft, growing harder to distinguish from the bank of the nearest island. From the back of the house came the soft trickle of water on dirt.

2. Poor York

My mother had lived in the house for so long I couldn't imagine her apart from it. I'd come to think of the place—the half-dozen rooms, porch and deck, lawn and garden beds—as an extension of her, or an appendage, necessary if not for her survival then at least for her stability, sanity, sense of purpose. She'd put so much of herself into the property, which had nearly sunk her when she'd first bought it, the year she and my father split. Thirty-eight and living on a paltry divorce settlement and then a receptionist's salary, she could have easily teetered into destitution, and the house almost dragged her there.

At the time, it was probably the only one she could afford, and when we moved in it was a wreck. Floors warped, window panes cracked, everything smelling like wet fur. Back then, in the mid-'80s, no one in that part of New Jersey wanted old houses like it, a turn-of-the-century bungalow with hardwood floors and covered front porch, and the ones that hadn't been leveled to make way for new construction were owned by retirees who let them fall apart as they aged. The only thing it had going for it was its lakefront property, a narrow backyard full of thorny weeds backing onto the water. Everyone told her she was crazy to buy the place, that it would cause her more problems than she could handle, especially without a man around to fix things. And there were plenty of problems those first years: the hot-water heater shorted out and left us with cold showers for a month; a hose on the dishwasher broke and flooded the kitchen; I fell through a rotten board on the front porch and gouged my calf on the splintered wood.

Still, nothing made her happier than sitting out back with her morning coffee, watching a breeze ripple the brown water of Lenape Lake. And it actually relaxed her to walk through the combined living and dining room, the three small bedrooms, the kitchen and bathroom, making note of each crack in the plaster, each water stain and leaking pipe, each section of crumbling linoleum she planned to tear out, each hideous light fixture she couldn't yet afford to replace. More than me, and certainly more than my older brother Kevin, who by then was already in high school, the house gave her something to focus on, something worthy of investing her resources and energy. I wasn't quite twelve when we moved in but had already begun to keep things from her, to live a secret life of my own. Kevin didn't want to switch schools, because the Lenape wrestling team already had a star in his weight class, so he stayed with us only on weekends. My father paid for our clothes and school supplies and gave us pocket money. Later, he'd pay for college. My mother was free to put everything she could scrape together into the house, and not a year went by when there wasn't some major improvement underway. At first she did all the work herself, painting, sanding and sealing wooden floors, affixing shower tile. She taught herself to use a hedge trimmer and a tiller, and by the time I turned thirteen, she could host a bar mitzvah reception on the cleared back lawn surrounded by tiny shrubs and the first sprouts of a vegetable garden.

Later, occasional boyfriends would lend expertise with plumbing and electricity, and when I was out of the house and she was making a better living—having worked her way up to office manager at a sizeable medical clinic—she started hiring professionals. A new roof, a new furnace, a new tool shed, a flagstone path from the street to the porch. Each time I came home to visit, the place looked fresher, the garden more exuberant. As some of those houses built in the '70s and '80s fell into disrepair, a few sitting vacant for months after the housing crash of the past decade, my mother's grew only more and more appealing, until it was the gem of the neighborhood and the envy of most of her friends, even the wealthy ones, married to surgeons and investment bankers. My God, Eileen, they'd say. I wish I had your eye. She'd shrug and smile and feign modesty, and then after they'd gone she'd call me to report on the horrifyingly tacky additions they'd built onto their enormous, slap-dash, pseudo-mansions, whose siding was so flimsy flickers pecked holes in it and built nests in their attics.

CR

Is it any wonder, then, that I was shocked to hear, after thirty years, she'd put the place up for sale? And even more, that she did so without a second thought? She didn't agonize over the decision or even ask my opinion. She just let me know, casually, in the early spring of 2015: "I put the house on the market last week." She'd retired six months earlier, and now she'd agreed to move in with the man she'd been seeing for the past three years, a widowed neurologist who lived in one of the massive, ugly, cookie-cutter houses at the top of Union Knoll, a place she would have scorned at any other time, though now she said she found it "airy"; she could breathe more easily there after so many years in the bungalow's tight spaces. The doctor—Bob—owned a second place in Sarasota, with a lanai facing a pair of sand traps and the fourteenth green. They'd spend winters there for now, and after he retired, they'd move down to the sunshine for good. She was getting rid of most of the furniture, she added, and if there was anything I wanted to hang onto, I should let her know.

Two weeks later, she told me she'd gotten an offer on the house, one she thought she'd accept, and that night I bought a plane ticket to New Jersey, outrageously expensive, for the following weekend. When she picked me up in Newark, she said, "I don't see what the big rush is. It won't close until mid-May." And then, on the way to the parking garage: "You could have at least brought the whole family. I haven't seen the kids since Thanksgiving."

"I would have had to take out a new mortgage. Plus, Lani has ballet class on Saturdays. If I made her miss one a month before her show, she'd never forgive me."

My mother looked better than when I'd last seen her. In general, she'd always seemed younger than her age, and at sixty-eight she was still straight-backed, vigorous, and elegant, with a forceful way of pushing through the world that made her seem larger than she was. During her visit to Portland in November, however, she'd appeared more tired than usual, drained of energy. She complained about the rain, about being too cold, about the draft through the single-paned windows in the guest room. Hadn't I heard of weatherizing? My wife Mona and I, too, had bought an old house, one that had already been restored by the former owners. We expected my mother to admire it, compliment us on the original fixtures and oak floors. I was counting on her to comment on other things, too: our stable marriage, our healthy finances, our inquisitive kids. I didn't need confirmation that I'd achieved the sort of happiness she'd always wanted for me, only a sign of her pleasure in noticing it. And maybe I wanted her to tell me I deserved it, that it was sure to last. But she seemed to notice nothing other than her own discomfort. She'd lost weight, and her skin was sallow. I suspected she was mildly depressed leading up to her last days at work but feared it might be more serious. The day after Thanksgiving we tried to take her out to dinner, a little retirement celebration, but she begged off, saying she was still too full from the previous day's meal. The two of us should go out, she said, and she'd watch the kids. She hardly ever got to see them, after all. Why we had to live so far away, she had no idea.

Now she was planning to move even farther away, but she was cheerful, the color had come back into her face, and she'd put on a few pounds. Maybe the six months away from stale office air and fluorescent lights had done it, or the new, more serious turn her relationship with Bob had taken. "So, will there be some kind of, you know, ceremony at some point?" I asked as we pulled onto Lenape Road, snaking over the ridge of Union Knoll and down toward the lake, feeling both foolish and apprehensive the moment the words were out. But she just laughed and said, "Don't be so old-fashioned. He just wants someone around so he won't die alone. But maybe I'll get lucky and beat him to it."

Even talking about death she was more lively and lighthearted, and again I found myself puzzled that she wasn't devastated—or even, apparently, the slightest bit sad—to give up the house to which she'd devoted herself for so many years. I even wondered, with a touch of bitterness when we turned the corner and I spotted the realtor's sign in the front yard, with a "sale pending" sticker running diagonally across each side, if she'd be equally casual about giving me up, too.

But as we pulled into the driveway and I caught sight of the yew hedge, trimmed and tidy but beginning to put out fresh growth, the front porch railing with scuff marks on the paint, oak leaves gathered in the gutters and moss growing on the roof, I began, without yet being fully conscious of it, to understand her giddiness. It was relief. The place had been her lifeline, yes, but also a burden, one that must have seemed heavier and more onerous the older she got, the less she needed it to keep up her spirits. And it was a weight in another way, too—a reminder of the difficult turn her life had taken so unexpectedly, the loneliness of the years that followed.

And only then did I wonder if I might also feel relieved once the place was gone. Shouldn't I? It was the site of the most painful period of my childhood, evidence of my family's sudden splintering. For years I'd wanted nothing more than to get away, and when I did, I hated having to come back to visit. The house oppressed me all the way through college and my early twenties, when I wanted to think only about my own happiness and not my mother's. Back then, I would have been glad to say goodbye to it forever.

ℂℛ

I spent the afternoon on the lake, paddling around in my mother's canoe and debating whether I could ship it to Oregon. I kept telling myself there was nothing special about the place, certainly not in comparison to where I lived now. The lake was artificial, the banks dug out and the brook that fed it dammed up not long before the house was built, in order to stock iceboxes in Lenape and Union Knoll and adjacent towns. The trees—oak and birch and pitch pine—would have looked stunted next to the majestic Douglas firs I now saw every day in my Portland neighborhood, the lakeshore made ugly by residents' desire for a perfect view from their bedroom windows. Just two miles away traffic snarled up Route 10. The place was mundane and suburban and conservative, nothing alluring about it, and even my mother's tasteful house and luxurious garden looked bleak from the water, surrounded by the blight of overconsumption.

And yet, it was a view so deeply ingrained in my psyche, I didn't know how I could possibly do without it. Nor without the sound of my feet in socks across the entryway, the smell of the wood oil my mother used on the furniture, the feel of the nubby cushions on the window bench, where I'd spent so many hours reading comic books and doodling my own strips into loose-leaf notebooks. I needed these things, I thought, and not just in memory, where they'd fade too quickly. I did my best not to appear gloomy while I helped pack boxes, not to reveal any misgivings about how little time I spent here over the past decade. I tried to match my mother's jovial mood, telling her about Lani's role in her ballet company's upcoming production of *Peter Pan*—she was one of Peter's lost children—and Eliot's newfound love of worms. "He rescues them whenever Mona turns them up in the garden," I said. "Has a little worm hospital by the back fence."

I managed to keep up a breezy front all the way through dinner. Bob came over with take-out Thai food and wine, and his presence did genuinely cheer me. He was a big smiley man with a white beard and a two-inch ponytail, who muttered jokes as he struggled to uncork the bottle and after he splashed his shirt with red curry. He talked about his grandkids, about the boat he kept at his Florida place for fishing in the Gulf, about the Spanish mackerel he'd caught on his last trip down. What could be better for my mother than to find a bit of comfort late in life, with someone who'd look after her financially, relieve her of the responsibility she'd borne—with little complaint—for so long? How could I begrudge her that, after all the years she'd had to worry about paying bills and keeping herself busy enough to stave off the pain of disappointment? Bob was gentle with her, affectionate in a bumbling and endearing way. He was five years her junior but seemed much older, not far from doddering. At one point during the meal, she leaned toward him and with her napkin dabbed a speck of sauce from his chest. He blew her a kiss and then gave me a wink. "She doesn't miss a thing, does she?" he asked. "If it weren't for her, I'd go around with half a steak hanging off my chin."

After dinner, a couple from down the street came to visit. They were afraid they'd never see me again once my mother moved away, they said, and they couldn't let the opportunity pass. The truth was, I hadn't seen the Schechners in nearly a decade by then and had no particular interest in seeing them now. Dr. Schechner had been my dentist for most of my childhood, and I'd carpooled to Hebrew school with their kids, whom they now reported on in great detail: Gillian was in Virginia, taking golf lessons now that her kids were in school; Aaron was an investment banker, living in Weehawken, right up on the Palisades, divorced again but with a new girlfriend every time they visited. "They'll be so excited when we tell them we saw you," Mrs. Schechner said.

I'd told Mona about the Schechners once, years ago, when she was pregnant with Lani but before we'd gotten married. I wanted her to know how ridiculous my childhood had been, and perhaps to give her a warning about what it might be like to spend her life with me. Her morning sickness was brutal, lasting well past the first trimester. I did my best to feed her bland foods she mostly threw up, and afterward she'd lie on the couch, with her head in my lap. This time I'd just gotten off the phone with my mother, who'd mentioned seeing Dick and Marilyn—they'd asked about me and were delighted to hear I'd soon be a parent—and my mind flooded with images of them. Dr. Schechner was a bushy-haired, mumbly guy whose hands shook. When he had to pull a tooth, he'd stab me in half a dozen places and fill my face with Novocain, and still when he touched my gum I'd cry out in pain. My mother knew he was a lousy dentist, but she kept sending me to him because he was cheap, and because she didn't know what she'd say to Marilyn the next time they played mah-jongg. Plus, how would she get me to Hebrew school every Monday and Wednesday afternoon if she couldn't count on Marilyn driving me?

But the carpool was worse than the cleanings and check-ups. Mrs. Schechner was a terrifying driver, small and hunched over the wheel as if she were getting ready to leapfrog through the windshield. She'd fiddle with the wipers and the heat and the defroster, and the car would drift all over the road. Sometimes she and Gillian would fight over the radio knob—Gillian would keep turning it until she found "Like a Virgin," which made Mrs. Schechner close her eyes and mouth a prayer—and once they spent so long slapping each other's hands away that the car jumped the curb onto someone's lawn, its grille pointing straight at one of those big wooden mailboxes people in the neighborhood would put at the end of their driveways, a miniature barn with a tiny weathervane on top. We would have hit it, too, if the older girl sitting next to me didn't scream. The car jerked to the left, thumped back onto the road, and Mrs. Schechner turned to glare at us. "I don't appreciate being yelled at while I drive," she said, and the whole time Gillian kept singing about being shiny and new and touched for the first time.

When I reached this part, Mona's eyes were closed, but she was laughing hard. It was the most genuinely joyful sound I'd heard from her in months, and I wanted to keep it coming. "I can't believe the way you grew up," she said. "It might as well have been a different planet."

"From a backwoods Oregon commune? Definitely a different planet. I can confirm that."

"Not even the same solar system."

"I traveled a long way to find you. Hope you don't mind having been impregnated by an alien."

"So that's what's making me so sick."

"It's probably the lizard genes," I said. "And the radioactivity."

"I hope that other girl stopped riding with you, at least. She must have been traumatized."

"No chance. She stayed with us until her bat mitzvah. Probably another year and a half."

"Are you kidding?"

"Carpools were hard to arrange. Not many people available to drive into Chatwin at four o'clock on a Wednesday."

"Right. Better to risk your child's life than leave work an hour early."

"Or skip aerobics class."

"Of course. Kids come and go, but the abs are with you forever."

"I'm pretty sure she went to Dr. Schechner, too. If I remember right, she was missing a couple of molars on her lower—"

"Stop," Mona said, really cracking up now, "you're killing me," and then her face changed, a fierce accusatory look passing over it, as if I really had poisoned her with my alien sperm, fostered in a dark, cold stretch of the galaxy, and before I knew what was happening, she'd pushed herself up from the couch and was running for the bathroom. She came out pale and drawn and lay back down, this time with her head on a cushion. "No more stories," she said. "I need to rest."

⊂⊃

Now the Schechners were sweet and subdued, a pair of small, wrinkled, white-haired elders who seemed to think of me as someone they could be proud of, as if they'd had a hand in the positive trajectory of my life. They recalled moments we'd spent together that I'd long forgotten—a Labor Day barbecue, a fireworks display, a graduation party. What I remembered was Gillian's DUI arrest, a week after she'd gotten her driver's license; the fistfight Aaron got into with a kid on the swim team, after Aaron dumped his sister two days before the prom; the time the Schechner kids and their friends nearly set the neighborhood ablaze with a bonfire that got out of control in the woods to the west of the lake.

But I didn't mention any of that. We exchanged pleasantries for longer than was comfortable, and as I showed them pictures of my kids, my mother, impatient to get back to sorting and packing, stood and thanked them for dropping by. Only when they were heading toward the door did I realize that Dr. Schechner, retired for more than a decade, had trouble walking. He'd shuffle one foot forward and then get stuck. Mrs. Schechner tossed a coin on the floor in front of him, and he managed a couple more steps before she had to bend down, retrieve it, and toss again. She glanced up before I could turn away. "Parkinson's," she said. "Gets worse in the evening."

"So great to see you," I said when they finally made it across the front porch and down the steps. "Say hi to Aaron and Gillian for me."

After they left, I asked my mother how long Dr. Schechner had been sick. "He got the diagnosis last fall," she said. "But who knows. Probably had it for years." She shrugged, as if it were all the same to her. I didn't remind her of his shaky hands and the needles he stuck into me and all the years she kept sending me to him to avoid risking the carpool. What did it matter now?

Bob settled in front of the TV, turning it to a crime drama played too loudly, and my mother went back to work, finishing with the kitchen and then moving on to the basement. I'd already named the couple of items I wanted to take home with me—a painting one of her friends had made of the house with the lake behind, a vase I thought Mona would like—but I had the odd feeling I was overlooking things I'd regret leaving behind. That's when I forced myself to reckon with my old bedroom, which no one but my kids had stayed in since I'd moved out at eighteen. Whenever I visited, I slept in the guest room, where my brother had stayed on weekends when I was still a kid. Kevin and I had since agreed never to visit at the same time; our relationship was healthier when we saw each other on our own, separate from our parents. His room felt like a neutral space to me now, one where I could maintain some distance from those years I'd spent weekdays alone with my mother, the two of us eating dinner together in near silence broken only by her questions about school and friends I refused to answer. My own room was too fraught, even though my mother had long ago cleared out most of my stuff, pulled down my Clash posters, scraped anarchy stickers off the built-in bookshelves and painted over the ones she couldn't remove.

Still, there was the desk where I'd struggled with algebra and written manifestos on teenage liberation; the bean bag where I'd lounged for hours with headphones on, doodling in notebooks; the bed where I'd had awkward sex for the first time with a girl named Melanie, whose skin was cold in weird spots—on her ribs and the backs of her thighs—and who cried inconsolably afterward. I didn't find anything interesting in the dresser drawers or on the shelves, nothing I needed to hang onto. In the desk were a couple of mixed tapes, not bad ones, my handwriting on the covers neater than it was now, with some slashing flourishes meant to look menacing. But I no longer owned a tape deck, not in my house or in my car, so there was no point in reclaiming them. The desk itself—my name carved into it crudely with a pocketknife— might have been useful to Eliot in a few years, but to haul it across the country seemed frivolous.

I didn't want to indulge nostalgia for its own sake, or so at least I told myself. But I was left with the nagging feeling of having missed some crucial detail, something that would help me reconcile the mixed emotions I experienced as I visited the house for the last time, the irritation and impatience as I listened to the sound of the TV through the wall, the lump in my throat as I tossed the mixed tapes onto the desk. In the closet I found mostly linens, quilts my mother never used, extra pillows, but also some clothes that must have hung there since I finished high school. A leather jacket with chrome studs, a pair of slacks I'd worn to a cousin's wedding, my graduation gown—green and gold, the colors of the Union Knoll Mallards. More stuff I could happily never lay eyes on again.

On the shelf above the clothes rack was a shoebox. I pulled it down carefully, as if there might be fragile treasures inside. But when I set it on the bed and opened it, all I found were papers and photos and yearbooks from junior high. The last I flipped through quickly, recognizing almost no one, those few who did spark hazy recollections people I wished I could forget. Among the photos were some of me with my brother and father, none with my mother. I'd spent far more time with her than with either of them, but who would have taken our picture? At the bottom of the box was an envelope, a big square one with glossy paper, my full name printed formally: Jeremy Alan Moss. Inside was a slip of paper, too small for the envelope, cut to look like a ticket to a circus or carnival. On one side, the same formal print announced, "On the occasion of your bar mitzvah, IOU: one visit to the nearest House of Ill Repute. Your big bro, Kev." On the back was a crude drawing of a busty figure straddling a scrawny guy in glasses, with an appendix scar across his middle. And beneath, in hastier script, "Germ Becomes a Man."

I'd hated that nickname at first, which both my brother and kids at school used to torment me for years: I was a disease, an infection, someone to be avoided at all costs. But when I made it to high school and changed my look—skate shoes and shaggy hair and a denim jacket with hand-drawn images of Johnny Rotten on one arm and Joe Strummer on the other—it sounded dangerous enough to earn me some respect, especially during the year or so I sold quarter bags in the woods behind the football stadium, including to Gillian and Aaron Schechner. I even considered changing my name legally when I turned eighteen, dumping my father's last name while I was at it, along with any claim he had on me. But when the time came, I was too lazy to bother. Or else I was just so happy to be heading off to college, where no one knew me as Germ, that I became Jeremy Moss again, as if for the first time.

I left the shoebox on the desk with the cassettes, all items for the landfill, and joined Bob in the living room. The show he was watching was hard to follow, with urgent clipped dialogue and too many quick cuts, and anyway Bob was nodding off. I tried to imagine how my life would have been different if he'd been my father, a benevolent white-bearded figure who'd never have dashed his family to pieces the way Kevin's and mine had, before burning through two more marriages afterward. But I couldn't really. I knew my mother's tastes and habits too well. True, she'd accept Bob now, when she was winding down. She'd grown less particular, less demanding. Even ten years ago, though, she would have deflected his offer, kept him at arm's length before cutting him loose.

And just as I thought so, she bumped through the basement door, clattered loudly in the kitchen, dropped a big cardboard box near the sliding door to the deck. Bob sputtered and jerked upright, blinking and wiping away drool with a sleeve. Then she stood in front of me, blocking the screen, and held something up. "Want to keep this?"

Backlit by the TV, she was nothing but a flickering silhouette, and I couldn't read her expression. Nor could I make out the contours of the object, which was entirely in her shadow. I must have given a puzzled look, because she took a step closer, and then its shape became clear: narrow and pointed at one end, rounded at the other, with a bumpy ridge down the middle. A skull. A little one, not quite the size of her hand, with huge eye sockets and oversized incisors. I reached out, and my mother let it roll into my palm. It was lighter than I expected, the surface gritty with old dust, and even though I knew what it was, recalled cleaning and polishing it and thinking I'd put it in a prominent place in my old room, I had the feeling I shouldn't handle it much with my bare fingers, as if it were something ancient and precious, unearthed from a civilization long buried. I couldn't believe it had sat in the basement, without my realizing it, for nearly thirty years.

"Why would I want this?" I asked.

"Don't you remember it?"

"Sort of," I said, though I remembered it perfectly, the exact spot where I'd found the dried-up carcass near the water heater the day we moved in, the hours I'd spent soaking it to get the last bits of fur off, the sense of purpose it gave me during those first disorienting weeks in the crumbling house. And then, as if it had been clear all along, I knew why I'd been so uneasy since I'd arrived, or rather, since my mother had first called to let me know she was selling the place. More than the house itself, or the time I'd spent here, or even my mother's struggles, this was why I was so torn to see it go: because it reminded me there was a time when I believed life could only get better. The cracks in the plaster, the sagging ceiling, my absent brother, the cruel kids who taunted me— how strange, that out of all the misery of those years, what lingered most was the sense of expectation that kept me focused on the future.

"I can't believe you hung onto it."

"Maybe Eliot would like it."

"I don't need it," I said, and thrust it back toward her.

But she didn't take it. Instead, Bob sat forward and plucked it from my fingers. He held it out in front of him, on a flattened palm. "Poor York," he said. "When did you turn into a rat?"

"Opossum," my mother said.

"You telling me I don't know my Shakespeare?"

The skull caught light from the TV and threw a flash of color onto the rug, refracted in my suddenly blurred vision. It was true. Life had only gotten better. But I knew it couldn't go on that way forever. And now I spent most days braced for the moment when everything would begin to fall apart. My mother snatched the skull from Bob, who made a show of offense and told her to give it back. "That's my rat," he said, tried to push himself out of the chair, couldn't manage it, and fell back hard. "Oh, fine. Stick him back in the ground, Horace."

How did they do it? How did they go on like this, without constantly searching for new cracks that might have appeared when they weren't paying attention? How did they deal with the ones they couldn't yet see?

My mother stuck her hand out toward me again. It had hardly any more flesh on it than the skull. I didn't know when it had become so bony and cramped—arthritic, maybe?—with a slight tremor in the lean fingers that made me picture Dr. Schechner's halting shuffle to the door.

"You sure?" she asked.

"Sure," I said, and took one last look at the hollow eyes and bleached jaws and fanged grin before she swept them away.

Acknowledgments

I am enormously grateful to Antonya Nelson for selecting my manuscript for the Jordan Prize; to Allen Gee and his terrific team at Columbus State University Press for their care and attention in bringing this book into the world; and to Donald L. Jordan for the generosity that made it possible. Thanks also to my colleagues and students at Willamette University and the Rainier Writing Workshop who have taught me so much; and to my family for putting up with the many hours I spend with people who don't exist. I am also indebted to the excellent editors of the following publications, where some of these stories first appeared:

museum of americana: "Gray on Green on Brown"

Crazyhorse: "Loyalists"

Five Points: "While It Lasts"

Blue Mountain Review: "Have You Seen Stacey?" (as "Whatever Comes")

Westchester Review: "The Withered Hand"

Waccamaw: "Driftwood"

LitMag: "A Theory of Harmony"

Southern Indiana Review: "Lucky"

New Voices: Contemporary Writers Confronting the Holocaust (Vallentine Mitchell): "Babenhausen, 1947" (as "What Comes Next")

Subnivean: "A Minor Blues"

Baltimore Review: "Among Thorns"

Aethlon: the Journal of Sport Literature: "The Downs"

Finally, I am grateful to Princeton University Press for permission to quote excerpts from Peter Cole's translations of Yehuda Halevi's poems:

Republished with permission of Princeton University Press, from *The Dream of the Poem: Hebrew Poetry from Muslim and Christian Spain, 950-1492*, by Peter Cole, 2007; permission conveyed through Copyright Clearance Center, Inc.

About the Author

Scott Nadelson is the author of a novel, a memoir, and five previous story collections, including *One of Us*, winner of the G.S. Sharat Chandra Prize for Short Fiction and *The Fourth Corner of the World*, named a Fiction Prize Honor Book by the Association of Jewish Libraries. He teaches at Willamette University and in the Rainier Writing Workshop MFA Program at Pacific Lutheran University.

The Donald L. Jordan Endowment was established in 2016, in part, to facilitate the formation of Columbus State University Press, which was officially formed in 2021. CSU Press is pleased to recognize Mr. Jordan as the founder of the press, which serves as the publishing venue for the Donald L. Jordan Prize for Literary Excellence, and DLJ Books has been installed as a permanent imprint at the press. Mr. Jordan's foresight made CSU Press a reality, and we are grateful for his generosity. Mr. Jordan is a businessman and the author of novels, short stories, and works of non-fiction.